W9-DDF-644

JERRY ENGELS

JERRY ENGELS

A NOVEL

THOMAS ROGERS

HANDSEL BOOKS

an imprint of
Other Press • New York

The author gratefully acknowledges permission to reprint from the following: "Lay Your Sleeping Head, My Love," copyright 1940 and renewed 1968 by W. H. Auden, from *Collected Poems* by W. H. Auden. Used by permission of Random House, Inc.

Production Editor: Robert D. Hack

Text design: Kaoru Tamura

This book was set in Janson Text by Alpha Graphics of Pittsfield, NH.

10 9 8 7 6 5 4 3 2 1

Library of Congress Cataloging-in-Publication Data

Rogers, Thomas, 1927-

  Jerry Engels / by Thomas Rogers.

    p. cm.

  ISBN 1-59051-149-2 (hardcover : alk. paper) 1. Young men—Fiction.

2. College students–Fiction. I. Title.

  PS3568.O456J47 2005

  813'.54–dc22

                              2004018868

JERRY ENGELS

CHAPTER 1

From where he stood on Thompson Street, Jerry Engels could see them dancing in the Sigma Pi house. Couples circled and dipped to a tune that leaked faintly into the frosty air. Then the front door opened, letting out a burst of music and light. A couple emerged, hatless, coatless, laughing, and went running off to Delta Upsilon where another party was in progress. It was Saturday night in State College, Pennsylvania. December, 1951.

Jerry shifted on his feet and continued to stare grimly into the Sigma Pi party room. His usually reliable informant in the Kappa sorority had told him his girlfriend—check that, his *ex*-girlfriend— Pat Gaheris would be dancing this evening with Ken Moomaw. Jerry wanted to confirm those evil tidings. He wanted to see it with his own eyes. Though why did he want to see it? What masochistic impulse kept him standing there in the cold, waiting for pain?

Never mind, there she was in her red dress with the tight waist.

A bubble of grief burst in his heart. His eyes closed, and on the retina of memory he saw Pat in the two-piece Queen of Sheba costume she wore in last year's Greek Week pageant. He had been her Nubian slave in diaper and shoe polish who followed her around on stage holding an umbrella over her head. They were the hits of the show, and after the last performance, as cast and crew celebrated in the tent, he turned to Pat—she had not been his girlfriend then—and said, "I want to kiss your navel. Let me kiss your navel." Without a word she raised her arms, lifting her high breasts higher, exposing yet more midriff. He dropped to his bare knees on the trodden spring grass and pressed his lips to her warm skin. That had been the sweet beginning, this—his eyes opened—the bitter end.

Only moments had passed, but now his view of Pat was blocked by Moomaw's broad shoulders and thick head.

Jerry had fraternity brothers who believed you should challenge anyone who even *tried* to take away your girlfriend, but they could be wrong. They often were. Beating up Moomaw (assuming he could do it) would not bring back Pat, and anyway Moomaw had not taken her away. She had left under her own steam, slinging his fraternity pin back at him like a murderous little boomerang. And now there she was in Moomaw's arms, seen through the glass darkly.

So what did he do about it? Slink away crushed? Heave a rock through the window? Or just howl? He howled. Looking up at the crescent moon he let loose with one of those sustained ululations of erotic sadness or sad eroticism that sometimes rise along fraternity rows. Then, lungs empty, heart heavy, he turned away and started up Thompson Street toward the Deke house where there was no party that night because the chapter was in trouble again with the Dean of Men and the Interfraternity Council. No parties for six weeks. Fall rushing privileges suspended. Could things get worse? Probably.

Jerry was mounting the grand staircase when Mildenhall came out of the Trophy Room to say they needed a fourth for bridge. Jerry just shook his head. This was no time for cards. He proceeded to the room he shared with Jeff Begler.

He found Begler lying on his bed dressed in the anti-magnetic, self-winding, shockproof, waterproof Swiss watch he wore all the time, even in the shower. Begler had evidently just had one of his long, hot showers. His lean body looked pink and hairy. He was smoking one of his Upmann cigars.

Jerry sank onto the edge of his own bed and sat looking first at Begler, then at the nail-scarred wall above Begler's bed where hung the mighty lacrosse stick with which Begler had knocked out the teeth of an enemy at Lawrence Academy in the days before he came to Penn State, indeed in the days before he was expelled from Lawrence. Begler finished high school in Cooperstown, New York, where his father, the Reverend Jeffrey Begler, had a rich parish. Mr. Begler wanted his son to go to Yale, row for his college, and prepare for the ministry, but Jeff had inherited enough money from his mother to do what he pleased. He had chosen Penn State for its Hotel and Food Management major. Begler planned to own and operate a ski resort one day. He had his future all mapped out.

"Well, she's down there dancing with Moomaw," Jerry said at last.

Begler said, "What did you expect?"

"Am I dancing?" Jerry asked. "Have I gone out with anyone?"

Begler didn't answer. He continued to smoke. He smoked the way he did everything, with artistry. First he rolled the cigar be-tween the tips of his fingers while blowing gently on the coal. Next he put the cigar to his rosy lips and inhaled. Then came a suspenseful moment before he released the smoke. Sometimes Begler blew smoke rings, but tonight he was not trying for special effects. When he exhaled, the smoke rose in a fragrant blue plume to be instantly dispersed by the cold wind blowing through the window. Begler was a Spartan. He kept the window open all winter, never wore pajamas, and scorned any man who even owned a hat or an umbrella.

Jerry said, "In high school we studied a poem about what to do when your mistress some rich anger shows. Did you study that one?" Begler seemed to shake his head. Jerry went on. "Well, the poet says you should imprison her soft hand, and while she raves you feed deep, deep upon her peerless eyes, but that's crazy. I mean, if I'd done that with Pat she'd have kicked me in the shins."

Begler tapped ash into the saucer resting on his flat stomach. "Well, you gave her crabs," he pointed out.

Normally, to protect their reputations, Jerry didn't talk about the girls he had affairs with, but this was a special case. At Thanksgiving he had gone down to Haverford to see his old pal Phil Forson, only that weekend Phil had to finish a paper on The Decay of the Weimar Republic and the rise of National Socialism, and so on Saturday night Jerry had gone into Philadelphia alone and picked up a young streetwalker who gave him crabs. He had never had them before, and didn't realize anything was wrong until after he had spent an evening with Pat in a motel in Port Matilda. Only then did he remark to Begler as they were going to bed one evening that he had been itching a lot recently. Begler took a look and said, "You've got crabs," and then it had all come out as Jerry realized he had exposed Pat.

"I suppose I could grovel at her feet," he said.

Begler puffed gently on his cigar.

"Only what good would that do?" Jerry asked himself. Pat was not an understanding or forgiving girl. That was part of her attraction. She was one of those quick people. Quick to love and quick to hate. And when she hated that was the end. Curtains. Finito Benito. "My goose is cooked," Jerry concluded.

Begler checked his watch. "Tell you what. I can get us down to Altoona by eleven."

"I don't want to go to Altoona."

"What you need is to get your ashes hauled." Begler was a great believer in the therapeutic effects of sex.

"That's the *last* thing I need."

"Your trouble," Begler told him, "is that you get all emotional over these sorority babes and lose your perspective."

"I know a lot more about my trouble than you do."

"So what are you going to do, sit here and moan?"

"Have I moaned?" Jerry asked.

"That was probably you outside caterwauling a while ago."

"What if it was? I have a right to howl."

Begler was up and dressing. He was a man of action. "So are you coming with me or not?"

"To the Knights of Corassen?" Jerry said scornfully. The Knights was an Altoona dance hall and pickup joint.

"So if you don't like the Knights we can stop in Bellwood and check out the Paradise Bar and Grille."

Jerry didn't think much of the Paradise either. "Is that the best you can do?"

Begler frowned in thought. "Well, there's that joint in Juniata. We haven't been there in years."

"The Brown Derby!" Jerry exclaimed.

They went in Begler's MG.

"There should be a pint in the glove compartment," Begler said as he pulled on his driving gloves and adjusted his goggles. Jerry got it out, a fresh pint of Jim Beam. They each took a hefty swig. Then Jerry capped the bottle and put it away, Begler gunned the motor, and they were off with a roar. Begler always drove like the wind that poured over the windscreen.

These night rides with Begler had been going on since they were both freshman, and by now they had seen all of Centre County and most of Blair and Clearfield and Huntington counties as well. They had seen frozen cornfields glittering in the moonlight and town squares deserted except for bronze doughboys flanked by cannons and symmetrical piles of cannon balls. They had seen courthouse clocks registering the unearthly hour of four a.m. Owls on fence posts had turned their heads in solemn disapproval as Jerry and Begler flashed by, and deer waited nervously at the side of the road getting ready to jump in front of the car. Once they had seen what they thought was a bear. "That looked like a bear," Begler said, as they raced down Route 45 toward Water Street. "I think it was a bear," Jerry replied, and Begler had shaken his head. "We're really in the boondocks out here." But in fact they both loved these hills and valleys and little towns of central Pennsylvania.

They stopped to warm up in a roadside bar just beyond Warrior's Mark. They ordered boilermakers. "Go to State?" the bartender asked, as he put their drinks in front of them. They went to State, they said. "Know Dorsey Struble?" They knew who he was. A great wrestler. Jerry had seen Struble working out in the weight room at Rec Hall. "Comes from around here," the bartender said. "That's his uncle." The bartender pointed at a heavy-set, balding man in overalls drinking alone at a table for two. Begler and Jerry looked with respect at Dorsey Struble's uncle, then downed their drinks and went out into the cold. "You were right," Jerry told Begler, "I needed this." When they stopped in Tyrone for another boilermaker, he added, "I mean, I'm heartbroken, but I've got to go on living."

You couldn't talk easily in the open cockpit of the MG.

The Brown Derby was a raunchy Juniata bar near Bedbug Row and the main gate of the Altoona mills. Jerry and Begler had come upon it by accident when they were freshmen, new to the region, and exploring in every direction. They filed it away then as a possible pickup spot, though they had seldom visited it because once when they were sophomores they had trouble getting served at the bar. Now, as juniors, they had proof they were of age, though no proof was asked. The bartender served them their boilermakers without question.

Begler downed his shot, and then, beer in hand, went off to talk to a woman studying the selections in the Wurlitzer. Jerry just sat for a while, toying with his shot glass, thinking the long, long thoughts of youth. Pat was the fourth girl he had lost in as many years, and as he thought of them all he wondered if there was something really wrong with him. Aside from his promiscuity. Did he lack grip? Did girls just sort of trickle through his hands because he was weak? Should he try to be more the caveman sort? But that didn't seem to fit his personality. He was not cavemanish. Maybe he was sort of weak. In fact, his weakness and his promiscuity were probably connected, twin facets of an easy, light-hearted, somewhat negligible personality. He felt fresh sadness gathering at the edges of his mood. He could get quite sad thinking about his negligible personality, but he was not there for sadness. Shaking himself mentally, he began to look around.

There were no beauties in the bar, but then he had not expected beauty. Beauty was not the point, the point was fun, adventure, excitement. He wondered about two enormous women drinking beer together at a table in the back. They seemed to be having a great time, bantering with the regulars, and hoo-hawing over jokes of their own. They were whoppers, but jolly. Jolly whoppers. Jerry smiled in their direction, and one of them shouted out, "Hey, Handsome, come on over."

He went on over. One of them was named Phoebe, the other Sandra. Sandra got right to the point. "Which of us would you rather take home?" she asked.

"I'll take you both home," Jerry said.

They howled at that. "Sure you're man enough for us both?" Sandra asked.

"Just feel my muscle," Jerry said, flexing his right arm. Sandra laid a fat hand on his biceps. That made Phoebe clamor that she wanted a feel, too, so Jerry flexed his left arm.

"Aren't you the man?" Sandra said. "Can you sing?"

"No, but I know some poetry," Jerry told her.

"Let's hear it," said Sandra, so Jerry recited a Shakespeare sonnet that Phil Forson's grandmother once bullied him into memorizing. It began, *Shall I compare thee to a summer's day?* When he finished, Sandra said, "It makes you want to cry, doesn't it?" Phoebe said she always wanted to cry when she heard poetry. "But you're too young to know what tears are," Sandra told Jerry.

"I am not," Jerry declared.

"When have you ever cried?" Sandra challenged him.

"Yeah, when have you ever cried?" Phoebe echoed.

"I've cried lots."

"Pete! more beer!" Sandra yelled toward the bar.

"Let me pay for this," Jerry said. He hauled out his money and paid for the pitcher when it came. Then he filled glasses all around. "There you are, ladies."

"Who you calling a lady?" Sandra asked.

"Yeah, who you calling ladies?" said Phoebe.

"Well, anyway, there you are," Jerry said, "and don't tell me I don't know about tears. I cried buckets over Rosalind."

"Who's she?" Phoebe asked, looking around the bar suspiciously.

Jerry said, "She was the most beautiful girl in my high school. She had everything. She was blonde and rich and beautiful and kind, and she got good grades. Everyone loved her. You'd have loved her, too. Girls didn't even feel jealous of her, she was so nice."

Sandra seemed touched. "So why'd you cry over her?"

"I lost her," Jerry said. "I had her and I lost her, so I went out in the garden and cried, and then I went out to the Shores and tried to drown myself."

"That's the saddest story I've ever heard," Phoebe said.

Sandra patted Jerry's shoulder. "But you'll find another, good-looking like you are."

Jerry shook his head. "I've lost three more girls since Rosalind."

"And you tried to kill yourself every time," Phoebe prompted him.

"No, I didn't," Jerry said. "When Marie left me for another man, I stole a car and started to drive back to Indiana to avenge myself."

"That's the spirit," said Sandra.

"I'm not so sure," said Jerry. "If someone doesn't love you anymore, what good does it do to kill her, or kill yourself, or kill the other man?"

"Makes you feel better."

"Not if you're dead."

"So what happened?" Phoebe asked.

"When?"

"When you stole a car to go kill the trollop that jilted you."

"She was no trollop. She was going to a beauty school in Gary. She wanted to be a hairdresser. I met her on the beach at Indiana Dunes State Park. Have you ever been there?"

"Been where?" Sandra asked.

"She loved presents," Jerry went on. "She had a charm brace-let." He held out his arm to show his wrist to Sandra and Phoebe. "She wore it here," he said, "and I used to buy her charms to put on it. Silver charms. And when I went away to school, I gave her a platinum pin. I spent every buck I earned that summer on that pin. And then she never wrote me, and she started going out with this steelworker . . ." He shook his head.

"I was right," Phoebe said, "she was a trollop."

"I'd kill her," said Sandra.

"I wanted to kill him," Jerry confessed, "but I ran out of gas. There wasn't enough gas in the car I stole, and I'd forgotten to take any money with me. I mean, I was distraught."

"You poor thing." Sandra patted Jerry's leg.

Phoebe turned the pitcher upside down. "There's no beer left," she announced.

"Let me get this one," Jerry said.

"You got the last one."

"Then let me get the next one."

"I'll tell you what I'm going to do," Sandra said, "I'm going to take you home and make things all right for you."

"And she's the girl that can do it," Phoebe assured him.

Jerry said, "I don't know. How can it be all right if no one loves me and wants to marry me anymore? I mean, Pat and I were going to get married. She'd even decided that we'd honeymoon on the Gaspé peninsula. Now I'll probably never see it."

"Well, who wants to see it?" Phoebe asked.

"It's supposed to be very beautiful."

"Honey," Sandra said, "I'll show you beauty. Now finish up that beer, and we'll go around the corner."

Phoebe frowned. "Wait a minute! Why do you get him?"

"I saw him first," said Sandra. "I called him over here, didn't I?"

"Don't quarrel," Jerry told them.

"Yeah, but I'm younger than you are," Phoebe said to Sandra. She explained it to Jerry. "I should get you because I'm more your age."

"I'm twenty-one," he said.

"She's forty," said Sandra.

"It's a lie," said Phoebe. "I'm hardly thirty."

"When she's drunk, she forgets her own name," Sandra said to Jerry. "Now you come on. We're wasting time," and the next thing Jerry knew he was out in the cold, with Sandra beside him. She steered him around the corner and up the steps of a double house that looked quite ordinary from the outside. Inside it looked very strange. A sofa stuck out at an angle from the wall, chairs lay on their sides. An upside-down coffee table reminded Jerry of those dead groundhogs and raccoons you saw laid out on the highway, their little legs stiffening in the air. It was as if Sandra had just thrown furniture into the room, but before Jerry could take it all in, Sandra dropped her coat over an empty birdcage and said, "This way."

Then they were in her kitchen, a nightmare kitchen, and Sandra was rummaging in her refrigerator for a bottle of gin. She slopped gin into two glasses, handed one to Jerry, and said, "Here's to us." Then she swayed forward for a kiss and an embrace that caused Jerry to spill some of his gin down her backside. The cold gin got to her. "Whoops!" she cried. "Naughty, naughty." She gave Jerry a love tap that sent him reeling against the stove, where there was a dead geranium on one burner.

Next they were upstairs advancing across a carpet of discarded clothes toward a bed with a naked mattress. The sight of that mattress sobered Jerry. This adventure was threatening to get sordid. "There's got to be a sheet," he declared.

"Oh! Yeah! I know there's one somewhere," said Sandra.

It proved to be underfoot. Jerry extricated it from the maelstrom and began to tuck it in. Aside from goosing him as he bent over, Sandra was no help. Instead she moved away to look at herself in a mirror. When Jerry finished tucking in the sheet Sandra was still teasing her spit-curls and running a wetted fingertip along her plucked eyebrows. He had seen her do the same thing in the bar. He felt he was beginning to understand her rhythms. Basically this was a very fat, slightly crazy, and possibly self-destructive woman who needed quiet moments from time to time to take care of her looks. "Okay, the bed's ready," he called out.

Sandra turned from the mirror and fixed him with a bright smile. "Well, here goes," she said, pulling a rip cord somewhere. Her dress came slithering off like a tarpaulin from some public monument, revealing what Jerry had surmised in the bar. Sandra had nothing on underneath. She raised arms like great sausage links and did a shimmy that set up wave motions on her surface. "Like it?" she asked.

Jerry had never met a woman he couldn't like. "You're terrific," he told her.

"Aren't you sweet?" Then, lowering her arms, Sandra began to tramp forward, caught her foot in something on the floor, and came cascading over Jerry, who had been sitting, still clothed, at the foot of her bed.

He was under her then, smothered by her, drowning in her. Her weight pinned him to the mattress. Then she found his mouth and cut off his wind. He was only saved by the bell of an alarm clock that suddenly went off on the floor beside the bed. "That damn clock!" Sandra exclaimed. "Always going off at the wrong time." She looked for it, failed to spot it, heaved herself up, and went stalking out of the room. When she returned she was feeding shells into the breech of a shotgun. "I'll fix it," she said.

"Hey, no, wait!" Jerry cried, but she paid no attention.

"Goddamn fucking clock," Sandra muttered.

"Don't do that," Jerry said, as Sandra pulled the trigger, producing an explosion that filled the room with acrid smoke and brought down some plaster. The clock continued to ring. Madness reigned. On the far side of the common wall, neighbors banged in protest. Sandra banged back with her hip. Then the alarm began to wind down. "That's better," Sandra said. And at that point she eyed Jerry, still in his clothes. Pointing her blunderbuss at him, she said, "Get your things off, hunh?"

He had never undressed so fast in all his life. His alacrity pleased Sandra. "Aren't we going to have fun?" she said, dropping her gun and throwing herself on Jerry.

Again he found himself struggling around under Sandra, trying to make sense of an anatomy that didn't give a man many guidelines. There were creases and folds, crevices and dead ends Jerry had never encountered before, and despite her boast that she could make things all right for him, Sandra gave him no help. She just lay atop him, crooning in his ear. He would have to get her on her back, he decided.

"Hey!" she exclaimed as he finally turned her over. Then she began to croon on a new note, and all seemed to be going well until a fresh sound intervened.

"I think someone's at the door," Jerry said.

Sandra stopped her crooning and listened. "It's those fucking neighbors again," she decided, and once more she showed herself to be a woman of action. She threw Jerry off her, grabbed her shot-gun, and went thundering downstairs.

Jerry waited for the sound of another gun blast, but none came. Instead some kind of argle-bargle developed. He could hear several male voices mixed with Sandra's. Then she reappeared, all of a twitter so to speak. "Hide, will you?" she said. "He's got his cop cousin with him. I could lose my alimony if they find you here." Then she snatched the sheet from the bed, draped it around herself, and left, saying she would hold them off. This time she seemed not so much to descend as to tumble downstairs. First came the sharp crack of breaking wood, then a sustained, majestic crashing that shook the house.

Jerry looked over the broken banister. Sandra, tangled up in her sheet, was being helped to her feet by two men, one of them in uniform. She was cursing vigorously and seemed to be unhurt. Deciding that he had better not appear, Jerry withdrew to Sandra's bedroom, dressed almost as rapidly as he had undressed, and then climbed out the window. It was an easy drop to the roof of the back porch, and another easy drop from there to the ground.

Twenty minutes later he pushed his way into HARRY'S EATS, the rendezvous he and Begler always used when they got separated in Altoona. Begler was not there, but that was all right. After a bout with Sandra, Jerry felt in need of sustenance. At the counter he ordered a milkshake and a hamburger. When they came, he took them off to a corner table, because Harry—if it was Harry who tended the counter at night—had a tendency to talk about the Pittsburgh Steelers, a flop team he seemed to love. Jerry understood the phenomenon. At home in Chicago he had friends who rooted for the White Sox, who hadn't won a pennant since 1918. People learned to love teams that always disappointed them. They were actually attracted by the pain of losing. Jerry himself was. He dwelt almost lovingly now on his loss of Rosalind Ingleside, for whose sake he had tried to drown himself when he was seventeen. He considered it one of the most beautiful if painful episodes in his life, but the point was that you loved your own losses, not other people's. He did not want to hear how the Steelers had blown yet another game.

Once settled at his corner table with some much-needed nourishment inside him, he began to reflect on recent events.

Though no philosopher, Jerry had intuitively arrived at Nietzsche's dictum: *Whatever does not kill me makes me stronger.* He felt stronger for having tried to drown himself after losing Rosalind, stronger for stealing that car, stronger even for having grappled with Sandra. For a moment he sat there in HARRY'S EATS feeling good and strong. Then the troubling question arose: what was all this strength *for*? He didn't want to end up a professional strong man, just showing off his muscles. What did he want to end up as?

He frowned thoughtfully. He went to the counter to get himself a cup of coffee. Back at his table he stirred in cream and then gazed at the brown surface that gave back no reflection and suggested no answers. In the absence of insight he wondered if he should just volunteer for active service in Korea? It was the patriotic thing to do, and now that he had lost Pat and was about to be kicked out of his major in Petroleum and Natural Gas Engineering there was nothing to keep him at Penn State. Yet did he really want to fight in Korea and maybe get killed there like Jimmy Kaplan, one of his high school pals? Though on the other hand was life so safe here in Pennsylvania with people like Sandra—and Fred—spraying bullets around?

He began to think about Fred, a rural lunatic who had turned up one night when Jerry was with a semi-pro named Dolly. He and Dolly had been in each other's arms when they were interrupted by the sound of a furiously driven car coming to a gravel scattering halt outside Dolly's trailer in Slab Cabin Park. Dolly raised up and looked out the window. "Shoot," she had said, "Fred's back." Then it was shoot indeed as Fred fired into the night sky. "Whore! Whore! I know you're in there, whore," he yelled in a hoarse voice. "He's got no right to call me that now we're separated," Dolly said. She had opened the window and shouted, "You're drunk, Fred Brummel. You go home and go to bed." Fred yelled, "Lousy whore!" "Stinking polecat," Dolly replied. Then Fred fired a second time, and Jerry pulled Dolly away from the window. "We should get on the floor," he said, but Dolly seemed more indignant than afraid. "He'll see! I'm going to get an injunction against him coming out here and bothering me," and at that point Fred had shattered a window with his third shot, then leaped into his car, and gone careening off into the night. "He's dangerous," Jerry said. "Fred was at Saipan," said Dolly, and from her tone it sounded as if she were proud of him. Jerry had made a little poem out of the affair:

> A veteran raves beneath the harvest moon
> Calls his wife whore,
> And knocks with bullets at her trailer door.

He was thinking of his poem and wondering if he could add some lines to it when Begler came into HARRY'S EATS, looking pleased with himself. Begler seldom failed to score on these excursions. He came over to Jerry's table and stood looking down benignly while Jerry gulped his remaining coffee.

"So how'd it go, Herman?"

Jerry stood up. "I got shot at again. I'll tell you about it in the car." Only in the MG there was too much wind for storytelling, and besides Begler had only a limited interest in other people's experiences.

CHAPTER 2

That was Saturday night. On Sunday morning Jerry did his laundry, took Rex, the house mascot, for a run, and then settled down to write his weekly letter home.

Dear Mother and Father, he wrote,

I've seen my advisor, and he says I'll be dropped from PNGE next semester unless I get all B's this semester, which is impossible. I'd have to get a perfect grade on the final in Mechanics 11, and my cumulative in Chem. 40 already means I can't get higher than a C plus. The only course I'm doing well in is Geology 481. I know this is a big disappointment to you both, but now I think that I chose Petroleum and Natural Gas for the wrong reasons, because you two are both scientists and because Daddy works for Standard Oil. It was never the right major for me.

I've checked around, and I think I should go into psychology. The Psychology Department only requires that students have a 2.0 grade average, which I can handle, and it's a subject I'm interested in. Maybe I could become a youth counselor? I already know a lot about youth. Anyway, we can discuss it at Christmas.

Phil has the Chevy this semester. He'll pick me up on the 19th, so I should be home sometime on the 20th. Be seeing you soon. All my love.

Jerry

P.S. It's all over with Pat. I feel heartsore, but you don't have to worry that I'll do anything silly like I did after Rosalind. I've grown up a lot since then.

He went off to mail that at the post office in town—he liked his letters to get on their way as soon as he finished them—and then he went on to the weight room in Rec Hall. Swimming had always been his sport and remained his first love, but he had been disappointed with Penn State's swimming program. The university had no natatorium. The team practiced in town at the Glennland Pool, which was a goofy length, and so shallow at one end that the team had to install a bulwark three-quarters of the way down the pool so racers could do flip turns. It was just embarrassing to host visiting teams at a facility like that. Jerry's University of Chicago High School had a better pool than Penn State. So when the university downgraded its swimming program from a varsity sport to a club activity, Jerry quit in protest and took up weightlifting instead.

He had found the weight room dominated by what he thought of as Old Timers. One was a mailman, another delivered beer for a local distributor, a third owned a gift shop in town. These were men in their late twenties and early thirties, some of whom had never been students. A few had connections in York, Pa., the capital of American weightlifting. One of them had actually lifted with the great John Grimek himself. They were serious power lifters who looked askance at Jerry when he first started turning up. A man named Dunkel took Jerry aside and said, "Kid, if you want to lift, I'll help you train. But forget about it if all you're after is that body-beautiful crap." Jerry said he wanted to lift—at that point he really didn't know what he wanted—so Dunkel took him in hand and showed him how to clean and jerk, and curl, and bench press. He advised Jerry on the amount of weight he should train with, and the number of different repetitions for each movement. "See, lifters go for maximum weight. We're not interested in hundreds of repetitions. That's for the body-beautiful crowd. What we want is to get that old iron up there, see? So you put as much weight on the bar as you can, and do five reps. Only five. Then you rest. Then do another five. Rest some more. Then try for three or four. See? Three sets, five reps max. You walk into a gym and see a guy going up and down, up and down, up and down like some goddamn oil rig, you know right away that all he's interested in is how he looks, not how much he can lift. Posers, that's all they are."

Jerry accepted Dunkel's teaching and in turn had been accepted by the Old Timers, who now welcomed him into their window-less sanctuary that smelled of chalk and liniment and old sweat. The weight room had a hushed, almost priestly calm to it, with Old Timers sitting about as if in prayer much of the time while they collected all their inner force for some maximum lift. After a lifetime spent swimming and floating along, Jerry found the slow, thick atmosphere of the weight room strangely appealing. He thought it had had a good effect in solidifying his character, to say nothing of strengthening and defining his muscles. He loved the place, and after a year of lifting he had begun to experience what Dunkel and the others referred to as "the Pump," a mildly plea-surable overall erection that came from pumping blood into your muscles.

On Sunday after his workout he sat for a while just savoring his pump. Then, inevitably, his thoughts drifted to Pat.

Up to now he had always been able to rationalize his losses and so make them easier to bear. He had told himself that Rosalind Ingleside was just too good for him, and that Marie Promojunch hadn't been good enough. He told himself that he and Laura Smith could have lived together happily ever after were it not for Bucephalus, her damn horse. Laura had brought Bucephalus to campus with her, boarded him at Jodon's stables, and spent all her time currying him and schooling him over jumps. She looked wonderful in jodhpurs and hard hat, but riding Bucephalus had taught her to keep a tight rein not just on horses but on men as well. Jerry could only kiss her, and hold hands, and very occasionally cuddle a bit. It finally drove him so crazy that in his sophomore year, when Laura's parents were up for Homecoming, he got drunk and made such a spectacle of himself that the next day Laura returned his Deke pin. Five months later he gave it to Pat Gaheris.

She had seemed ideal. She was unusually liberated for a sorority girl. She actually liked sex, and moreover she appeared to have a tolerant attitude toward male promiscuity. She admired her father, a Wilmington banker whose habit of going off to conventions with one of his secretaries had sent Mrs. Gaheris into a permanent depression. "But she's wrong," Pat told Jerry. "He's never wanted to leave her. He just likes to have some fun." When he heard that, Jerry thought he had at last found his soul mate. And now that he had lost that soul mate he felt he had reached some sort of crisis or turning point in his life. Despite his promiscuity he had always assumed he would eventually end up a monogamous and happily married man like his father. But if he could not keep Pat, who could he keep? What decent woman would ever want to marry him? Only if he didn't marry, what would he do? What became of men like himself? Were there happily unmarried men?

He could not answer any of his own questions. They frightened him a little, and rather than mull them over, he got up from his bench in the weight room and made his way to the steam room, where the first person he saw through the pearly mist was brother Harold Collins sitting on the marble slab with his eyes shut and his pores open.

Jerry slid in next to Collins, who opened his eyes and said, "Oh, hi, Jerry, been working out?" Collins ran an experienced eye over Jerry's body. "Looking pretty good," he said.

"How about you?" Jerry asked, and together the two of them studied the still-red stitch marks across Collins's right knee.

"It's fine," Collins said. "Doesn't hurt at all unless I put weight on it."

Considering that Collins must weigh about 280 pounds, that didn't sound good to Jerry, but he forbore to comment because the sight of Collins had awakened him to one of his duties in the chapter. Jerry was Rush Chairman, and since the chapter's fall Rush privileges had been suspended, it was particularly important to have a good spring Rush. He said to Collins, "Listen, tell me what you think of Jack Murger."

Murger was a hard-hitting linebacker on this year's freshman squad, an almost sure starter on next year's varsity, and while DKE was not an athletic fraternity, it was felt that the chapter should always include at least one Nittany Lion. Collins had been that Lion until he wrecked his knee in the Villanova game. Since then he had been sitting around the house reading old copies of *Esquire* when he wasn't up at Rec Hall getting whirlpool treatment for his knee and trying to shed weight in the steam room. He understood the importance of Jerry's question. With himself out of action, probably forever, the chapter would need another Lion to carry on the tradition.

After due thought—Collins neither moved nor spoke without conveying the impression that some effort went into what he did—after due thought, Collins said, "Well, Jack's a terrific hitter. He really hits. And he's a great guy, one of the best. Only he may not be polished enough for us." Dekes thought of themselves as polished. Even Collins had the mysterious conviction that he, too, was polished, one of nature's Dekes, who just happened to be twice as big as everyone else and to look good in check suits and pointy, two-toned shoes.

Jerry said, "Maybe we put too much emphasis on polish?"

Collins closed his eyes to ponder the matter, and while Collins pondered, Jerry leaned back against the wall and watched a drop of perspiration slide down his gleaming torso to lodge, eventually, in his belly button.

Finally Collins opened his eyes and said, "Well, I like Jack, and he's a real hitter. Maybe we could polish him up."

"Of course we can," Jerry said. "We can polish him, and he can toughen us."

Collins said, "That's a real nice idea, Jerry."

Jerry acted on it that evening. After supper he called an impromptu meeting of his committee in order to start gathering names for the spring Rush. They met in the Trophy Room, the committee sitting in leather armchairs, Jerry standing on the empty hearth. Above him, filling the whole chimney piece, hung an oil painting of a ship under full sail in a tremendous storm. Along the horizon you could see a streak of light, indicating that if the sailors could just hold on long enough the skies might eventually clear. No one knew who had painted the picture, or where it came from, but everyone accepted it as valuable. It was like the books that filled the built-in bookcase. They, too, were thought to be valuable, and from time to time Jerry had paused to read their titles: Stoddard's *Lectures*, Ingersoll's *Sermons*, Guizot's *History of France*, and Motley's *The Rise of the Dutch Republic*, all in matched sets, together with a miscellaneous collection of what appeared to be the complete works of Henry Van Dyke. Some day, if they ever found the key to the bookcase, Jerry meant to browse through those books to see what they were like.

He called the meeting to order with a few well-chosen remarks about the urgency of having a good spring Rush. No one disputed it. Then they began to throw names into the hat. A few names were well received by everyone. Indeed, no real disputes broke out until Jerry threw in the name of Jack Murger.

"He's got no front teeth," Bill Houser objected.

Jerry reminded Houser that you had to look below the surface. Murger was a terrific hitter who would improve the image of the chapter. Dekes were thought of too much as lightweights, mere dancers and ladies men. They needed a Murger or two to toughen up their image and make them seem more virile to the world at large. To this Houser replied that he was perfectly satisfied with his own virility and did not need to live with a berserk linebacker to prove it. That shocked Jerry, who said that it showed very bad taste to call Murger berserk, but Houser would not back down. He was only stating the obvious. Murger was dangerous, aside from the fact that he looked awful.

Jerry said, "Collins thinks Murger is a great fellow, one of the best."

"Well, what does Collins know?" Houser said. "Look at him."

"What's the matter with him?" Jerry asked.

"What's the matter!" And Houser began to enumerate Collins's flaws, beginning with his haircut, going on to his clothes, and ending with his behavior at parties—to which he never brought a date. Instead he spent his time at the bar talking football with other men between fixing their dates Sazeracs, Butterflies, Lizard Breaths, Texas Stingers, and other exotic cocktails that he had learned to mix at his uncle's bar in McKeesport. "Christ, Engels," Houser concluded, "I've never seen Collins with a woman. I think he mates with bears in the hills."

"What's that got to do with it?" Jerry asked.

"Murger couldn't hurt Collins. He'll kill the rest of us."

"That's plain wrong," Jerry said, and he pointed out that Collins was as vulnerable as everyone else. Look what had happened to his knee. Everyone was vulnerable. Even Murger. Murger could be wrecked in any game. "It's unfeeling to talk that way about people," he told Houser.

Houser said, "So you want another crocked-up football player sitting around the house bringing down the grade point average?"

"That's not what I want at all," and Jerry went on to explain what he wanted. He wanted the Dekes to present the best, the most balanced, the most ideal image of young American manhood that could be assembled, and, in his opinion, they could improve on their present mix by introducing some rough diamonds like Jack Murger and polishing them up a bit. Murger, he argued, could very well turn into a hero of sorts. He was very strong and completely fearless. He might well bring glory to the Dekes. "He could be another Teddy Roosevelt," Jerry asserted. T.R. was still the greatest of the Dekes.

"Not without teeth he couldn't be another Roosevelt," Houser said.

"Teeth aren't the issue at all," Jerry declared. "It's picayune to keep harping on Murger's teeth. He can get false teeth."

"The issue," said Houser, "is that you're trying to fill up the chapter with crazies and screwballs like yourself."

Mildenhall intervened. "If you two are going to start this again, I'm leaving."

"It's Houser who always gets personal," Jerry replied. To Houser he said, "And you've got no grounds to call me a crazy. *I* don't have a stuffed deer head hanging over my bed. *I* don't play the 'Battle Hymn of the Republic' on my trumpet at three a.m."

"No," said Houser, "you get picked up by the police for running naked up to Rec Hall."

"That was on a bet," Jerry said.

"And who got hauled up the flagpole the night we beat Nebraska?"

"I was drunk."

"Do other drunks take off all their clothes and persuade people to run them up the flagpole by their ankle?"

Mildenhall said, "I'm not going to listen to this anymore."

"Yeah," said O'Dana, "let's keep to the point."

"That's right," said Jerry, "and the point is tolerance. I think this chapter is too conservative and intolerant. I think we should go after men like Murger. I think we should broaden our base and take in all kinds of men and not keep it closed up and exclusive."

"Now you're talking about dropping the restrictions," Houser said.

"Are you for keeping it restricted?" Jerry demanded.

"That's not the issue at all," Houser replied. "Murger isn't Jewish, he's a maniac."

"Shall we try to stick to the point?" O'Dana asked.

Jerry said, "The point is that we should stop paying so much attention to what men look like and where they're from and what they wear and what church they go to, and start paying attention to what's inside them."

"Blood!" said Houser. "That's what Murger has inside him, lots of good red blood. You want to brotherize him so he can shed yours?"

Mildenhall said, "I don't think either of you is making much sense."

"I'm not giving up on this," Jerry declared. "I vote we rush Jack Murger. All in favor say aye."

The nays had it three to one.

"All right, but this isn't the end," Jerry said. "I'm going to open up this chapter. I'm going to bring in fresh blood. I'm going to change things." And on that note the meeting broke up.

Every Monday afternoon, and usually on Wednesdays and Fridays as well, Jerry posed for Life Drawing classes in the Art Department. The job brought in some money, which he always needed, and more than that it gave Jerry several hours a week of intense, alert freedom, though he could not say freedom from what. Yet when he appeared in class, and stepped up onto the platform, and took off the robe he wore between dressing room and studio, he felt as if he were removing some great weight or impediment. It was like swimming, it was like slipping into water, and since childhood he had loved the water. Naked, except for his posing strap, he felt somehow reborn, as if by removing his clothes he had peeled off some wrinkled old hide to reveal his true and original self.

Popular opinion in the chapter held that Jerry posed to show off, and to attract girls, but that had nothing to do with it, or at least very little. Until he lost Pat he hadn't needed to attract anyone, and now that he had lost her, he felt she could hardly be replaced, especially by an art student. They seemed to want him to keep his distance. During breaks when he got down from his posing platform to see their work, many girls clutched their sketch pads to their chests, or blocked his view of their easels. "Go away," they said, or, "I don't want you to see." He wore his robe during these breaks, but even so he seemed to make girls nervous. The only one he had gotten friendly with was Anne Player, a tubby little Kappa with frizzy red hair, and he had had a speaking acquaintance with her to begin with. Now, of course, she had become his chief informant about what was going on in the Kappa suite.

He spoke to her on Monday between poses. "You were right. Pat was with Moomaw Saturday night. I couldn't believe it."

"Why not?"

"Well, would you go out the week after you'd broken up with someone?"

"I don't know," Anne said. "I've never had the chance to find out."

She had already told Jerry that her only boyfriend in high school was the class sissy. Thank God for sissies, she told him. Otherwise girls like herself would never get dates. At the time it struck Jerry as one of the saddest things he had ever heard. Now, looking down at Anne, he made up his mind about an idea he had been toying with for several days. The Pan-Hellenic Christmas Ball was scheduled for Friday. He no longer had a date. He was pretty sure Anne didn't have one. Why shouldn't he take her to the ball?

"I want to ask you something," he said.

"What?"

"Not here. Can you go to Baroutsis with me afterward?"

"I guess so," she said.

So after class he walked Anne to Baroutsis, where they ordered hot chocolate. He delayed popping his question. When their orders came he watched Anne pick up her cup with what struck him as stubby fingers. Then he hated himself for reacting this way. After all, had he not argued with Houser that appearances should not matter so much? Leaning across the table, he said, "Listen, Anne, would you go to the ball with me Friday?"

Her head came up sharply. "The Pan-Hellenic?"

He nodded. "I know it's late to ask, but I've lost my date, and I thought maybe you'd be free."

"I'm free all right, but what about Pat?"

"If she can go out with Moomaw, I should be able to go out with you."

Anne said, "She'll think it's pretty funny you're taking me to the ball."

"Why? What's funny about it?"

"Oh, this and that." Anne tugged at one of the tight little curls by means of which she tried to give body to her hair. She ran a hand down her solid waist.

Jerry said, "I don't know what you mean."

"Like heck you don't."

"Okay, maybe you're not as tall and slim as Pat, but appearances aren't that important."

"There speaks somebody who's never known what it's like to be short and fat."

"You're not fat," Jerry told her. "Anyway, it's personality that counts."

"Haven't you noticed that funny-looking people develop funny personalities to match?"

"What do you mean 'funny'? You've got a good personality. I like talking to you."

"You don't really know me all that well."

"So what are you saying?" he asked. "Are you turning me down?"

"Not on your life! You're in for it."

Jerry shook his head. "You shouldn't think that way. You shouldn't feel that way. I'm not in for anything. I want to take you out. I like being with you."

Anne shifted in her seat without replying to that. She sipped at her hot chocolate. Feeling more confident now that he had taken the plunge, Jerry pursued his theme. "Sororities and fraternities overemphasize appearances," he said. "I mean, look at me."

"I am looking at you."

"Well, they made me Rush Chairman just because they think I look right for the job. I'm their face man. I mean, that's how the Greek world works, and I think it's wrong."

She said, "Have you any idea what you really look like?"

"What do you mean? Of course I know what I look like."

"You look like Michelangelo's *David*. Without the expression."

This was a new one. "What expression?"

"David's looking over at Goliath and figuring out how to kill him. You're beautiful without having murder on your mind."

Jerry glanced at the neighboring table, and then lowered his voice. "Don't say *beautiful*. I mean, you shouldn't say a man is beautiful."

"Why not—if he is?"

"You just don't say it, especially in front of him."

"Well, you are beautiful," she said. "Why are you so embarrassed about it?"

"Who's embarrassed?"

"In class you're not embarrassed," she went on. "I've seen lots of male models. Some are show-offs, most of them are self-conscious, a few of them are embarrassed. You're none of those things. When you undress it's like the sun coming out. You glow."

Again he looked at the neighboring table—two Chi Omegas with their heads together. God, what if they were listening to this? "Will you shut up?" he whispered.

"I think it's very funny the way men like you go around pretending only women look beautiful. That's what you think, isn't it?"

He decided all was lost, the fat was in the fire, and further coyness on his part would only spoil a very interesting conversation. He said, "No, I know I'm beautiful but I don't like people to say so."

"Why not? You say it to girls, don't you?"

"That's different. They don't mind. Anyway, some girls really are beautiful clear through. I've known at least one girl"—he meant Rosalind—"who was beautiful right down to the bottom. She was perfect, but men never are. We've always got an ugly side."

"Tell me about yours."

She was smiling at him. He smiled back. "Well, I'm lecherous for one thing."

"Is that what broke it up with Pat?" Anne asked. "She won't talk about it. She just says you turned out to be a rat."

"Well, yeah, I did," Jerry agreed, feeling almost exhilarated by this conversation. "Listen, would you like to see a movie tonight?"

The question seemed to surprise her.

"Or what about dinner?" he continued. "Let me take you to the Tavern."

"You've just bought me hot chocolate," she protested, "and invited me to a dance this Friday."

"Yeah, but you're right that we don't know each other that well. We should spend time together this week. Are you busy tomorrow afternoon? Do you like to ice skate?"

"No, I hate it."

"Do you bowl?" he asked, "or ski? I could get a car, and we could ski up at Black Moshannon."

"I'm terrified of skis," she told him.

"No, don't be," he replied. "I thought I'd be scared. I mean, I'm from the Midwest. It's flat. But Begler took me out skiing and showed me how, and it's really terrific. In fact we're leaving Saturday for the Poconos to ski at Split Rock."

He could see a bemused expression on Anne's face.

"What's the matter?"

"Nothing," she said, "I just didn't realize what dating you might entail."

"You don't *have* to ski," he assured her.

"Don't worry, I won't."

She was an unusual girl. He thought about her all week, so that by the time he arrived on Friday, corsage box in hand, to pick her up for the ball, he had grown to feel more intimate and familiar with her than the facts warranted. "You know?" he told her, "I don't even know where you're from, or what your father does." They were on their way across campus to the Armory. "I mean, I grew up in Chicago and Northern Indiana. My father's Director of Research of Standard of Indiana. That's why I came here to major in petroleum and natural gas, only it hasn't worked out." He bent to look into Anne's face. "So what about you?"

Her father, he found out, owned a little printing company in Philadelphia. Her mother ran a decorating business in Merion, where they lived. Originally they sent Anne to Shipley, but after a month among the sub-debs she pleaded with them to take her out and let her go to the public school where eventually she found a few kindred spirits. Coming to Penn State had been her idea. Joining the Kappas had been her mother's. "She buys me all my clothes," Anne said, "and I think she prays at night that I'll grow another four inches and lose weight. She'd love for me to be the belle of the ball."

"That's natural," Jerry said.

"At twenty? Looking the way I do? It drives me crazy that she won't accept what I am."

He understood that. In fact he understood it from the inside. "My family is that way, too," he said. "They're all Phi Beta Kappa. They'd like me to be a good student."

"*Familles, je vous hais,*" Anne said.

"What?"

"Family, I hate you."

"I love mine," Jerry said, "only I hate disappointing them, don't you?"

"It's more than that," Anne said. "I mean, I say it drives me crazy that mother won't accept what I am, but I don't accept it either."

"You mean you don't like yourself?"

"No."

"You should."

"Why?"

"Why?" he echoed. It seemed to him self-evident. "If you don't like yourself, who are you going to like?"

"Yeah, but how can you like yourself if you hate the way you look?"

"I don't know," he admitted.

"So don't sound-off about what you don't understand."

"You're a funny date," he told her.

"You asked me to this dance, I didn't ask you."

"Listen," he said, "I'm enjoying this. It's just that dates don't usually argue so much, or talk back the way you do."

As at Baroutsis, Jerry felt excited just talking to Anne, but taking her out and dancing with her was another matter. At the Armory when he turned to pin his corsage to her dress, she flinched away. And to make matters worse his corsage consisted of coral rose buds that looked terrible against her blue dress. "Gee, I should have asked you what you'd be wearing," he said. And as for the dancing, well, she was too short to begin with, and when he held her close he could feel her stiffening in his arms. If he relaxed his hold on her, she got out of step with him. Then, most of all, he couldn't feel the intoxication he felt whenever Pat was in his arms. He thought Anne had probably done all the things Pat did before a date—wash her hair, dab perfume behind her ears, and so on—but Anne wasn't at the right level for him to bury his nose in her hair or brush her ears with his lips. He found himself looking down at the top of her head, about the least erogenous zone a woman had. In fact he couldn't ever remember getting excited about the top of a woman's head. He had touched, caressed, fondled, kissed, nibbled, or licked virtually every other part of a woman's body, but never the top of a head. If Anne's hair had been thick and lustrous and beautiful, things might be different, but that was not the case. There were just those frizzy red curls to look at. The sad truth was that Anne presented about her least attractive side to a dancing partner.

And as if this were not enough, he kept seeing Pat in a slinky, cream-colored gown, dancing first with Moomaw, then with some other jerk, then with Moomaw again. As always, Pat stood out at a party, royally enjoying herself (at least when Jerry was looking her way), whereas Jerry could not be sure Anne was having a good time at all. He had arranged with various brothers to exchange dates, but each time he relinquished Anne, he felt she left him apprehensively, and when he reclaimed her she never floated back to his arms—as Pat always had—on a flood tide of social and sexual success.

During a break between sets he said to Anne, "Enjoying yourself?"

"Are you?"

"Want to know something? I'd like it better if we were side by side on the front seat of a car."

The idea seemed not to appeal to her, but he persisted. He had a brother who would lend him a car. They could drive somewhere. Get something to eat. Talk. Have a good time. Lots of people left these dances early. See, there was a couple going now. Sometimes people left early, and then came back. Anyway, it wasn't so early now. Why didn't they go? Unless, of course, she'd really like to dance some more.

Half an hour later, at the wheel of O'Dana's Studebaker, Jerry pulled off the road into the parking area on top of the mountain behind Pine Grove Mills. Through a fringe of bare trees he could see out into the dark valley with the clustered lights of State College in the distance. "It's beautiful up here," he told Anne, killing the car lights, and reaching to draw her closer to him.

"Now cut this out," she said.

That jarred on his mood. "I'm not trying anything," he protested. "I just want you closer to me."

"I'm near enough."

"We can't cuddle if you're going to sit way over there."

"I don't want to cuddle."

"Why not?"

"I just don't want to."

"Well, but why not?" he persisted. "I mean, you think I'm beautiful. You said so."

"Sunsets are beautiful, but that doesn't mean I want them pawing me."

Feeling in the dark in more ways than one, Jerry said, "Well, I think you're wrong."

"It's wrong not to neck with you?"

"I didn't say that."

"What are you saying?"

He said, "I'm just saying that if you like someone and he likes you, it's natural to hug and kiss a little."

"Well, maybe I'm not natural," Anne said.

Jerry had been thinking. "Listen!" he said, "have you ever necked with anyone? I mean, you said that in high school you only went out with a sissy. I bet he didn't try to neck with you."

Anne said nothing.

Sounding stern all of a sudden, Jerry said, "Have you ever been kissed?"

Anne remained stubbornly silent, sitting as far from him as possible.

"At least let me kiss you just once."

"No."

"I'll think you don't like me."

"Think what you want."

He said, "Girls who go out to balls expect to be kissed before the night's over."

No answer.

"I mean, how are you ever going to fall in love and get married if you won't even kiss?"

"Will you leave me alone?" she said.

"Leave you alone? On a date?"

"Just stop pestering me."

It was like being back in high school. "I'm not pestering," he said.

"Then what are you doing?"

Yes, what was he doing, he wondered. Was he trying to start up a new love affair? On the whole he thought not. So what was all this about? He said, "I guess it's just sort of automatic with me."

"Well, stop being an automaton."

"The thing is," he told her, "I don't feel natural if I haven't got someone I can hug and be in love with."

"Well, find someone else."

"I guess I'll have to," he said, and the next day he did.

CHAPTER 3

On Saturday he and Begler left early for Split Rock and skied until dark. Then they took hot showers, put on good clothes, ate dinner together, and settled down comfortably in the bar-lounge. Begler lit up a cigar. Jerry's foot tapped in time to the polka being played by a three-piece band in the next room, but he could see no one to dance with. All the women here seemed to belong to mixed parties like the one at the next table where a lively blonde with a crutch was entertaining everyone with an apparently hilarious account of how she had hurt her ankle. She sounded like fun, though not to dance with.

"There's one," Begler said.

His unerring eye had spotted a single woman across the room from them, sitting at a table for two. She looked interesting, framed by the black window against which she sat. Moreover, once he began to focus on her, Jerry had a curious sense that he knew her. Then she raised her glass, and it all came back to him. "That's Mrs. Whittington!" he cried.

"Who?"

"My freshman English teacher." On days when she returned a batch of themes, all bleeding internally with red ink, Mrs. Whittington used to lift her chin just like that woman. It had to be her! He couldn't be wrong.

"Your English teacher?" said Begler.

"I'm positive. I wonder what she's doing up here?"

"Go find out," Begler suggested. His own interest in her had cooled.

"She wouldn't remember me," Jerry said, still looking her way. "Anyway, her husband's probably with her."

"I don't see him."

Neither did Jerry. Furthermore, though he could not have said how, Mrs. Whittington looked alone. He said, "Some guys in class hated her, but I thought she was great." He thought of her as the Passionate Grammarian. She once gave him the most bizarre grade he had ever received—an F plus for a hastily written essay about the Cold War. Only an unusual woman could have come up with a grade like that.

"So go say hello."

"I really should," said Jerry.

She saw him coming, and now that he could see her full-face all his last, lingering, irreducible doubts vanished. Definitely it was Mrs. Whittington gazing at him with her calm, somehow far-seeing eyes that didn't seem to focus completely on things close up. He felt a smile forming on his face as he came to a halt beside her table. "You won't remember me," he said, "but I was in your class a couple of years ago. My name's Jerry Engels."

For a moment nothing happened. Then she said, "I do remember you. You wrote an essay about Lake Michigan."

Jerry smote his brow. "What a memory you must have!" He had gotten an A minus on that one.

"But I've forgotten your name. What did you say it is?"

"Jerry Engels," he repeated. "I just wanted to say I thought you were a terrific teacher."

She took that with a gracious nod. "Thank you. What grade did I give you?"

"Well, you didn't like all my papers as much as that one about the Indiana dunes. I got a final C."

"I'm sorry," she said.

"Oh, that's all right," Jerry assured her. "I never expect to do well in English."

She frowned at him. "You should."

"I know I should," he hastened to say. Then, repairing his slipping smile, he said, "Well, I just wanted to say hello. I couldn't believe it was really you up here."

"Why not?"

"Well, I mean . . ." He gestured around at the predominately collegiate crowd. "I mean . . ." He meant he didn't think English teachers liked to ski.

She said, "I remember you better now. You sat in the front row. You were always smiling."

Jerry nodded. "I smile too much," he admitted, "and I'm not even that happy."

That seemed to amuse her. "What are your secret sorrows?"

"I don't have any *secret* sorrows," he said, and then, since they seemed to be talking, he asked if he could sit down.

"Yes. Do sit down. And please tell me your name again? I'm terrible about names."

"Jerry Engels," he repeated. She nodded. He said, "I'm surprised you like to ski."

"For heaven's sake!" she exclaimed. "I grew up in Montana where we skied all winter."

"Montana!" Jerry could not keep the astonishment out of his voice.

"Is there something the matter with Montana?"

"No, but you don't look like someone from Montana."

Again he seemed to have amused her. "What do people from Montana look like?"

"And you don't sound like a westerner, either." She didn't. She had a pure, clear voice that went with her pure, clear complexion. Montanans, Jerry was convinced, had leathery skin.

"Actually, I'm not very western," she admitted, and then she explained that her parents were from New England, but had gone west to run a dude ranch. They sent her back east to school.

That sounded more like it to Jerry. "I was sure you were eastern."

She said, "I bet I can ride and ski as well as you can."

"I bet you can do better." She looked fit. "I'm terrible on horseback, and I only started skiing when I came east."

"You call this east?" she said.

"It's east of Chicago."

"Well, yes, but . . ." She let it drop. "And so are you still at Penn State?" He told her he was, and asked if she was still there. She was, she told him, though she might be looking for a new job next year. She had just finished her Ph.D. dissertation on William Blake.

"That's terrific," he exclaimed. "You should celebrate."

"I *am* celebrating." She explained that she was treating herself to this weekend.

"Alone?" he blurted out, and then said, "I'm sorry, that was rude."

"Yes, it was a little."

"But you do seem to be alone," Jerry pointed out.

"I am. I've divorced my husband."

He was not surprised. He had already checked her ring hand. Feeling more and more at ease with her, he said, "Can I buy you a drink? To celebrate with?"

She folded her hands over the top of her highball. "Thank you," she said, "I'm fine."

"Why don't we dance?" Jerry asked. She thought that over, and while she was thinking, he added, "I'm not just being fresh."

"I hope not."

"Only maybe you don't want to dance with a student?"

She gave him a pleasant enough smile and said she was comfortable where she was, and there, for the moment, things rested. To get them going again, Jerry said, "Blake. I like Blake." Then he recited:

> And we are put on earth a little space
> That we may learn to bear the beams of love.

She looked interested. "You know that poem?"

He nodded. "When I was growing up I knew this old German lady who thought everyone should be accomplished. You know— sing or play the piano, and have beautiful handwriting, and recite Goethe and Shakespeare. She made me memorize poems."

"Good for her."

"Now I like poetry." Jerry smiled. "I even make up poems myself."

"Do you?"

"Would you like to hear one?" he asked. Then, without giving her a chance to say no, he fixed her with his eye and explained that these were some lines composed on top of Mount Nittany when he climbed it to bury his Deke pin after a girl returned it to him. With that preamble, he cleared his throat and intoned:

The low sky and rising smoke of autumn leaves meet here,
On this mountain-top where I have climbed to lay my
        love to rest.
"You've changed," she said, handing me back my pin,
Which now I leave beneath the laurels and the leaves.
Love dies, but love is not dead.
It grows from every seed that sprouts or heart that yearns.

Silence followed his recitation. Mrs. Whittington moved her shoulders uneasily. Her chin came up as it used to in class when she was about to hand back papers or bawl the class out about something. The long line of her exposed throat and the tilt of her nose gave her an imperious beauty that went straight to Jerry's heart. He'd forgotten how striking she could be. Feeling oddly apologetic, he said, "The girl was named Laura, that's why I put in that bit about laurels. Actually there aren't any laurels up there."

"I know that."

Still smiling, Jerry said, "I guess you don't think my poem's very good."

She said, "Please don't take this the wrong way. It's just that I *can't stand* bad poetry."

For a moment he felt frozen with astonishment. Then he let out a yelp of laughter. "Wow!" he exclaimed, feeling his cheek as if she had slapped him.

She said, "I hope I haven't hurt your feelings."

"That did hurt." He laughed again. "What's funny is that I've recited that poem to girls who thought it was beautiful."

Again she moved her shoulders restlessly. "Well, now you've recited it to a girl who doesn't think it's beautiful."

"You're no girl," he observed.

She agreed with that. "In fact, I've been a woman for a long time," she told Jerry.

Not quite sure what she meant by that, he said, "In class you had some of the fellows buffaloed. You intimidated them."

"I'd like to have done more than that. I could have wrung some necks."

"Were we so bad?"

"It's the same thing as with your poem," she explained. "I hate sloppy thinking and bad writing."

"Then you must have hated me."

"I expect I did at times." She said it quite calmly and without animus. "But you were different."

"Different how?"

"Well, you sat there in front looking happy and eager all the time as if someone were about to give you a puppy to play with."

"Ouch!" he exclaimed.

"Have I hurt your feelings again?"

"Well, that's not very flattering," he pointed out.

She said, "Then, when I'd given you a low grade on some paper, you'd get a sweetly resigned look like St. Sebastian being shot through with arrows."

"Who?"

"St. Sebastian. He's the first Christian martyr. He's generally portrayed as a beautiful young man with arrows stuck into him at inviting angles."

Jerry said, "Oh." Then, feeling that she owed him something, he said, "I really wish you'd dance with me." This time she agreed.

She was as tall as he was, and broad-shouldered for a woman, but graceful, and light on her feet. He held her at a respectful distance—this was not a woman to get fresh with—and for a while neither of them said anything. Finally he said, "Tell me what's wrong with my poem."

Without missing a beat, she said, "It's lax, it's flaccid, it's sentimental. The feeling isn't earned. It comes from you and your life, not from the words themselves. It's a classic example of bad poetry."

"Well, what's good poetry?"

"*Tempt not the lord thy God, he said and stood.*"

"What?"

"Milton," she said. "There are thousands of lines of great poetry. *Foodless toads within voluptuous chambers panting, crawled. . . . My God where is that ancient heat towards thee/ Wherewith whole shoals of martyrs once did burn,/Besides their other flames?*"

He seemed to have touched a spring and let something loose in her. He could feel excitement in her body, and hear it in her voice. He remembered moments like this in class, but none in which she seemed to have so far forgotten herself. Almost chanting, she went on and on. Some of it seemed more like prose than poetry, but it was all exciting, and somehow violent. "*He asked for water, and she gave him milk; she brought him butter in a lordly dish, She put her hand to the tent pin, and her right hand to the workman's hammer, And with the hammer she smote Sisera, she smote through his head. Yea, she pierced and struck through his temples. At her feet he bowed, he fell, he lay. At her feet he bowed, he fell; Where he bowed, there he fell down dead.*"

Then, as if she were running out of gas, she said, "Oh dear!"

"Go on!" he urged, "don't stop." But he could feel her stopping herself, and falling back into the tame rhythm of the polka music to which they were dancing. "That was wonderful," he told her. "I wish I had your kind of memory."

She said, "It's nice of you to say so, but my memory isn't so perfect. You'll think I'm a complete fool, but will you tell me your name again?"

"Jerry Engels," he told her for the fourth time.

"Engel! Angel. I'll remember that," she promised.

"And what's your name?" he asked.

At first the question seemed to surprise her. Then she said, "Oh! Of course. I'm not Mrs. Whittington anymore. I'm Miss Grant again." Was he going to have to call her Miss Grant? Jerry wondered. Then she relieved him by saying, "Elizabeth Grant."

That night, as they lay side by side in bed, she told him her story.

The dude ranch in Montana barely broke even throughout the Depression. Her father's checks to the Oak Grove school in Vassalboro, Maine, often arrived months late, but Elizabeth had never been made to feel poor or unwanted by the Owens, who ran Oak Grove. They belonged to the Society of Friends. Mr. Owens was a state senator. They were wonderful people, and their school had been a perfect place for Elizabeth. Oak Grove was healthy, high-minded, and practical, all at the same time. It had its own stables and bridle paths. It emphasized winter sports. It prepared girls for college as well as for secretarial jobs. Elizabeth had loved it, and in common with half the girls in school her generalized love of Oak Grove had become focused into a particular crush on Mr. Mason, who taught English, coached tennis, and directed plays put on by the girls. Mr. Mason was a vigorous, curly-haired, cheerful, manly young man, happily married to his pretty wife, a former Oak Grove girl, who helped out in the office. Mr. Mason's love for his wife just added to his many attractions and made him seem even more ideally unattainable. At seventeen Elizabeth had adored him.

That winter, the winter of 1940, the girls of Oak Grove were putting on *Romeo and Juliet*. Elizabeth played Mercutio, partly because of her height and athletic skill with swords, and partly because she actually preferred Mercutio to Romeo. One day after rehearsal Mr. Mason asked her to stay behind and help him straighten up. Also he had something to say to her, though when it came to the point he simply kissed her with his customary energy and warmth. She had been too astonished to respond. "I'm afraid I'm in love with you," he told her with a smile. And at that point, as she saw her idol crumbling into human dust, she shoved him away from her with all her strength, which was considerable, and went storming off to see Mrs. Owens. Mrs. Mason, then seven months pregnant, was typing letters in the outer office. The sight of that wronged woman simply added to Elizabeth's indignation, and without asking permission, saying only, "I must speak to the Headmistress," she marched straight into Mrs. Owens's sanctum.

There, in scalding words made all the more passionate for having to be hushed so Mrs. Mason wouldn't hear, Elizabeth denounced her fallen idol so violently that at first Mrs. Owens believed that Elizabeth had actually been assaulted. And to Elizabeth it had been an assault from which she was still reeling. She told Mrs. Owens that Mr. Mason would have to be dismissed before he pawed some other girl. Mrs. Owens said, "He pawed you?" "Yes! And he kissed me on the lips!" Elizabeth cried out, bursting into uncontrollable tears. It was her first kiss.

"I feel sorry for Mason," said Jerry, eleven years later.

"Don't you think I do now?" said Elizabeth. "I think I ruined his life. He had to leave Oak Grove, and of course everybody thought something much worse had happened. The rest of that year was just a nightmare. The girls were all expecting me to get pregnant, and I was beginning to feel guilty over exaggerating it so."

"He picked the wrong girl to kiss," Jerry said. "What happened to him?"

Elizabeth groaned. "That's almost the worst part. He was killed in the war."

"Golly!" said Jerry, and he lay for a moment looking solemnly at the ceiling of Elizabeth's bedroom. Then he turned on his side to study her classic profile. "So how did you get from there to here?" he asked.

She sighed. "You really want to hear my whole life?"

"I certainly do," he told her.

"Well. . . ," and she began again.

From Oak Grove she went to Radcliffe on a full scholarship. The war killed the dude ranch. Her father managed to get a minor job with the Interior Department in Boise, Idaho, but he had not been able to help her at all. She was on her own in wartime Cambridge where she fell deeply in love with a sweet boy from Ozona, Texas, who was at Harvard studying in the Army's intensive Japanese language program. They shared a love of horses and nature. Elmer— that had been his name—was almost physically homesick for the dry air and wide open spaces of west Texas. He and Elizabeth went riding on hired hacks and sometimes picnicked in the woods around Lexington or Concord. She would recite lines from Thoreau, and Emerson—*If the red slayer think he slays, or the slain think he is slain*— and he would talk to her about the starry skies and the wind and the vast, empty landscapes he loved. He made love to her for the first time in the Concord woods, not far from Walden Pond. "It was scratchy, but nice," Elizabeth told Jerry.

It was her understanding that they were engaged to be married sometime in the future when the war was over. She looked forward to a life beside him in west Texas. It gave her something to hold onto when he shipped out, and it made her whole senior year at Radcliffe seem quite unreal. She would look at the old chestnuts and elms in Cambridge and think that in her future life she would never be sheltered by such trees, or walk on old brick sidewalks, or awaken to misty Cambridge mornings, or see ducks paddling on the still waters of the Charles. It lent a special topspin to the honor's thesis she wrote on John Donne's elegies. She graduated summa cum laude and for the summer went to stay with her parents in Boise, where, in September 1945, she got a letter from Elmer informing her that at last he was home in Ozona and about to marry a childhood sweetheart. He hoped she would understand.

"Did you understand?" Jerry asked.

"Oh, when I finished crying I guess I did. He was much simpler than I am. That's probably why he picked a local girl. He thought I wouldn't fit in, but I loved him so much I would gladly have spent the rest of my life in Ozona." Then she smiled reminiscently. "I almost did go there. I actually had a ticket. I was going to turn up at the wedding and when the minister invited anyone present to speak now or forever hold his peace, I was going to speak up and forbid the marriage, as in *Jane Eyre*."

"But you didn't go?"

"No, I didn't go."

Instead she went back to Radcliffe, where she began graduate work in English, and where she met Anthony Whittington, a Junior Fellow at Harvard. "He wasn't as beautiful as you are," Elizabeth told Jerry, "but he was a *much* better poet." He had already published in *Poetry* and in *Partisan Review*. F. O. Matthiessen had been heard to say that Whittington could be the American Dylan Thomas, or a new Hart Crane. Everyone expected great things from him. He expected them from himself. He cut a conspicuous swath through Cambridge in those immediate postwar months. Elizabeth felt flattered when he began to ask her out. When he proposed marriage, she was frankly surprised. She had not realized he loved her. She was not sure she loved him. He persuaded her, however, and they got married one March weekend in 1946. Their only witness was the wife of the J.P. who performed the ceremony. Then they ate dinner at the Vendôme in Boston and afterward went upstairs to the wedding suite, which Whittington had reserved for the occasion. He had a grand streak. They had dined on pheasant under glass and drunk Dom Perignon. Elizabeth's wedding preparations had consisted of buying herself the fanciest nightgown she could find in Filene's Basement. Wearing that nightgown and feeling almost virginal (Tony had never made love to her), she had emerged from the bathroom with her hair down, only to find Whittington stabbing the wedding bed with a knife. There were rents not just in the bedding, but in the mattress itself.

"But why?" Jerry asked.

Just what Elizabeth had wanted to know, but Whittington could not explain. He felt awful about it. When he saw her standing there in her new nightgown and long auburn hair, he dropped the knife and collapsed into a shaky huddle. She had to comfort him and soothe him before he could talk, and even when he began to talk he didn't make sense. They agreed to postpone their wedding night. The next day Whittington visited Father Feeney, then at the height of his influence as Catholic chaplain at Harvard. Whittington was a lapsed Catholic. Feeney soon fixed that. Next Father Feeney began to have private talks with Elizabeth, urging her to join the Church. His fundamental message was *extra ecclesiam nulla salus.*

"What?" Jerry said.

Elizabeth translated for him: Outside the church there is no salvation. Father Feeney believed it and preached it until his Catholic superiors shut him up. "He was a fascinating man," Elizabeth said, "all tense and passionate and packed into that hard shell of belief like a bomb about to go off." She was repelled by

Feeney's narrowness and fanaticism, but at the same time attracted by the strength of his convictions. At Tony's urging she continued to see him and to take steps toward being received into the Church so that she and Tony could have a proper Catholic wedding. All her undergraduate work on Donne and the other metaphysical poets had familiarized her with traditional Christianity, and though she found it hard to give up the Friend's Meeting House, late in the summer of 1946 she converted to Catholicism. She and Tony were quietly married a second time by Father Feeney himself. They honeymooned on Cape Cod.

By then she was already looking upon Tony as her cross to bear. Little did she know how heavy a cross. He was an alcoholic, something she had not noticed during all the evenings they spent together during the previous year. He could drink prodigiously without showing it. Then he would escort her back to her dormitory, kiss her a little clumsily and unsatisfactorily, and go cruising off into the night to pick up some young man. He was homosexual, something he confessed to her during their honeymoon.

"What a terrible time to do it!" Jerry exclaimed.

"Oh, he could make love to me," Elizabeth said, "but it was . . ." She searched for the word. "Never like this," she concluded.

"You should have left him."

She tried once, and it drove Tony to such despair that she feared he would kill himself. She was his one hope for a normal life. She was bound to him by a sacrament. She had to stay with him. He could not live without her. He loved her. He loved her more than he had ever loved anyone. Didn't she believe him? Couldn't she understand it?

"Do you think he really did love you?" Jerry asked.

"Love has a million shapes," Elizabeth said.

In any case she stuck with Tony for almost three years, the worst years of her life. They left Cambridge abruptly that winter when Tony got in trouble with the police for urinating in public and exposing himself in Harvard Yard. They went to Palm Beach and stayed for some months with Tony's mother, a lady who welcomed Elizabeth with the poised charm of a cobra about to strike. Then Tony's father, a regular army Colonel with a hog bristle mustache, came home from the wars, and they had another outbreak of bed stabbing and visits to priests. From Palm Beach Elizabeth and Tony went to Los Angeles, where Tony had his only job during the marriage, writing scripts for Metro-Goldwyn-Mayer. Tony's father had gotten to know someone in MGM during the war. Family pull got Tony the job, but the first treatment he turned in lost it for him. It was in doggerel verse and entirely obscene. "Tony could be very vulgar when he felt like it," Elizabeth said.

From Los Angeles they fled north to Sausalito, where Elizabeth worked in a lawyer's office supporting them while Tony wrote poetry. By then she was saving money to run away from him, only at that point an admirer who liked Tony's looks and believed in his talent gave them five thousand dollars, and Tony persuaded her to go off to Mexico with him. He would stop drinking; he was going to write an epic poem on the conquest of Mexico; everything would be different. Half believing him, she went along.

He tried to kill her in Cuernavaca. He was drunk. She easily knocked him out with the leg of a chair he had broken earlier in the evening. He liked to break things. They never had enough dishes.

And so that was it. She searched their rented house until she found Tony's secret cache of money. They had spent her running-away funds on the new used car they had bought to get to Mexico, and the five thousand dollars was in American Express checks made out in Tony's name, but Elizabeth knew that just as she had been hiding money from Tony, so he had been hiding money from her. His came to him from his mother and from various magazines where he published book reviews and poems. She unearthed it eventually and was relieved to find enough to get her back to Cambridge. While Tony slept it off on the floor, she packed two suitcases, and wrote him a note saying she couldn't go on any longer. Then she simply walked out. "I felt I wasn't helping him, and that I couldn't help him, and that living with him was just destroying me." She looked over at Jerry, "And do you know? I felt guilty. I still feel guilty about leaving him."

After a bit, Jerry said, "Boy, you've lived."

"You sound surprised."

He ran his hand through her hair. "Well, it's hard to imagine you conking a drunk." He kissed her. "You're wonderful," he told her. "You shouldn't feel guilty about leaving Tony. I mean, how many women would have put up with him for as long as you did?"

"You don't understand," Elizabeth said. "He could be charming, and he was very attractive." She turned on her side to look at Jerry. "Besides, it was my fault, too. I should never have married him. I knew I didn't love him the right way."

"What is the right way?" Jerry asked.

Her answer came as a quotation:

> Lay your sleeping head, my love,
> Human on my faithless arm;
> Time and fevers burn away
> Individual beauty from
> Thoughtful children, and the grave
> Proves the child ephemeral:

> But in my arms till break of day
> Let the living creature lie,
> Mortal, guilty, but to me
> The entirely beautiful.

"That's good," said Jerry. "I had an affair like that. She was the entirely beautiful to me, only I knew she wouldn't be true, and that I wouldn't be either."

"You understand Auden," Elizabeth remarked. "I didn't, then. I never accepted Tony the way he was. I was always trying to reform him and improve on him." She ran a hand over Jerry's chest. "It's easy to love perfection, only you can't find it in life. So we have to make do." She smiled. "When we have the chance," she added. "Do you know? You're the first man I've slept with in fifteen months."

"Fifteen months!" That explained something about her energy in bed.

"He was a colleague," she went on. "I thought maybe he'd ask me to marry him, but he didn't." She went on stroking Jerry's chest as she talked. "There have been other young men like you who have attracted me, but it wasn't mutual. It's hard for a woman, especially as she gets older."

"You're not old," Jerry told her. "I bet you're not even thirty."

"I'm almost twenty-nine. That's a big difference." She smiled at him. She ran a finger along the line of his jaw. "I've loved being with you tonight, but I don't expect you to marry me—if you're worried about that. In fact, I don't expect anything more. You've been perfect, the entirely beautiful, and you've listened to me like an angel, and I just want to thank you."

"Are you trying to get rid of me?" Jerry asked.

She smiled. "I'm trying to say goodnight."

"You want me to leave?"

"Well, it's very late, isn't it?"

It proved to be three a.m. Downstairs they had danced and talked until midnight. Then they had been making love and talking for hours upstairs. "It is late," Jerry admitted, "but I'll see you in the morning, won't I?"

She stretched her bare arms luxuriously. The sheet slipped, half exposing one pink and white breast. "The morning!" she said. "*Full many a glorious morning have I seen.*"

Jerry frowned slightly at this fresh outbreak of poetry. "I could spend the rest of the night here," he pointed out. "No one will know. You can kick me out at dawn before the maids get busy."

"No! No!" she said. "Go now. You've been wonderful. Good-bye."

So he went back to the room he shared with Begler, feeling slightly puzzled. It almost seemed as if she meant this to be a one-night stand.

CHAPTER 4

That was exactly what she meant it to be. When he called her room at ten o'clock Sunday morning, a cleaning woman answered. The party had checked out, she said. Was she sure of that? Jerry asked. Of course she was sure; did he think she wasted her time doing rooms that were going to be messed up again? Jerry hung up and hustled down to the desk. Yes, Miss Grant had checked out, the clerk told him. Well, had she left a message for Mr. Engels? "Let's see," said the clerk. He checked, and produced a sealed envelope with "Jerry Engel" written in a familiar, bold hand across the front. "Here you are," he said.

Jerry went into the coffee room, ordered himself breakfast, and then slit open his letter with a table knife.

Dear Jerry, it began,

It is six a.m. now, and for the last hour I have been sitting at the window of my room looking out at the dark trees and the snow glowing in the moonlight. When I finish this letter, I will pack up and leave here. Probably by the time you read this I will be halfway back to State College. I don't want you to follow me, or try to see me when you return.

I haven't slept since you left me. I've felt too happy to sleep. At times I've felt like rushing outside to make angel wings in the snow. You've made me feel young again, and silly, and I'm writing this letter to thank you once more and to explain why we should not see each other again.

I am too old for you, but it is not just that. My life is set now in an academic groove. I've worked off and on for six years to get my Ph.D. I want to teach poetry to young people, and maybe some day to write it myself. Poetry means more to me than anything but love. It's like what Keats said about the bursting of joy's grape within one's mind and heart. Maybe one day you'll know what I mean, because your feelings are keen and quick, but you are not literary in any way, or interested in books. My life of reading and writing and teaching has no place in it for someone like you, and you belong in other groves than those of academe. I think of you now as a sort of Pan, fresh from the blueberry patches and woods and lake you wrote about so feelingly in that essay on your hometown. You belong in that world, not in mine, and so I am bidding you a fond and loving farewell. Please accept it as my gift to you, a gift of freedom in exchange for the sweet gift of pleasure and happiness you brought me.

She signed herself "Elizabeth" without any "yours truly," or "love," or "sincerely."

Jerry read the letter while he was waiting for his bacon and eggs, read it again when he finished breakfast, and then read it a third time back in the room. Well, what about this? he thought. For want of anything better to do, he read the letter a fourth time. He had never had a letter like this. Rosalind had sent him a couple of sweet little notes when she was parting from him, but Marie never wrote at all, and Laura and Pat spoke what they had to say—which had nothing in common with what Elizabeth Grant had to say. *Pan?* he thought, a Midwestern Pan? How did you like that?

So what did he do now?

He was sitting on the edge of his unmade bed across from Begler's bed, also unmade. By then Begler had been out on the ski slopes for hours, leaving behind his keys, his comb, his pocketknife, and other objects one didn't necessarily ski with. They formed a trusting pile on the table between the two beds, in arm's reach of where Jerry sat. Jerry reached out for the key case. Its leather had a smooth, soft feel to it, soft and smooth as a baby's behind. —Of course, he could go find Begler on the slopes and tell him they had to leave now, but the odds of persuading Jeff to quit Split Rock early were approximately a googol to one. And the mere effort of trying to persuade Jeff would lead to arguments and backchat that Jerry just didn't feel in the mood for. So he wrote a little letter of his own that morning.

Dear Jeff, he wrote,

Something's come up, so I'm taking the car. I have to be in State College today. Maybe you can get a bus back. I'll call you tonight, and if necessary I can come pick you up tomorrow. Sorry if it's inconvenient, but it's something I can't help.

He signed it "Thanks, Jerry," left it on the bedside table, and then packed his overnight bag. Next he returned his rented skis. By noon he was on his way back to State College, rather enjoying this rare opportunity to drive the MG. Begler was very stingy about lending it.

At three o'clock that afternoon Jerry arrived at the Deke house. "Jeff's been calling every half hour," O'Dana reported.

"Yeah?" said Jerry.

"He claims you've stolen his car."

"He's crazy. I only borrowed it."

"Yeah, well you better call him at Split Rock. He sounds mad."

Jerry nodded and went into the phone booth, where he looked up the number of Miss Grant. She lived, he noted, on Fraser Street, almost in the center of town. Deciding it would be better to visit her than to telephone, Jerry left the booth. O'Dana was still hanging around. "Listen," said Jerry, "I'm going out. If Jeff calls again remind him that Weigert's in Shamokin for his birthday. He'd probably be glad to bring Jeff back."

"I'm not going to tell Jeff anything," O'Dana said. "You better call him."

"I can't talk to him now," said Jerry. "I'm too busy," and with that he went upstairs to brush his hair and freshen up after the drive. *Pan* he thought again, as he looked at himself in the dresser mirror. First David, now Pan. He shook his head. Then, thinking he really ought to dress up a little, he got out a new, pink, button-down shirt he had bought a few days before. He was still taking the pins out of it when Gossage, the chapter archon, stuck his head in the room to say that Begler was on the line. Jerry said, "Tell him to call Weigert in Shamokin."

"He's calling you, here," Gossage said.

"Oh, all right!" Jerry went to the second-floor telephone, grabbed the dangling receiver, and said, "Look, Jeff, I can't talk to you now, but Weigert's at home in Shamokin. Get him to pick you up, okay?" Then he hung up.

Gossage was sitting on Begler's bed when Jerry got back. "So what did Jeff say?"

"Nothing." Jerry slipped an arm into his new shirt. Down the hall the telephone began to ring again.

Gossage said, "I hope we're not making a mistake about tomorrow." Tomorrow the Dekes were going to celebrate Bob Weigert's twenty-first birthday by getting him drunk early in the evening at the Rathskeller, and then at midnight presenting him with a girl to be brought up from Altoona specially for the occasion. "You think old Bob can handle it?" Gossage asked. Jerry was considered an expert on these matters.

"Don't you?" Jerry said.

"Well, he says he's not a virgin, but he's got to be very inexperienced."

"She'll be good for him."

Houser stuck his head in the room. "Begler wants you on the phone, Engels."

Jerry, tying his necktie by then, said, "I'm not here."

Gossage said, "And I'm not sure I like the idea of bursting in on Bob at midnight. What if he's jacking off when we bring her in? Mildenhall says he hears Bob's springs squeaking every night." Gossage shook his head.

Houser joined in the discussion. "We're telling Bob to expect a surprise at midnight."

Gossage said, "A naked babe on a litter carried by four brothers in their jockstraps could be too much of a surprise."

Jerry left them arguing about it. As he passed the phone on his way out he replaced the dangling receiver on its hook.

Elizabeth lived in a boxy wooden building almost across from the Justice of the Peace. Originally it must have been a one-family house, but additions everywhere had turned it into an apartment building with a rusting fire escape running down one side. The lobby had damp rattan matting and four mailboxes. Elizabeth's was numbered Three. Evidently she lived upstairs.

The sight of the stairs awoke unpleasant memories in Jerry. It was a straight staircase with a strip of brown linoleum covering the steps. It looked just like the staircase leading up to the dentist office in Whiting, Indiana, where Jerry had his teeth straightened when he was a boy. For five years Dr. Vulmer tightened Jerry's braces every Thursday afternoon. Sometimes, despite all of Vulmer's meticulous care, there would be a wire just a tiny bit out of place that chafed the inside of Jerry's mouth for the next few days. He had hated his braces. Furthermore, the atmosphere in Dr. Vulmer's office disturbed him. Vulmer, a good-looking, fussy, finicky man, had some kind of neurotic relationship with his dental assistant, an ugly, middle-aged woman named Miss Tolan. Dr. Vulmer nagged at her and criticized her all the time, sometimes reducing her to tears, yet she never quit and he never fired her. They were like an unhappily married couple. And now, just when he didn't want to be thinking about them, they had popped back into Jerry's mind. Why?

And why was it so dark in the upstairs hall? And why was he trembling now as he looked at the metal 3 screwed to Elizabeth's door? To calm himself he breathed deeply. That made him notice that the hall smelled of soup and soap. Next he focused on a crack in the plaster above Elizabeth's door. He began to suspect this whole day was turning into a mistake. He rang the bell.

Nothing happened. Wasn't she home? Had he done all this for nothing? Then he heard footsteps. Thank God, he thought, she *was* home. Only what if she got angry that he had disobeyed her instructions not to try to see her in State College? Yet what kind of airy arrogance did it take to kiss a man off the way she was trying to kiss him off? And suddenly, as the door opened, Jerry felt very angry with Elizabeth.

"Why'd you leave?" he demanded. "Why'd you write me that letter?"

"Oh dear," she said, "I thought this might happen, but not so soon."

"You've ruined my whole day," he told her.

"You better come in," she said, stepping aside.

He preceded her down a short hallway into her main room where his first impression was of ugliness and disorder. All across one wall he could see books arranged higgledy-piggledy on long shelves. More books lay stacked on top of what looked like her dining-room table, a round, pedestal affair with lion's-paw feet. A couch, messily covered with a blue cloth, divided the room in half. The walls, where one could see them, were mud brown. It was a terrible room. "How long have you lived here?" he asked, turning to her.

"Why have you come?" she said.

That brought him to order. "Your letter!" he said, "that letter! What kind of letter is that to write someone on the morning after? You didn't even get my name right. It's Engels with an ess."

She seemed to grow an inch in height and to put on a fresh layer of dignity as she responded. "I was trying to be kind and considerate of your feelings."

"Considerate!" he cried. "I loved you last night, and you loved me."

"I wrote that letter in a spirit of love."

"Some love," he replied, "telling me not to try to see you again."

"I explained why."

"You explained nothing," he told her. "If you love someone, you don't tell him to go jump in the lake and blow on his Pan pipes. I mean, that was a terrible letter to write me, and this is a terrible room."

She said, "I'm trying to be patient with you, because . . ."

He interrupted, "I'm trying to be patient, too."

"You're evidently very angry," she said.

"No I'm not, but I'm upset. You've upset me."

"I'm very sorry it's ending this way," she said.

"Ending? Nothing's ending," he said. "You don't think I'm going away, do you?" She had begun to move toward her door as if to escort him out. "I'm not going," he announced.

She said, "I think you're forgetting where you are and who you're talking to."

"I'm in the apartment of the woman I slept with last night," Jerry said, "and I don't see why you keep it so dark here." The day, over-cast to begin with, was fading toward dusk, but the only light Eliza-beth had on was a desk lamp beside the typewriter on which Jerry could see she had been working, maybe writing another of her great, loving letters. And, as if to annoy him even further, she was wearing a brown cardigan. He hated cardigans.

She said, "I've had some experience in dealing with young men who presume too much, and try to go too far. I would hate to have to treat you the same way, but I will unless you leave."

Without a word Jerry sat down at the book-piled table.

She looked at him a moment before she burst out, "You fool! You utter ass! To force your way in here and spoil the memory of something beautiful that we shared."

"Memory!" he yelled. "Memory?" He still had marks of her fingernails on his back. What did she mean *memory*? "That's no memory," he told her.

Bitterly, she said, "You're certainly doing your best to destroy it."

Jerry said, "You talk like love is a one-night stand. Is that your idea? People meet, hop in bed for the night, part in the morning, and share a beautiful memory for the rest of their lives? Well, it's not my idea."

In acid tones she asked, "And what is your idea of love?"

He couldn't answer her, because in his anger he couldn't speak of love. Only after a tongue-tied moment, and then in a quite different voice, he said, "This. This is love. Wanting to see you again, wanting to be with you. That's all I want. Let me stay. Don't make me leave."

It was seven o'clock before thoughts of Begler, stranded at Split Rock, began to bother Jerry. "Oh, say, listen," he said to Elizabeth, "is it all right if I use your phone for a minute?" Then, with her permission, he rolled out of bed, found her telephone on the kitchen wall, and dialed the Deke house. Weigert answered on the second ring. He frequently answered the phone for reasons no one understood, since he got very few calls of his own.

When he heard it was Jerry, he said, "Wow, is Jeff mad! He's looking for you right now."

"So you picked him up?"

"Lucky I was that close, hunh? But you better watch out. He's after your hide."

"Tell him I'll see him later," Jerry said. He hung up, checked the refrigerator, and went back to Elizabeth's bedroom.

The room, lit mainly by a shaft of light shining through the open door to the bathroom, was full of shadows and dark corners. He could see a hump in the bedclothes over Elizabeth's feet and legs, but her head was in darkness, and as he looked at her from the doorway to her main room, Jerry could not even be sure she saw him. Then she said, "It's Sunday night, but I'm thinking of lines from 'Sunday Morning' about how *wakened birds, before they fly, test the reality of misty fields by their sweet questionings*. I feel like that, as if I ought to put my hands on the window pane, or touch the ceiling to be sure I'm in this room."

"You're here," he told her.

"Well, I'm glad you think so."

He moved forward, and sat on the edge of her bed. Their hands met. "I hate to say it," he told her, "but I'm hungry. Aren't you?"

She said, *"For he on honeydew hath fed, and drunk the milk of paradise."*

"I need something more substantial," Jerry pointed out. "We both do. How about if I make us an omelet? You've got eggs."

"An omelet," said Elizabeth. "'The Omelet of A. MacLeish.'"

"You're slap-happy," he told her.

"It's ridiculous," she agreed. "I feel boneless."

"Well, we're both empty," he pointed out, "and you haven't had any sleep. I'm going to make an omelet." Without further parlaying he went back to her kitchen.

It needed almost as much work as her main room. Dirty dishes were stacked in the sink. The garbage had not been taken out recently. Elizabeth would be having cockroaches if she didn't watch out, and he doubted she would find some poem to celebrate them. Though maybe she would. If anyone knew a beautiful cockroach poem, it would be Elizabeth. She had a line for every occasion. Being in bed with her was her was like being in bed with *Bartlett's Quotations*—though more fun. He set to work.

He was busily stirring up the eggs in a big saucepan when he heard her behind him. He looked over his shoulder, and saw her standing in the doorway in a belted robe, her hair combed and pulled back into a ponytail. "It'll be ready in a minute. I've set the table," he told her. "You can go sit down."

She said, "You're wearing my apron."

He said, "Well, listen, have you ever cooked without anything on? It can be very painful."

"It's so sweet to see my apron strings touching your bottom."

"Go sit down," he told her again. "You're distracting me."

"I shouldn't let you do everything."

"You can clean up," he told her. On second thought, he said, "Or maybe you can't."

"Hmm. Do I detect some criticism of my housekeeping?"

"Oh no!"

"Don't you know that *a sweet disorder in the dress kindles a certain wantonness?*"

"We're not talking clothes, we're talking garbage here, and dirty dishes, and rotting tomatoes in the refrigerator. I couldn't find coffee, either. I'm making us tea."

"I could kill for a cup of tea," she said.

Their meal consisted of a light omelet, crackers, cheese, some apples, and a pot of tea. He was glad to see that when it came to the point, Elizabeth ate her share with a healthy appetite, though several times she paused to say, "This is heavenly. Being loved, being fed, being waited on. I can't tell you how I feel."

He said, "When I've got time I'm really going to do something about this apartment. Doesn't your landlord give you a decorating allowance?"

She was eating an apple. "I don't know. I don't think so."

Jerry said, "In Chicago good landlords generally allow tenants the equivalent of a month's rent every year for repapering and painting and so on. You should get something off your rent to pay for painting these walls."

"They are awful," she agreed. "That's why I've tacked up so many pictures and postcards."

"They look awful, too," he told her. "It's cluttered here."

She gave a long, luxurious sigh. "Well, I can't worry about it now. I can't worry about anything, even what's going to happen to us."

But just saying that made them both think about their future. Jerry was the first to bring it up. "What would the university do if they found out about you and me?"

She said, "Well, this isn't Oak Grove in 1940, but even so it would finish my chances for tenure. Teachers have been fired for sleeping with students."

Jerry said, "It's always love that gets people in hot water. If you look out for yourself all the time and never go overboard about anyone else, you can sail right through life and end up rich and respected."

Elizabeth smiled across the table at him. "What makes you say that?"

"I believe it," he said, "I think it's true. Love's not understood in this country, and lovers aren't respected. You know how I was described in my high school yearbook? *Swimmer, dancer, lover. Everyone's favorite goof-up*. I mean, my best friends wrote that about me. *Goof-up!* I was very pained."

"*The lunatic, the lover, and the poet*," Elizabeth murmured.

"Exactly," said Jerry, "and we're always in hot water. My roommate's going to kill me for taking his car this morning."

"You took a car?"

"To follow you. I mean, I don't have my own car this semester. It's in Haverford."

Elizabeth nodded dreamily. He felt she wasn't listening. "Can I stay here tonight?" he asked. "I just don't feel like fighting Begler this evening."

That got her attention. She said, "Well, I'm afraid my landlady lives in the building."

"She won't know I'm here."

Elizabeth looked uncertain.

"Anyway, you can't keep kicking me out and kissing me off."

"You are a little hard to get rid of," Elizabeth conceded.

"So it's all right if I spend the night?"

She didn't say *yes*, and she didn't say *no*. She let him stay, but when they were back in bed again, she said, "How long do you think this can last?"

He had never been asked that before. He said, "I used to think a love affair would last forever."

"We all begin that way," Elizabeth told him.

"You're making me feel very sad."

"Don't! Don't!" and suddenly she was holding him tightly. "No, don't," she said again, "don't let me make you sad when you've made me so happy."

On Monday morning he went straight from Elizabeth's apartment to class. He stayed on campus all morning, eating lunch at the Temporary Union Building. Afterward he killed some time playing pinball. He told himself he was not afraid of going back to the Deke house to face Begler's wrath. Begler could not really hurt him. Jeff boxed better than Jerry did, but Jerry was stronger. He could always wrestle Jeff to the ground and pin him. The worst that might happen would be a black eye or a bloody nose, and what difference did they make? A black eye even lent a certain distinction. It made a fellow look like the man with the eye patch in the Hathaway shirt ads. A patch or black eye showed that you had lived. He wouldn't even mind getting his nose broken, Jerry decided, but somehow he just didn't *feel* like fighting. He wondered why.

It could be that he was afraid of what Elizabeth might think if he turned up scarred by battle. Now that she loved him—or at least had learned his name—he would have to be on his best behavior. He felt a rush of gratitude toward Elizabeth, and toward love itself. He felt that already love was at work on him, making him into a finer, nobler person. Abruptly he abandoned his pinball game with one ball left to shoot. Outdoors, in an ecstasy of sorts, he scooped up a handful of frozen snow and rubbed his forehead and the back of his neck. Then he headed across campus toward the Sparks Building.

Elizabeth shared an office with three other teachers. Jerry walked by the open door, and saw her at her desk in a far corner with a student in his ROTC uniform sitting beside her, their heads bent over a paper. Jerry stood with his back to the wall, beside the door, out of her sight, hoping to hear what Elizabeth was saying, but all he could hear was a middle-aged woman instructor at a desk nearer the door, talking to a Theta Jerry knew slightly. The subject seemed to be *Oedipus Rex*. The lesson of that play, the instructor said, was always to tell adopted children that they are adopted. If Oedipus had known he was adopted everything might have worked out differently. For one thing he would have been more careful about marrying an older woman like Jocasta.

Yet there were reckless people, Jerry thought, gamblers, and drivers like Begler, who almost courted danger. Danger was a sort of woman. There was something alluring and seductive about danger. Men like Begler, who didn't really love women, loved danger instead, and perhaps got as much a thrill from danger as other men got from women. Oedipus could have been that sort.

The Theta came out of the office and went to the water fountain across the hall. Jerry joined her there to say hello. Then he resumed his place beside the office door.

He could hear Elizabeth now. She was summing things up. The paper she was discussing with her student had been written backward and upside down, she said. She couldn't possibly give him more than a D plus for it. She sounded regretful, as if she yearned to give him a C minus. Jerry could hear the fellow getting to his feet. Elizabeth had a parting shot for him. She advised him next time to do his thinking beforehand rather than afterward. Moments later he came out looking hot and bothered.

Should he go in just to say hello? Jerry wondered. On the whole he thought not, yet it seemed dumb just to hang around without saying anything to her. He should really go in, he felt, but just then a tall male instructor came down the hall and turned into the office. Elizabeth said, "Hello, Mark," and Mark said hello to Elizabeth and to the other woman in there, and it seemed to Jerry that he might be interrupting a social moment if he dropped in now. He walked past the open door again, but Elizabeth was talking to Mark and didn't look around. She was busy. Her time was fully occupied. She had already told him she would be working all evening, and that he couldn't come see her. "Anyway, we both need to sleep tonight," she said with a smile, and it was true. He had not been getting enough sleep. He felt less peppy than usual. He checked his watch and decided there was time for a quick workout in the weight room before he had to model in Life Drawing. A workout always refreshed him.

An hour and a half later he was sitting in the dressing room models used, oiling his torso and limbs. Anne Player had told him he glowed when he undressed. Well, he had a surprise for her. That glow came from the baby oil he used, not some inner radiance. Would she be disappointed by the truth? How did she feel about him, anyway? He realized he had not given her much thought since Friday.

Normally he didn't think at all as he posed. Part of the whole excitement and pleasure of posing came from not having to think as he grasped a spear, or crouched on one knee, but this Monday as he assumed first one position and then another, Jerry could feel some kind of little buzz going on in the back of his mind, like a fly in a closed room, as thoughts about Anne Player contended with his usually mindless, purely physical performance on the platform.

When class was over he approached Anne and said, "I'm sorry I offended you Friday."

She said, "*I'm* sorry I was so negative."

He smiled in response. "Wait while I dress," he told her, "and we'll go to the Creamery." Then, a short while later, as they walked side by side up Shortlidge Road, he said, "I should have understood you didn't mean anything by saying I'm good-looking."

"I said you're beautiful, and I meant it," Anne replied.

"That's my point," he told her. "It's *all* you meant. Normally a woman would mean more."

"Like what?"

"She'd mean she's attracted, or that she thinks I'm sexy. I mean, for most women a good-looking man is nothing like a sunset. He has arms and legs, and a body. She's not just being an art critic when she tells him he's beautiful."

"Well, I can't help what other people mean." Anne sounded annoyed.

"It's natural for them to mean more."

"It shouldn't be."

Jerry said, "You're just not attracted to men, but if you were attracted, you'd know what I'm talking about."

Anne stopped and looked up at him. "Why do you say that?"

"Say what?"

"That I'm not attracted to men."

"Well, are you?" Jerry asked.

She said, "Just because I didn't want you to grab me and kiss me Friday night, you think I don't like men?"

"Well, do you?"

"I just don't want to be pawed," she said.

"All right! Okay!" said Jerry. They resumed walking, but Anne wasn't finished with the subject.

"It's very unfair of you to say I don't like men. I do. I like you."

"I know you do."

"Then why do you bring this up?"

Speaking carefully, he said, "All I meant to say was that I should have realized you like me and that you think I look great, but that you're not physically attracted to me."

"You think I *ought* to be?"

"Wow!" Jerry raised his arms in surrender.

"What's that mean?"

"It means I want to buy you an ice-cream cone." They had arrived at Borland.

"I don't feel like one."

"Don't you want anything?"

She said, "I want to go back to Simmons." She pivoted, and started back down Shortlidge. When Jerry turned to follow her, she stopped. "You don't have to come with me."

"I want to."

She started to say something, stopped herself, and struck off at an angle across Shortlidge and out into the fields. Jerry kept pace with her. Finally he said, "Look, if you're upset about something, why don't you tell me?" He got no response to that. "It's about not being attracted to men, isn't it?"

She said, "Please leave me alone, Jerry."

"You shouldn't be alone," he answered. "Are you worried that you're attracted to women?"

That stopped her. "How can you ask a thing like that?"

"Well, are you?"

Her expression seemed to shatter in a dozen different directions as she said, "I don't know!"

That didn't make sense to him. How could she not know something like that? "You must know," he told her, and then he realized she was so choked up by feeling that she could hardly speak and that what she needed was to be hugged, not talked to. "Hey, Anne," he said, putting his arms around her, "it's all right." She resisted him at first, and then suddenly she was hugging him back and weeping in his arms.

Fifteen minutes later she had calmed down enough to talk to him more or less coherently and rationally. For years she had been more and more afraid of her reactions to other women. She should never have let her mother persuade her to go out for a sorority at Penn State. She should have stayed in the kind of social group she had made for herself in high school, a mixed group held together by their fears of the same sex rather than by attraction to the opposite sex. "I'm so afraid," she kept saying. "I'm just so afraid." And now here she was at Penn State actually living with girls like Pat Gaheris, watching them wash their hair, and shower, and even shave their armpits as they got ready for dates. "I hate them!" she cried. She should never have accepted the bid they had made her—a bid made because of her clothes, because of her intelligence, because of her family, and because every sorority seemed to need at least one ugly duckling to set off the beauty of the swans. "I'd like to die," she said at one point. She did die every weekend as her sisters dolled themselves up and went off to dance and to have a good time. She died as she heard them gossip about boys, and exchange knowing tidbits not meant for her ears. Or, sometimes, meant for her ears alone, because she had become a kind of good sister Anne to some of the prettier and dizzier Kappas. Her role was to listen to these popular sisters describe the complications of their romantic lives and then to give them sensible advice, the kind of advice an unmarried librarian aunt might be supposed to come up with. "I hate it!" she cried, "I just hate it!" She hated it because she wanted to be popular and to have a good time herself. Most of all she hated it because her sisters had what she wanted for herself—long legs, slim waists, perfect skin and hair. "They're so beautiful!" Anne moaned.

"You should tell them," Jerry said.

"Are you crazy?"

"Well, it doesn't help to tell me I'm beautiful."

Anne touched her forehead as if to check whether she was feverish. "I can't believe this conversation is happening."

"It's good for you."

"I don't know why you're so understanding," she said.

"My freshman roommate fell in love with me," Jerry explained. "I mean, I know all about this."

Anne looked at him curiously.

"You can't tell how people will react," he went on. "You could have a sister who'd be glad to know how you feel. Who feels the same way."

Anne shook her head. "Jerry, I can't go around telling girls I think they're beautiful, and anyway I'd be terrified if anyone responded. I'm afraid. Don't you understand?"

He said, "You're not afraid of me, are you?"

"You?"

"Me."

She looked up at him as if she'd never seen him before. Then she looked away. "Oh, Jerry, I just don't know where I am. I'm so confused."

"Listen," he said. "We'll go out to dinner. I'll take you to dinner. Do you like lobster? We can go to Tyrone. There's a restaurant there that has live lobster."

She said, "Jerry, what are you talking about?"

"I'm talking about dinner. And then we'll see how you feel. Can you sign out till midnight?"

She nodded helplessly.

"I'll have to get a car," he went on, "but that should be no problem." Elizabeth wouldn't be using hers. "And we'll just see what happens," he concluded.

When she didn't respond to that, he said, "And nothing has to happen. I mean, that's the point. You're safe with me. You've got nothing to be afraid of."

"I've never felt this way before," Anne said, "like I'm going to pass out or something."

"You'll see. It'll be fun. We'll have a great evening."

He hit a slight snag, however, when he telephoned Elizabeth from the lobby of Simmons Hall to ask if he could borrow her car for the evening. "My car?" she said. He explained that something had come up. A friend of his was in trouble and had to be cheered up and taken out. He needed a car for the night. He was a very safe driver, he added. He had been driving since he was fourteen, with only one serious crash to blemish an otherwise perfect record, and the crash had been the fault of the other driver.

His words didn't seem to convince Elizabeth. "Well, I don't know," she said.

"If you'd rather not lend it, I could probably borrow one somewhere else," he said, "only you told me you'd be working this evening, so I knew your car would be free."

"Yes, but why do you need a car?" she asked.

"To take out this friend. She's terrifically upset and I want to buy her a good dinner at La Villa in Tyrone."

In tones more doubtful than ever, Elizabeth said, "It's a girl?"

She couldn't be jealous, Jerry thought. Jealousy was beneath her. He said, "She's someone I know from one of my classes, and she's going through a kind of crisis. I mean, she really needs help, but if you're afraid about your car . . ."

"It just seems a little strange," Elizabeth said.

"But you'll lend it?" he said, on a rising note of hope.

She agreed to lend it, though when he dropped by her apartment to pick up the key and to find out where the car was parked, she made him sit down for a minute. "Was that you walking back and forth in front of the door to my office this afternoon?"

He frowned at the question. "I wasn't walking back and forth."

"Why were you there?"

He said, "If you saw me, why didn't you look at me?"

"You could see I was busy."

"And I didn't interrupt you," he pointed out.

"You looked in, and then you must have stood by the door for a while, and then you went to the water fountain, and then you stood by the door again before you finally went away."

"So you knew all along that I was there?"

She said, "You can't behave this way, Jerry. I can't have you hanging around my office, and calling up and dropping by here to borrow my car.

"If you don't want to lend it . . ." he began.

"No, I agreed." She handed him her spare key. "But we'll have to talk about this," she added, in tones that reminded him so strongly of how his mother began her reproofs that he instinctively straightened up and assumed a look of hurt innocence.

"I'm not a child, you know."

She gave him a considering look. "No, you're not."

He had left Anne at the New College Diner while he went to pick up the car key from Elizabeth. He reclaimed Anne and piloted her back around the corner onto Fraser Street to the car Elizabeth had pointed out to him from her front window. It was a clunky-looking old Hudson. "I haven't been in one of these for years," he said to Anne. He helped her in, and then spent some time studying the dashboard and trying out the gears and lights and the feel of the brakes. "These used to be good cars," he said, "but . . ."

The engine started up with a clatter of tappet valves. Elizabeth needed some Bardahl in her motor, and he felt pretty sure the clutch cable should be adjusted. More work for him to do when he got the time. Then he flicked on the lights, eased out from the curb, and turned west onto College Avenue.

Beside him, Anne said, "I know I can't eat a thing tonight."

CHAPTER 5

Jerry ordered her a lobster dinner anyway. Then, as the waitress was about to leave, he said, "And bring us martinis now. You like martinis, don't you?" he asked Anne. She didn't know, she had never had one. "You'll love them," Jerry assured her. "Very dry," he told the waitress. "And make mine a double." Then, when the waitress was gone, he smiled at Anne. "Well, isn't this better?"

"Better than what?"

"Better than eating with your sisters at Simmons."

Anne looked around La Villa, shrugged at what she saw, and said that she guessed so. Jerry said, "I know it's better for me. I love my brothers, but it's hard for men to be really intimate. There's too much competition and argument and punching each other. That's why I like women better. Women are nicer than men. They're more lovable."

Anne said nothing.

"In fact, it's probably natural for women to like each other more than they like men," Jerry went on, "so you shouldn't blame yourself."

"Jerry, can we talk about something else?"

"We can talk about anything you want, only why don't you want to talk about that?"

"I just don't."

"It's good to talk about things that trouble you. I used to tell my sister everything." He beamed at Anne. "Her name is Anne, too. And if I didn't tell her, she'd worm it out of me."

"I don't want you worming things out of me."

"I already have."

"Well, aren't you satisfied? Do you have to go on?"

"No, but there's something I want to say. I mean, you don't know much. I mean, you're a virgin, aren't you? You don't know what it's like to be with a man. You know what I mean?"

"I get the idea."

"So if you want to find out—if you're ever curious—just tell me, and I'll show you. You know what I'm saying?"

A hitherto silent customer at the next table seemed to know exactly what Jerry was saying. He burst out, "That's outrageous! That's the worst thing I've ever heard! What a terrible thing to say!" It was a middle-aged man who had been quietly sipping after-dinner coffee with his wife while apparently drinking in Jerry and Anne's conversation. Now he swiveled around to glare at Jerry.

Who said, "This is a private conversation."

"It's a disgusting conversation." The man shifted his attention to Anne. "Does your father know you're going out with a boy like this?"

The man's wife said, "Don't talk to them, Henry."

Henry looked back at Jerry. "If she were my daughter I'd fix your wagon good."

Mrs. Henry was getting to her feet. "Henry!" she said again. Reluctantly Henry rose to follow her toward the cashier's desk. He had a parting shot for Jerry. "You should be ashamed of yourself."

Then he was gone, leaving behind a pool of silence eventually rippled by Anne, who said faintly, "They were horrible!"

"Well, I should have lowered my voice," Jerry admitted.

"But to talk to you that way!"

"I've been talked to worse than that."

It seemed to surprise her. "You have?"

"By the police. By fathers. Even by girls. You should have heard Pat."

The Henry interruption changed the atmosphere, so that when their drinks arrived things proceeded in a more normal way. Jerry saluted Anne with his martini. "To us!"

Anne took a cautious sip. "Yuck!" she said. "It tastes like medicine."

"I thought so too the first time, but you get used to them fast."

"What's the point?" Anne asked. Then she said that in high school she had a friend who loved to drink. He regularly stole whiskey from his father's liquor cabinet. Sometimes he had whiskey with him at school. Once during lunch in the school cafeteria he offered her Scotch. "I thought I'd die," she said. It had taken her forever to swallow the mouthful she incautiously accepted, and then she was terrified the teachers would smell it on her breath. "There's the story of my life," she said. Everything she did frightened her.

"Yeah, but you go ahead anyway," Jerry pointed out.

Anne shrugged.

"You're actually pretty brave," Jerry told her.

"Rah! Rah!" Anne took another sip of her martini, and made a face.

"You don't know how to take compliments, do you?"

She admitted she didn't. Her high school crowd spent its time wisecracking about themselves and each other, and making fun of the athletes and popular boys and girls. They had not sat around bandying compliments.

Jerry said, "I was the sort of person you made fun of. I was an athlete. I was popular. And now here we are together."

"I don't know why you're being so kind."

"Because I like you."

Anne shook her head dubiously, as if there were no accounting for tastes.

He said, "You're down on yourself for no reason at all. You can draw. You're talented. You're smart. You're probably a lot smarter than I am. You have no reason to feel bad about yourself."

"Will you stop it?" she said.

"No! Listen!" Then he declaimed:

> Never fear the thing you feel,
> Only by love is life made real.

"Did you just make that up?"

"No, it's by Ella Wheeler Wilcox."

"Who's she?"

"I don't know. A poet. I found that in an anthology, and it's right. Love makes life real. And it's right to love beauty. You should be glad you find girls beautiful."

Anne said, "I thought we were going to get off this subject."

"Well, it's just that I think people should talk about what's interesting. I mean, I hear guys telling their dates about football games and cars and I feel sorry for the girl."

With a return of the spirit he liked to see in her, Anne said, "You can talk to me about cars all you want. I'd be grateful for a little boredom tonight."

Their meals arrived—two platters of lobsters red with anger at being boiled alive. "You want bibs?" the waitress asked. They let her fasten bibs around their necks. Jerry ordered another round of martinis. Anne refused a second martini so he ordered her a glass of white wine instead.

Then for a while eating occupied them almost to the exclusion of conversation. Anne cracked the claws of her lobster and emptied its body of meat more efficiently than Jerry did. He was impressed. She obviously knew her way around inside a lobster. At one point he said, "I didn't know there was any meat in there." Anne was finding meat in what he thought of as the head of the lobster. She explained that there was good meat at the base of each leg. They cleaned their platters at almost the same time. "So you did have an appetite," Jerry said with approval.

He ordered them slices of hot pecan pie for dessert. Then, as an afterthought, he told the waitress to bring them Benedictine. Benedictine was a recent discovery of his. "You'll love it," he promised Anne. In the event, she disliked it even more than she had disliked her martini. Jerry had to finish her Benedictine as well as his own. Then he called for the check, at which he stared in a puzzled way for a minute or two.

Anne leaned forward and lowered her voice. "Is something the matter?"

"I don't have enough money," Jerry admitted. It was all those drinks that had undone him.

"I have some."

Jerry was not surprised. He knew that in the Kappa suite girls all advised each other to take money with them in case their dates passed out or got rough and they had to take cabs home. "How much?" he asked.

"Ten dollars."

"Good." They wouldn't have to do dishes, or whatever the Villa made you do when you couldn't pay. Jerry actually had a dime left over, which he gave to the waitress on his way out. Smiling apologetically he said, "This is all I have left."

Then they were outdoors in the cold night air scented by the Tyrone Paper and Pulp Works. Jerry inhaled deeply. Tyrone always reminded him of Whiting, Indiana, where he'd spent his early years. He liked industrial smells. There were few sensations he didn't like, or at least find interesting enough to provide food for thought. Even not having enough money to give the waitress a real tip intrigued rather than embarrassed him. He had just realized that being poor was like being naked and exposed. It quickened one's senses. "What do you want to do now?" he asked Anne.

"Aren't we going back to campus?"

"You signed out till midnight," he reminded her.

They crossed the street and got into the Hudson, where he sat for a moment behind the wheel without starting the motor or turning on the lights.

"Are you drunk?" Anne asked.

"No. I never get drunk." Then honesty compelled him to admit, "Well, I do, sometimes, but I'm not drunk now. I just don't know where to go."

"I think we should go home."

He didn't. "I think we should talk." Some of his best, most intimate talks had been at night, driving around with high school buddies, or with girlfriends. "Let's just drive," he said, "and talk some more."

Anne said, "Jerry, if you're going to start up again about sex, I'll scream."

"All right, you choose what to talk about."

He started to drive slowly out of Tyrone on the road to Seven Stars. Beside him Anne maintained her silence. Ahead the widening cone of Elizabeth's headlights lit up the leafless underbrush and low snow banks along the highway. Finally Jerry said, "This car belongs to a woman I met at Split Rock on Saturday."

"And she already lets you borrow her car?"

"Well, yeah. Why not?"

"I don't know. I don't think I'd lend a car to someone I'd just met."

"Well, we spent the night together," Jerry explained.

"Oh." Then after a moment Anne said, "You've slept with Pat, too, haven't you?"

"I'm not sure you should ask me that."

"Well, haven't you?"

"I don't even see why you want to know."

"Because I don't know anything!" she burst out. "And you do. You said you do."

"And you said you didn't want to talk about sex."

Anne didn't reply.

"You see?" he said. "Sex is interesting. You're curious. You want to know."

"So all right, tell me. What's it like to sleep with a woman?"

Jerry mused for a while. Finally he said, "Well, it's wonderful. You're in each other's arms. There's nothing between you, nothing separating you anymore, you're together. Sometimes I feel like I'm her and she's me. We're one." His voice changed. "Only that doesn't happen all the time. I mean, I feel sorry for a lot of girls. They don't feel that way. They're afraid. They feel guilty. I was at the Delaware shore once at a party where a Goucher girl seemed to like me, so I went out on the beach with her and we began to neck, and finally

she asked me to spank her. That's what she wanted, a spanking."
He shook his head over the memory. "I felt terrible doing it."

"You did it!"

"Maybe I shouldn't have." He gave a sigh. "I mean, I didn't get
much out of it, but she did. It excited her. She began moaning,
Daddy, Daddy, Daddy. I felt sort of embarrassed."

"That's the worst story I've ever heard," Anne told him.

"Well, you asked me."

"I didn't ask to hear something like that."

"I guess I shouldn't have told you that," Jerry agreed.

"What about your nice experiences?"

He thought about them. He felt shy of telling her about Rosalind
or Marie, and anyhow those affairs had ended badly, so after a moment he began to tell her of an occasion when he got tired of waiting for Begler at HARRY'S EATS in Altoona. He was hitchhiking
back to State College when a woman driving a messy Plymouth
picked him up. "It wasn't a nice car," Jerry said. The ashtray overflowed with stale butts. Empty pop bottles rolled around on the
floor. And at first the woman hadn't seemed nice as she fumed
about her husband, a truck driver who was out on the road most
of the time while she stayed home feeding his hunting dogs and
taking care of his fish. He was crazy about tropical fish. Their whole
basement was full of fish tanks she was supposed to take care of,
and the first thing he did when he got home was to check on his
dogs and his fish. Then, if he were in a good mood, he might say
hello to her. What kind of life was that, she asked?

"So I told her," Jerry told Anne, "that I used to keep fish and
knew how to clean tanks." It was all he needed to say. The woman
took him home with her, and while he fed the dogs and the fish,
she fried up some scrapple for herself and Jerry. They ate in the
kitchen, and over coffee and scrapple she told Jerry she was so

lonely some nights that she just lay in bed crying. She hadn't gone out dancing or to the movies in more than a year. All she ever did was to get in the car at night and drive around smoking cigarettes and drinking sodas while she tried to get up her nerve to go into a bar alone, or to pick up a stranger on the road. And when she did have the nerve to stop for a hitchhiker, or to let a man pick her up in a bar, it usually led to a bad experience. Jerry looked sideways at Anne. "You know what she said to me? She said, 'You're not going to hurt me, are you?' I almost cried."

"So what happened?" Anne asked.

"Nothing. I mean, after we ate we washed the dishes and went to bed." Jerry paused to let Anne fill in the gap. Then he went on with his story. In the morning he had gotten up early and cleaned all the fish tanks. His hostess cooked him a hearty breakfast, and then drove him up to State College. Before they parted in front of the Deke house she kissed him on the lips and said that if there were more men like him this would be a better world. "I mean, that set me up for days," Jerry told Anne. "I still think of her. I wish I could make all women that happy."

Anne said, "How many women have you slept with?"

"Forty-three." Then he corrected himself. "No, forty-two." He decided Sandra didn't count.

After a moment Anne said, "Isn't that an awful lot?"

"I don't know. I mean, I've been reading the Kinsey Report. Have you seen it?" She hadn't. "Well, it's got graphs and tables and charts and statistics about almost everything except the average number of different partners men have. I mean, it treats sex as an individual experience." He shook his head over that anomaly. "But sex isn't individual. It's a kind of whole experience. I feel whole afterward. I can't even remember the last time I did it alone."

Anne still didn't say anything.

"I shouldn't be talking to you this way."

"Have you slept with other men?" she asked.

He had been wondering if she would ask him. "You mean with my roommate?"

"You said he fell in love with you."

"He said he was in love, but I was never sure. I mean, he felt bad about what we did, only how can love make you feel bad?"

After a moment Anne said, "I don't believe this. I just can't believe it."

"Believe what?"

"Well, I've never done anything and I feel guilty all the time, and here you go around spanking girls and sleeping with men, and you're not even ashamed of it."

"I know. My mother doesn't understand it either."

There was silence for a moment, then Anne asked, "Did you mean what you said in the restaurant when that man got so angry?"

"About sleeping with you if you want me to?"

"Would you?"

"Yes. Do you want me to?"

"No!" she burst out.

"You don't have to shout it."

"If I don't shout you'd probably pull off the road and reach for me."

He shook his head. "Now is that fair?"

"Well, you're so . . ." She couldn't seem to think of the right word.

"Promiscuous? I told you that at the start."

"Actually you're nice," she told him. "No one else would have taken me out to dinner and made me feel almost normal."

He got her back to campus before midnight and kissed her when they parted in front of Simmons. She saw the kiss coming and for a moment he thought she was going to turn her cheek, but in the event she held firm and their lips met. It was a brief kiss, but a real one. "I'll call you tomorrow," he said, and stood watching as she entered the lobby and signed in. Seeing her from behind somehow added to the tenderness he felt for her. Then he went back to the Hudson where he sat for a while reviewing his options.

At the Deke house they would be getting ready to deliver his birthday present to Weigert. Jerry had blithely agreed to be one of the jock-strapped litter bearers, but he found now that he wasn't in the mood. He decided to return the car to Elizabeth and see what mood she was in. Only when he parked the Hudson on Fraser Street he could see that Elizabeth's windows were dark. So she hadn't waited up for him, and he didn't think she was the sort of woman who would appreciate being woken up. Anyway he wasn't going to try. He had had bad experiences waking women up.

He sighed. He thought of Dolly out in Slab Cabin trailer park, but she would expect him to pay her something and he didn't have any money, besides which there was the hazard of Fred turning up again with his pistol and Jerry didn't feel in the mood for another Quaker State shootout. It began to look like a chaste evening. He locked the Hudson and crossed the street to drop the key into Elizabeth's mailbox. In the lobby of Elizabeth's building he fished an old envelope out of his pocket, and wrote on the back, "Thanks for the use of the car. Your engine needs some Bardahl. I'll come by tomorrow to put it in." He folded his note, and slid it into the mailbox after the key. Then he stood for a while letting his fingers wander over the mailbox grille. Finally he bent and kissed the grille. It had a funny taste, probably of Brasso and dust.

It was after midnight when he finally got back to the Deke house. Every light seemed to be on. Clearly no one in DKE had settled down for the night. Jerry circled the place and was about to enter through the back door when Begler came shooting out in his shirtsleeves, a wad of what looked like a woman's clothes in his hands.

Begler came to an abrupt halt at the sight of Jerry. "Son of a bitch!" he exclaimed. "I'll deal with you later." He shoved the clothes he was carrying into Jerry's hands and said, "Put these in the MG and come help me with the ladder." He went hurrying off toward the kitchen wing where the chapter had an extension ladder fastened to a rack on the outside wall.

The clothes in Jerry's arms seemed to consist of a woman's outfit, complete with shoes and overcoat. Feeling bemused, Jerry put them into the passenger seat of the MG and went to help Begler with the ladder. Begler explained what they were doing. They were rescuing Veronica.

"Veronica?"

"Weigert's birthday present, dummy. She's locked in his room. We've got to get her out."

What was Weigert doing to her that she had to be rescued? Jerry wondered. That didn't sound like brother Bob. And why was Begler carrying Veronica's clothes?

Begler explained it all as they lifted down the ladder, and carried it into position under Weigert's third-story window, the only dark window on that side. It seemed that Begler had smuggled Veronica into the house around 11:30 and taken her up to his and Jerry's room where she undressed and got ready. "Why our room?" Jerry interrupted.

She had to undress somewhere, didn't she? So she took off her things in their room, and then everyone tiptoed upstairs where Veronica stretched out on a litter in front of Weigert's door. Then four brothers, including Begler, lifted her up, someone flung open the door, and they surged into the room to deposit Veronica in front of Weigert. Everybody then sang "Happy Birthday, Dear Bob," before bowing out and leaving him to his pleasures—which had not lasted long. Minutes after the door closed on the happy couple, Weigert burst out of his room, and fled down the hall to take refuge in one of the toilet stalls, where, so far as Begler knew, he was still sitting, shame-faced and frightened, while some brothers exhorted him to take a cold shower, others advised push-ups, and still others plied him with strong drink and psychological advice. Meanwhile, yet other brothers had begun to say that if Weigert didn't want Veronica, they did. So she had locked herself into Weigert's room, and that was why Jerry and Begler were rescuing her.

They had extended the ladder to its full length by the time Begler completed his story. "You scoot up there, and help her down," Begler told Jerry, "while I get my coat and bring the car around here." Once more he disappeared into the night, and Jerry began to climb the ladder.

He had to tap several times before Veronica appeared at the window, a white figure with apple-shaped breasts seen through a wavy pane of glass. She yanked up the window. "You!" she said.

Jerry said, "Hello, how are you? I didn't know you were going to be here tonight."

"You son of a bitch," Veronica said, "you gave me crabs last time."

"I've been wanting to apologize, I've been wanting to explain that," Jerry told her. "I mean, I feel terrible about it. I mean, it's practically ruined my life. I gave them to my girlfriend, too, and she's axed me."

"Well, I'd like to push you off that ladder. What the hell are you doing on it, anyway? Trying to get in here like those lunatics at the door?"

In the background Jerry could hear banging on the door. "No, I'm trying to get you out. Begler and I are rescuing you."

Veronica stuck her head out the window. "Where is he?"

"Getting the car."

"And I'm supposed to climb down that ladder without anything on? I'll freeze my ass."

Jerry was getting out of his coat. "Here, put this on. Your clothes are in the car. Jeff's bringing it around."

Veronica accepted Jerry's coat. Then, with his help, she sat on the windowsill and cautiously transferred herself to the ladder. "This is the last time I do this," she remarked. All the way down she was in a bad humor, which she took out on Jerry specifically and the Dekes in general. They were a bunch of adolescent jack-offs and dumbbells who didn't even know enough to keep themselves free of crabs. "And you know what some of them wanted?" she asked Jerry. "They wanted me to stick a lighted birthday candle in my twat."

"Well, it *is* Bob's twenty-first birthday," Jerry pointed out.

"I wouldn't put a candle there if it was his hundredth birthday."

"Maybe it is a little tacky," Jerry admitted.

At that point a fresh noise broke out above them. Evidently the lock on Weigert's door had been picked, or else given way, and now heads were thrust out the open window above them. "She's escaping!" Houser yelled.

"Jerks!" said Veronica. She reached the ground where Jerry was waiting for her. "Ouch! I got to walk barefoot?"

Begler was backing the MG across the grass toward them. "I'll carry you," said Jerry, scooping her up. Her overcoat—actually his overcoat—fell open, and he could see her breasts, puckered with cold. Around her neck she had a black ribbon which he found very attractive. Then Begler came to a halt only a few feet away, and Jerry deposited Veronica in the MG just as some brothers, led by Houser clad only in his athletic supporter, came bursting out of the house.

"After them!" Houser yelled, but no one made a move to pursue Begler, who was now roaring off into the night. They knew no one could catch Begler. Instead, they closed around Jerry. "You helped her escape!" Houser said in a strangled scream of anguish.

"So what?"

"It's a frame-up!" Houser declared. "Jeff collects the money, gets the girl, brings her up here, and fixes it up with her to scare Bob into running away so he can screw her himself."

"That's absurd," Jerry said.

"And what are you doing here? How come you turn up to carry her out when you were supposed to help carry her in?"

"None of your business." Jerry started to shoulder his way toward the house, but Houser grabbed him.

"I asked you a question, Engels."

Jerry pushed Houser away from him. "Lay off," he said, but Houser, aching for action of some sort, came charging back, fists flying.

Their fight was short, but sweet. At the expense of a knuckle in the eye, Jerry landed a good solid blow to Houser's solar plexus, and then had the additional satisfaction of hearing Houser curse as he nearly broke his fist against the top of Jerry's lowered head. After that the surrounding brothers gripped both combatants and pulled them apart. Brothers were not supposed to fight, and anyway they should get inside. The chapter had enough trouble already without another citation for indecent exposure. Jerry led the way indoors. Houser followed, insisting that he wasn't indecent, and that he had every right to slug Engels. He wanted to resume the fight, but he and Jerry were made to give each other the grip. Then everyone went upstairs to see how things were going with brother Bob.

They found Weigert sitting naked on his bed, his hair still wet from the shower he'd been urged into taking. Someone had given

him a pint bottle of Wild Turkey. He looked sodden and stupe-
fied with beer and cold water and whiskey and mortification. He
was a broad-shouldered, heavyset young man with a slablike face
that normally didn't register much of anything. Jerry felt very sorry
for him.

The room was packed with brothers, all consoling Weigert in
one way or another.

"We scared you by bringing her in that way," someone said.

"We shouldn't have got you drunk first. No one can do it when
he's loaded."

"You've got to be in the mood."

"You have to have your faculties about you."

"You didn't have your faculties."

"I couldn't get it up," Weigert said. "I was scared."

"Nobody gets it up if he's not in the right mood."

"It's not your fault."

"There's nothing wrong with you, Bob."

"I ran away," said Weigert.

Collins, monstrous-looking in his athletic supporter, knelt beside the bed and laid a tender hand on Weigert's knee. "Bob," he
said, "there's nothing to worry about. You've done it before, and
you can do it again."

But Weigert had reached that stage of humiliation at which men
no longer try to protect themselves. "I lied to you," he said, "I never
did it before."

That silenced Collins, but Mildenhall spoke up. "That's all right.
I've never done it either."

"Neither have I."

"No one has."

"We all lie."

Weigert looked around at his brothers. "You all neck. I've never even touched a woman."

This was worse than Jerry expected. He had wedged his way into the room. Now he said, "Let's get some clothes on him."

Collins picked that up. Still with his hand on Weigert's knee, he said, "Bob, we're going to get some clothes on you."

"What do you fellows think of me?" Weigert asked.

"We love you, Bob."

"You're our brother."

Weigert said, "You think I'm a fairy, don't you?"

No one had ever looked less fairy-like. Collins said, "Bob! You're no fairy, you're a Deke!"

"That's right," everyone chorused, "you're a Deke."

Tears could now be seen sliding down Weigert's cheeks. He seemed to be dissolving before the horrified eyes of his brethren. Jerry said, "Get him up! Get him dressed!"

Collins relayed this to Weigert. "We're getting you up, Bob. We're getting you dressed." He stood to give Weigert a helping hand. Others reached out to pull Weigert up.

That seemed to be the last straw. Shamed beyond endurance and suddenly galvanized into action, Weigert leaped up, shouting, "Let me alone, let me alone, let me alone." He began to beat his way through the crowd around him. Brothers gave way. Jerry felt a thrill of fear as Weigert pushed past him. There was a commotion in the doorway, and then Weigert burst free and went running full-tilt down the hall and straight out the window at the far end.

CHAPTER 6

At four a.m. that morning, after the police left, after Weigert's body was taken away in an ambulance, after the Dekes had turned off their lights and gone to bed sobered and shaken by recent events, after all that, Begler returned to the house, made his way quietly to the room he shared with Jerry, and yanked Jerry's mattress out from under him. Jerry awoke with a crash. The room was dark, and for a moment he thought maybe he was still asleep, involved in some kind of violent nightmare. Then he heard Begler's voice saying, "Get dressed, you son of a bitch, we're going for a ride." So it was no nightmare, it was just Begler being himself, as usual.

Their first fight took place when they were freshmen, in and out of each other's rooms on the same floor of Irvin Hall. Jerry had borrowed one of Begler's ties without asking permission and worn it to the Phi Delt rush party. Begler turned up at the same party and said, "Where'd you get the tie?" Jerry said, "It looks good with this suit, don't you think?" Begler did not think. He asked Jerry to take it off then and there. When Jerry refused, he asked Jerry to step outside. Jerry couldn't refuse, so they went outdoors and traded punches on the lawn until the Phi Delts broke it up and told them they had damaged their chances of getting a bid.

On that occasion Jerry and Begler walked off together, agreeing that they had never wanted to be Phi Delts in the first place. Their next fight took place a few weeks later on the night they pledged DKE.

They were walking back to Irvin Hall, high and happy. On the wide lawn in front of Old Main, Jerry began to walk on his hands. He felt things dropping out of his pockets—coins and keys, pens and pencils. Let them go. He had everything he wanted—a new friend, a new brotherhood, a new life. Then he was on his back looking up at the Big Dipper. He could hear halyards rattling on a nearby flagpole. That nautical sound made him think of sailing with Rosalind on Lake Michigan, and for a moment his heart was flooded by erotic nostalgia. Then he saw Begler's head and shoulders outlined against the sky. "Help me up," he said. Only when Begler extended a helping hand, Jerry jerked him off balance.

They had lain together for a while on the wintry grass smelling each other's beer-laden breath. Then Begler stirred. "I figured you might be a fag," he said. "I'll show you what I am," Jerry replied, and they began to wrestle. It grew serious. At last, chests heaving, they separated. Begler brushed at the sleeve of his jacket. "We're ruining our clothes," he remarked. "Well, that's too bad," Jerry said, "but you insulted me." "For Christ's sake," Begler replied, "you were hugging me!" "I can hug you if I feel like it," Jerry declared. "The hell you can," Begler replied, and thus the ground rules were set for their whole subsequent relationship. Jerry regularly took liberties with Begler's person and his possessions, and Begler just as regularly retaliated by challenging Jerry to fight.

"Get up," Begler said again, as Jerry lay between his bed and the wall, still somewhat dazed by his rude awakening.

Jerry got up. "Listen, . . ." he began, but Begler was not about to listen.

"You're putting on some clothes, and we're going out, and I'm going to beat the shit out of you."

"Baloney," Jerry replied.

"Do I have to drag you out of here?" Begler asked.

When thoroughly angered Begler had a way of talking as if he could move mountains, dam rivers, and alter the course of the stars. Begler's assumption of omnipotence always annoyed Jerry. "All right," he said, "turn on the damn light so I can . . ." The lights came on. Jerry disentangled himself from his bedclothes, shoved his mattress back in place, climbed over his bed, and reached for some clothes. "It may interest you to know," he told Begler, "that Weigert's dead."

Begler, standing by the doorway, simply nodded.

"He jumped out the window upstairs."

"I'm waiting for you," said Begler.

"So I don't think we can exactly congratulate ourselves on the birthday present we gave him." Jerry had pulled on a pair of jeans. Now he reached for a sweatshirt. Begler continued to wait grimly by the door. Jerry said, "Gossage thinks this scandal may close us up for good."

"Get your shoes on," Begler replied.

Jerry finished dressing, and together they went down the back stairs and out into the night.

"In the car," Begler said.

"Why the car?" Jerry asked. "We can fight here."

"Get in the car."

"You sound like some character in a gangster movie," Jerry told him, but he got into the MG. Begler got in behind the wheel, and spent some time putting on his driving goggles. Jerry opened the glove compartment, and felt around for the pint bottle.

"I didn't say you could have any," Begler said.

Jerry unscrewed the top. "I'm going along with this bullshit of yours," he told Begler, "so you can at least offer me a drink." Then he took one. When he had drunk deeply, he offered the bottle to Begler. "You want one?"

"Put it away."

Jerry took another swig before putting the bottle away. Then they drove off.

Begler took the Benner Pike out of town, but soon turned onto the Puddintown Road. "Did you have a nice time with Veronica?" Jerry asked him. Begler didn't answer. "Houser was upset that you got her." Begler was driving slowly now, looking for a good open field for their fight. "That was before Weigert jumped out the window. After that we were all upset."

Begler slowed still more, and then pulled onto the berm. They were midway between Puddintown and Houserville. Begler spoke at last. "You've got to learn to keep your hands off what doesn't belong to you."

"Fine," said Jerry.

"You take my car and stick me with the whole tab for our room."

"Add it to what I already owe you."

"I've put up with your shit long enough."

"O.K., let's fight," Jerry said.

They got out of the MG, climbed through a fence, and walked out into the middle of a pasture covered with a light dusting of snow. "This all right?" Begler asked, sounding almost like a host now.

"I just want you to know," Jerry told him, "that you're behaving like a twelve-year-old asshole about your stupid car."

The fight, for as long as it lasted, had an edge to it that Jerry had never felt before. This time he wanted to hurt Begler. Normally he cared very little about their fights, regarding them as the natural, rowdy by-product of their kind of friendship. He knew Begler took these fights more seriously than he did, though there was never any hatred in Begler's fighting, and such pain as Begler inflicted had an educational purpose. It was to teach Jerry a lesson, or rather to drive home a lesson with a little salutary pain—like a father, spanking an errant son.

Only this evening Jerry wanted to teach Begler something. He wanted to rub Begler's face into the mud and manure beneath the snow crust. He sparred for a while, dodging most of Begler's blows, taking them on his shoulders and arms, waiting for his opportunity. When it came, he dived for Begler's legs, brought Begler down, and converted their fight into a wrestling match. Snow and wet earth soaked their clothes as they rolled around. The snow, and the half frozen ground beneath it, softened things, and gave their fight a cold, wet, increasingly heavy and squishy feel. Then at last Jerry had Begler where he wanted him, face down. Surprised by his own feelings, Jerry shoved Begler's face into the cold mud, and held it there. Then he thought, *what am I trying to do, kill him?* and he let up. He rolled off Jeff and sat beside him in the mud, watching as Jeff wiped muck from his eyes and his lips.

"Weigert just sort of lost his head," Jerry said, "and went running down the hall and right out the window. Nobody expected it. We couldn't have stopped him."

Begler seemed to hear it at last. "What?" he said.

"I've been telling you all along, only you're too self-absorbed to pay attention. Weigert's dead. He jumped out the window."

"When?"

"Right after you left."

"He's dead?"

"Yeah, we killed him by giving him Veronica. He was a virgin. He couldn't get it up. He thought there was something the matter with him. He asked if we thought he was a fairy. I mean, he just fell apart."

"You're not making this up?"

"And all you can think about is your precious MG," Jerry told him.

"Never mind that, you're not bullshitting me about Bob?"

"No. He landed on his face on the walk. His teeth were all over the place."

"Holy shit!" Begler exclaimed. Then, angrily, he said, "Why didn't you say so? Why'd you let me drag you out here?"

Jerry said, "I think I wanted to fight you."

"Oh my God!" Begler rose, a sorry sight, and slogged his way back toward the car. Jerry followed.

They killed the remainder of Begler's pint while sitting on the running board of the MG. Then Begler tossed the bottle into the ditch and said, "What are we going to do now?"

"Go home."

Begler was trying to brush mud off his pants. Then he put his fingers to his nose. "I don't think all of this is mud," he declared.

"Well, it's a cow pasture," Jerry pointed out.

Begler stood up and began to undress. "I'm not getting in my car with these clothes on, and neither are you."

They undressed beside the MG, tossing their wet and soiled

clothes into the ditch along with the pint bottle. Neither of them had on underclothes. Begler had dressed in haste to go get the ladder to rescue Veronica, Jerry had dressed hastily to fight Begler. So once they shed their muddied outer garments they were naked, their white bodies shivering in the cold, with nothing to wear but their coats. Begler had taken his off before the fight, and Jerry was pleased to discover that Veronica had left his coat in the car. They wrapped their shoes in Jerry's sweatshirt and stowed them in the trunk. "What a mess!" Begler said several times. "What a fucking mess." It seemed to Jerry a perfect commentary on the night.

The following day was not a whole lot better. Gossage spent half the morning with the Dean of Men, trying to save the chapter. The police revisited the house and took over the Trophy Room, where they went into business taking statements from one brother after another. The housemother, Mrs. McKinley, the widow of an Ag. professor who had been a Deke at Cornell, took it upon herself to telegraph flowers to the Weigerts in the name of the whole chapter and to offer the chapter's condolences in a letter she herself drafted and circulated for everyone to sign. She had nothing consoling to say to the brotherhood itself. When she learned about Veronica's presence in the house the night before, she sniffed and said that such a thing could never have happened in Professor McKinley's day. She wondered aloud what Delta Kappa Epsilon was coming to.

No one went to class. When not giving statements to the police, or signing Mrs. McKinley's letter, brothers gathered by themselves to talk it over. How could this have happened? How could anyone have done what Weigert did? What had possessed him? "Do you think he really was queer?" Houser said.

Jerry said, "Bob wouldn't have known a fairy if one sat on his lap."

"Well, why would he ask a thing like that?" Houser wanted to know.

"It's just the worst that Bob could imagine, that's all."

"Well, I think it's very funny he would ask that question."

No one was laughing, however; there was a mood of unrelieved gloom, heightened when Gossage reported that the Dean of Men took a very serious view of the case. He would hold off until the Coroner acted, and he would do some investigation of his own, but he told Gossage frankly that the least the chapter could expect would be temporary closure. The Dean spoke of banning the chapter permanently. He had been very severe, saying that he didn't expect this kind of behavior from fraternity men and that he was *not* going to put up with it. He said that the Dekes had given a black eye to the whole fraternity system and that if matters were entirely in his hands he would close the house instantly and order everyone in the chapter to withdraw from school. He was utterly disgusted by everything he had heard about the disgraceful and tragic events of the night before.

Gossage summed it all up. "We're in deep doo-doo."

From time to time brothers would go outdoors to stretch their legs and get some fresh air, but even that brought no relief. Jerry and Begler got down their lacrosse sticks and did a little passing on the lawn, but soon after they appeared men from neighboring fraternities drifted over to pick up salacious and gruesome details about the catastrophe. Finally, no longer able to stand the atmosphere either in or around the house, Jerry sneaked off to Rec Hall in midafternoon. He worked out longer than ever before. When, finally, he could not bench press another pound, he just lay on his back, feeling the blood course through his pumped-up muscles.

He felt guilty to be so alive and healthy when poor Bob was dead. He made himself visualize once more Weigert's broken body and scattered teeth. They had had to shoo away Rex, who tried to lap up Weigert's blood. There were still stains on the pavement, and there might be a missing tooth in the winter grass. But even with such macabre details in mind, Jerry just could not avoid his own sense of well-being. How unfair, he thought. Bob Weigert dies needlessly and gruesomely, and the next day Jerry Engels feels great after a long workout.

He got up and went to the showers. The saddest thing, he thought, was that no one in the chapter would really miss Bob. He had not been popular or well-liked. He was brotherized because he had a good car—his father owned the Dodge agency in Shamokin—and he dressed well, and played a decent game of golf, but aside from that no one could think of much to say about Weigert. He was one of those colorless, uninteresting people who talked a lot about business conditions in Shamokin and how many miles he got to the gallon. His dates often looked glazed with boredom. Girls went out with him because he spent money on them and took them to Deke house parties where they could dance with his brothers, but Weigert didn't have a real girlfriend on campus, or anywhere else. There'd been something lonely and loveless about him.

Despite the hot water pouring over him, Jerry felt himself growing cold inside as he thought of Weigert's lovelessness. He pictured the poor guy sitting on the edge of his bed the night before, his skin winter-white and somehow insensitive-looking, his whole body heavy and inert. How had he gotten that way? He couldn't have been born like that. So what made him turn lumpish and unresponsive?

Darkness had fallen by the time Jerry emerged from Rec Hall. Then, as he started down Burrowes Street under the arched elms, he realized he couldn't face dinner at the Deke house surrounded by all his glum brothers, with Mrs. McKinley sitting at one end of the table, radiating propriety and high moral standards. By the time he got to College Avenue he had made up his mind what he would do. He headed for the Esso station at the corner of Atherton and College to buy a can of Bardahl. Half an hour later he knocked on Elizabeth's door.

Her expression changed the moment she saw his face. "Heavens!" she exclaimed. "What's happened to you?"

"Listen," he said, "can you have dinner at the Diner with me?" It was the best he could afford with the five dollars he had managed to borrow that morning from O'Dana—part of which he had already spent on Bardahl.

"You've been fighting."

"You mean this?" He touched the black eye Houser had given him.

"And your lip's swollen."

"My roommate hit me."

Elizabeth said, "We have to talk."

"I want to talk. Let's go to the Diner."

"Come in here and sit down," she said.

He didn't like her tone, but he went in and sat down. She remained standing, which he didn't like any more than her question, "What were you doing just now under the hood of my car?"

"You saw me?"

"I was standing at the window," she said. Then she said, "Jerry, this can't go on."

"What can't?"

"Haunting my office, visiting me here all the time, borrowing my car, tinkering with the motor."

"I was putting in Bardahl. Didn't you read my note?"

"I don't even know what Bardahl is."

"It'll loosen up your tappet valves."

"I don't know what they are."

"They're what makes that rattling sound when you start up your motor." He stood up. Sitting down while she stood over him asking questions had begun to make him feel childish and sulky, a sensation he didn't like. "I think we should have a drink," he said, and without waiting for her agreement he went into her kitchen and mixed two highballs. She was still standing when he came back with a glass in either hand.

She accepted her drink. "What was your fight about?" she asked.

"There were two fights."

"Two?" She sighed. "This is just so . . ."

"Why don't we sit down?"

They sat. There was silence as they both drank. Finally Elizabeth said, "Try to understand, Jerry. I have my own life. I work. I teach. I have friends."

"I know that."

"And since meeting you I feel like I'm being sucked into some kind of vortex."

"Vortex?"

"Well, every time the bell rings, you're at the door. Every time I see you, you're up to something different. You chase me, you borrow my car, you fight, and now here you are mixing me a drink with my own bourbon."

"I saw where you kept it when I was here Sunday."

She studied him intently. "When we met at Split Rock you seemed young, and sweet, and a little passive, but you're not like that at all."

He was glad to hear it.

"I thought you were like that character in Murger's novel who walked backward through life with his eyes fixed on the day he became twenty-one."

Struck by the quotation, Jerry said, "I *am* like that. I think a lot about the past."

"*The glad live past that cannot pass away.*"

"You're right. The past is alive."

"That was Swinburne."

"Well, he's right, too."

Elizabeth said, "But your present seems to be even more alive."

That also could be true. Jerry nodded.

"In fact I think I've been misjudging you all along."

He did too.

She gestured at his black eye. "I certainly didn't expect this rough-neck side."

"This is exceptional," he said. "I mean, last night was exceptional." Then he told her what had happened at the Deke house. He shook his head sadly. "The Dean of Men is probably going to close the chapter."

"Good. I wish he'd close all of them."

It was like her response to his poem. He felt slapped.

"Well, what do you expect?" she asked him. "I hate fraternities."

"Just the same you could sympathize a little."

"Why? I don't even see why you're in a fraternity in the first place. You're not the type."

"What do you mean I'm not the type?"

"Fraternity boys are conventional."

"Don't you think I am?"

"If you were conventional you wouldn't be here. I don't appeal to conventional men."

That impressed him. He was thinking it over when she handed him her empty glass. "Here, get me another drink."

He refreshed his own at the same time. When he rejoined her, he said, "I don't think of you as so unconventional. I mean, you live in a kind of mess here, and you wear funny clothes, but that's superficial."

"What do you mean I wear funny clothes?"

"Well, you do. That sweater's terrible." She had on her brown cardigan again. "And your skirt doesn't go with it, and your shoes are wrong, too."

For a moment he thought he'd angered her. Then she burst out laughing. He enjoyed her laughter, though it left him slightly puzzled. When she had calmed down he said, "What's so funny?"

"We are. You. Me. You with your black eye and fat lip, and me in my dowdy clothes arguing about who's conventional."

"I don't think that's so funny."

"Well, you don't have much of a sense of humor, do you?"

"Don't I?" Then, before she could answer, he said, "Listen, there's some meatloaf in your oven."

"I know. I made it."

"Well, why don't we have dinner here?"

"I was going to suggest that myself."

During dinner she said, "Maybe I should know who you are? What's your family like? Where did you go to school? How did you get this way?"

He took the easy questions first. He told her that he'd gone to the University of Chicago schools, and that his parents both had advanced degrees in chemistry, and that his father worked for Standard Oil. As for how he'd gotten to be the way he was he really couldn't say. "I mean, I've always thought I was like everyone else, only now I'm beginning to wonder."

Elizabeth said, "I should think at Chicago you would have had to read the great books."

"I did."

"I don't see what effect they had on you."

"They had a lot," Jerry said. "I mean, Aristotle's *Art of Poetry* gave me a headache. I almost cried. And it's not even about poetry. It's about plays."

"And nothing you read meant anything to you?"

"The *Symposium* did, and St. Augustine's *Confessions* until he started to worry about what God did before he created the world. I mean, what kind of a problem is that?"

Rather than tackle the question, Elizabeth said, "And so what brought you to Penn State?"

"I wanted to go east with my best friend. He's at Haverford."

Elizabeth shook her head. "You still don't make a whole lot of sense to me." Her eyes narrowed. "For one thing, a boy like you should have plenty of girlfriends his own age. Why are you with me? And who was this girl you were taking out last night in my car?"

"Now listen, " he said, feeling on firm ground at last, "you don't have to be jealous of her. She's someone I know from Life Drawing class and she's afraid she's a lesbian and I was just trying to cheer her up."

Elizabeth frowned. "She told you she's afraid of that?"

"People tell me things. You told me your life story."

"And you're taking Life Drawing?"

"No. I pose for it. I have a good body—well, you've seen it."

Without saying anything Elizabeth got up and went out to her kitchen. She came back holding two bowls of canned pineapple chunks. "This is dessert," she announced. Seated once more, she gazed at him silently before saying, "When I let you pick me up I thought I knew what I was getting into."

Jerry nodded. "You thought I was just a good-looking young man you could sleep with and say goodbye to."

"I'm ashamed to say that's true."

"Don't be ashamed. Why be ashamed? You hadn't slept with anyone for a long time."

She nodded.

"Who was it? Was it Mark?"

"Mark?"

"That tall man you share an office with."

"Oh, Mark! He's a dear, but he's devoted to his wife. She's an artist who paints simply dreadful pictures."

Jerry smiled. "You can be pretty scathing."

"I can be terrible."

"I love that." He put out his hand. After a moment she took it. "Can I spend the night?" he asked.

Her answer was simply to squeeze his hand in response.

That was Tuesday. On Wednesday after Life Drawing he took Anne to the Creamery where, after getting their ice-cream cones, they sat down to talk. "You looked so funny on the platform," she said. "What's happened to you?"

With his free hand he touched his black eye. "You mean this?"

"And your lip."

"I got into a fight," Jerry explained. "Listen, you know about Weigert?"

Like everyone else on campus she had heard, but she didn't understand it. "Why did he jump?" she asked.

"He didn't really jump," Jerry said. "It wasn't a jump. He was just running away."

That didn't satisfy Anne. "Well, he had to know he'd kill himself if he ran right out a third-story window."

Sounding impatient, Jerry said, "He didn't *have* to know anything. People don't *have* to know what they're doing."

Anne looked surprised. "You sound angry."

"Well, it makes me angry that people don't understand. I mean, once I tried to drown myself. I didn't know what I was doing, only I was luckier than Weigert. He couldn't think things over while he was falling, but if you're a good swimmer it takes a long time to drown and I had time to change my mind."

"Why were you trying to drown yourself?" Anne asked.

Jerry shrugged. "I was seventeen. I'd lost my girlfriend."

"You make it sound ordinary."

"It is."

Anne thought that over. Jerry licked at his ice-cream cone. Finally Anne said, "Well, it still doesn't make sense that your brother jumped out a window for no reason at all."

"I tell you he *didn't* jump, and he had a lot of reasons."

"Like what?" Anne asked.

"Like humiliation, like shame, like lovelessness."

"I'm loveless," Anne said, "and I'm not about to kill myself."

Jerry's irritation melted. If he hadn't been holding an ice-cream cone he would have reached across the table to take her hands. As it was he said, "That's what I love about you. You're so honest."

Then on Monday, the 16th of December, the Dean announced his decision. In view of their reprehensible behavior and its grave consequences, he was withdrawing accreditation from the Penn

State chapter of Delta Kappa Epsilon for six months, beginning January 3rd. If, in July, the chapter applied to be reinstated with new officers, he would consider the request.

That evening the whole chapter met in the Trophy Room, Archon Gossage presiding, to discuss their future. Gossage opened the meeting by saying that he had talked to the heads of friendly fraternities. Some brothers could find shelter at Tau Kappa Epsilon and Sigma Alpha Epsilon. Lambda Chi Alpha and Acacia both had some space. Delta Upsilon was going to vote whether or not to offer its facilities for rump meetings of Delta Kappa Epsilon. "I think we'll be able to limp along," he concluded.

Jerry rose to his feet. "Can I say something?" Gossage recognized Brother Engels, who began by saying that he felt as bad as anyone about Weigert's death. "What we did was wrong," he went on, "but we meant well, and I don't think we should take this punishment lying down and scrambling for cover. I think we should show the Dean and the whole campus what sort of men we are. I think tomorrow morning we should all march down together to the recruiting center, and volunteer for service in Korea."

His proposal met with a moment of resounding silence before Houser said, "Why should we all get ourselves killed just because Weigert jumped out the window?"

Jerry turned to look directly at Houser. "This country's at war," he said, "and it's our country, and I don't know why college men like us are sitting around at home serving in the ROTC while other men are fighting for our hides."

Houser began, "Listen . . ."

"You listen," Jerry told him. "One of my best friends in high school was killed in Korea. His name was Jimmy Kaplan. He was Jewish, and he couldn't even make it into this fraternity. But he went over there and put his life on the line. How does that make you feel?"

Gossage said, "Let's not get all emotional over this."

"This is a very emotional issue," said Jerry.

"Order!" said Mildenhall.

"I move we all volunteer tomorrow morning," Jerry said.

"You can't make a motion like that," Houser told him.

"I just did."

"I second him," said Collins.

"You can't second a motion like that," Houser told Collins. "Anyway, with your knee they wouldn't take you."

"Let's not have personal remarks," said Gossage.

"Order!" said Mildenhall.

Jerry said, "Would Teddy Roosevelt have gone around to friendly fraternities asking if they had room for him? No. He wasn't that sort, and neither are we. I say we go enlist."

"Make him sit down," said Houser.

"I've got the floor," Jerry said.

"Order!"

"This country has given us everything," Jerry went on, "and now's the time to show our gratitude and let the world see what Dekes are made of. All in favor of my motion, say aye."

Collins and O'Dana and one or two others said aye.

"You're letting him take over the meeting!" Houser yelled at Gossage.

"Order!" said Mildenhall.

"What's the matter with you?" Jerry asked Begler. "Why didn't you vote aye?"

"I don't want to fight in Korea," Begler replied.

"You want to move into Acacia?" Jerry asked him.

"We can get an apartment."

Several voices called for order. Gossage, bemused by the whole situation, finally rapped his gavel. "Sit down," he told Jerry.

"I'm not going to sit down," Jerry replied. He looked around at his brothers. "Come on! Stand up for America."

"Sit down!" said Gossage again.

"Pull him down," said Houser. "He got us into this in the first place."

"I did not!" said Jerry.

"Whose idea was it to give Weigert a girl?"

"Order!!!!" half a dozen voices yelled. Others shouted, "Sit down!!!"

Still on his feet, Jerry said to Houser, "I said we should take Bob to that fancy knock shop in Pottsville. I didn't say we should serve him a naked woman on a tray with a birthday candle stuck in her."

"She held the candle, and anyway, what difference does it make how we gave her to him?" Houser asked. "It's the same thing."

"It's completely different," Jerry said. "You have to be really ignorant to think someone like Bob would respond well to having a naked woman dumped at his feet by a crowd of jerks in their jockstraps."

"He's insulting the chapter," Houser said. "I move Engels be censured."

"I'm telling the truth," said Jerry.

"You called us jerks."

"You are one."

"Are we putting up with this?" Houser yelled. He was on his feet. Mildenhall was on his feet, still calling for order. Half a dozen men had risen, and competing voices and motions could be heard from all over the room. Rising above everyone both in size and in the volume of his voice, Collins began to call for calm. "Men of Delta Kappa Epsilon!" he cried out. "Men! Men!" In the background Gossage hammered futilely with his gavel. During a brief lull in the commotion, Jerry heard Begler say to him, "Congratulations, Herman, you've scored again."

When the meeting finally broke up Jerry went straight to Fraser Street to throw himself into Elizabeth's arms, but once their first transports were over and he began to tell her about the meeting he had come from, she pushed him away.

"You what!?!?" she exclaimed.

"Now don't *you* get mad."

"You want to fight in Korea?"

"It's a patriotic thing to do."

"I don't believe this." She moved away from him. She looked him up and down.

Jerry put his hands out, palms up. "Don't be this way."

"Jerry," she said, "when I left Tony I left the church. I belong to the Society of Friends again, and we don't go along with war, or guns, or the kind of false manhood that revels in uniforms and marching around and saluting."

"What about bravery?" he said.

That seemed to make her even angrier. "That's the worst of it! Men think the only way to show bravery is to go out and shoot someone, or get shot. Is that what you want to do? Kill a North Korean to show what a man you are? Or get killed to show how much red blood you have in you?"

"I'm not going to get killed. That's a fallacy. Most soldiers aren't killed. Actually I think going to Korea could improve me."

"How?"

"Well, I'm sort of soft and gentle. Korea could make me tougher and more of a man."

"*Whoso would be a man must be a noncomformist.*"

"Who said that?"

"Emerson."

"I think he's right."

"Of course he's right."

Jerry said, "But even so noncomformists should be manly, and I just don't feel that I'm enough of a man. I think I'm too feminine."

"It's not going to change your nature to volunteer for Korea. You'll be the same there as you are here."

"But you know what I mean about myself?"

"Of course I know what you mean. It's what I love about you."

He felt a shock at her words, as if she'd touched him with a live wire.

But then later, when their argument was over, when they had gone to bed and made love, when she had finally fallen asleep, he lay awake thinking about what she had said. She had not said she loved *him*, she only said that she loved his femininity, so it was really a weakness of hers for young men like himself. Still, that was something. In fact, it was a lot. It was everything. He fell asleep feeling happy for the first time in days.

CHAPTER 7

On Thursday, the 19th, school broke up for the holidays, the Dekes began to scatter in all directions, and by midafternoon Phil Forson arrived in State College at the wheel of the prewar Chevy with real running boards that he and Jerry bought after their graduation from high school. Phil was Jerry's oldest and best friend, though gaps had begun to open between them now that they had been going to very different Pennsylvania schools for the last three years.

"Who tagged you?" Phil asked, when he saw Jerry's black eye.

"Houser. I've told you about him." Jerry dumped his suitcase in the back seat and got in beside Phil.

Who asked, "What was the fight about?"

"Nothing," said Jerry. "Let's go."

When Phil started up the motor, Jerry leaned forward to listen intently. "What's that whine?"

"Could be the generator."

"Don't you know?"

"All right, it's the generator."

"Well, why haven't you done something about it?" Jerry felt Phil neglected their car when it was in his keeping.

"It only just started."

"But if it's the generator we could break down."

Phil said, "Look, Jerry, the car's twelve years old. It's gone over a hundred and thirty thousand miles. We agreed after that valve job that we weren't going to put any more money into it."

"We could end up stranded in Ohio."

"Then we take a train."

Jerry didn't like the sound of that anymore than he liked the whining sound from the engine, but he settled back, and presently began to feel the soothing effect of being beside Phil in their old car. They had commuted in it to summer jobs on the Ash Gang at the Standard Oil refinery in Whiting, Indiana. And they had set off for college in it with their families gathered around them in the road at Indiana Shores saying, *Write*, and *Drive carefully*, and *Do you have enough cash with you?* and *Telephone us tonight; reverse the charges.* Linda Forson had made them a bumper sticker that read PENNSYLVANIA HERE WE COME, and their freshly simonized car had glittered in the September sun, packed solid with the clothes, the bedding, the dictionaries and typewriters and tennis racquets and golf clubs, and all the other things young men take to college with them. And when they finally drove off, honking, they had turned to look at each other as soon as they rounded the first bend. Jerry could remember the smile he and Phil exchanged then, the smile fellows have when they are setting off on their own for the first time, sure that their families have nothing to worry about, sure that nothing bad can ever happen to them.

"I'm going to miss this old crate when it breaks down," Jerry said.

"We've gotten our money out of it ten times over," Phil reminded him.

"Yeah, but I'm going to miss it anyway." Jerry had made love in the old Chevy, and as he thought of those steamy summer nights with the windows rolled up to keep out the mosquitoes while he and Marie Promojunch tossed around in each other's arms, Jerry let out a voluptuous sigh. "Do you ever wish things could last forever?"

"What do you mean?"

"I mean life is just so . . ." He couldn't finish.

Phil said, "You're in love again, aren't you?"

"How'd you know?"

"Who is she this time?"

So Jerry began to describe Elizabeth. Phil was privileged. Jerry had told Phil about all his great loves from Rosalind onward. It seemed natural to tell Phil everything, and yet it was hard for him to put Elizabeth into words. Finally Jerry said, "She's not like anyone else." He thought about it. "She reminds me a little of your grandmother."

"Granny?" Phil sounded surprised. Mrs. Yngling, his grandmother, had been a heavy, high-tempered, deaf old lady.

"You know how angry your grandmother could get?" Jerry said. "She blew up one afternoon when she found out I didn't know any poetry. *What are they teaching you in that school?* she yelled." Jerry's voice went up as he tried to imitate Mrs. Yngling. "And then she gave me a book, *Great Poems of the English Language*, and told me to *memorize* some of them. I mean, Elizabeth might do something like that. Actually, your grandmother scared me so much that I did memorize some poetry."

"Granny could be pretty scary," Phil agreed. "What I don't understand," he went on, "is when you met this woman. At Thanksgiving you were in love with Pat."

"Oh, well, listen," said Jerry. "I hope you got an A on your paper about the Weimar Republic so at least some good came out of that weekend."

"What do you mean?"

Jerry explained what he meant.

When Jerry had finished, Phil said, thoughtfully, "Crabs!"

"Have you ever had them?"

"No."

"Well, they're terrible. They dig in and itch like hell, but I just scratched without really looking to see what was going on down there. I mean, who wants to stare at himself? So I didn't do anything until it was too late."

"Pat must have wanted to kill you," Phil said.

"She was very angry," Jerry agreed.

They drove along in silence for a while. Then Phil said, "And so now you're in love with the woman who was your freshman English teacher?"

"Yes."

"Is she in love with you?"

"Well, she lets me sleep with her."

Phil thought that over. "I don't know how you do it," he said at last. "I haven't slept with anyone in I don't know how long. I just don't have time to be having affairs right and left."

"Well, I am failing out of my major," Jerry admitted.

"I don't know why you aren't failing out of school. Penn State must really be easy."

Annoyed, Jerry said, "Penn State can be pretty strict about some things." Then he told Phil that the Deke house was to be closed for the spring semester as punishment for importing Veronica and scaring Weigert to death.

"Holy mackerel!" said Phil. "What are you going to do?"

"I don't know. I've been thinking of volunteering for Korea."

"Korea!"

"That's what everyone says, but what's so wrong about fighting for your country?"

"South Korea isn't your country."

"Yeah, but you know what I mean."

"No, I don't."

"I mean it's good to be brave and patriotic."

"Listen, Jerry," Phil began.

"I know what you're going to say. *Don't do anything rash.*"

"Well, don't."

"Yeah, but I've been going to school all my life. I'd like to do something different for a change."

"Like getting killed?"

"I'm not going to get killed. Why do people think everyone who goes to war gets killed? Anyway you can get killed at home. You can get killed in bed. I was with a crazy woman who let off a shotgun in her bedroom."

Phil didn't react to that. He had evidently been thinking. "Anyway, if you've just fallen in love why do you want to leave her and go off to Korea? What does she think about it?"

"She's a Quaker. She hates it."

"Well, there you are."

"I'll tell you where I am. Nowhere. I'm going nowhere."

"We all feel that way sometimes."

"I bet you don't."

"I get discouraged," Phil admitted.

"That's not what I mean," Jerry said. "I'm not discouraged, but I'm just going in circles, having an affair then losing the girl and starting again. It's like school. It just goes on and on. You know something? I'm actually glad this is happening, that the dean's closing the house."

"Yeah, but Korea," Phil said.

"Listen, if Elizabeth would marry me I'd drop Korea like a shot. That's what I really want—to get married and start a real life."

"Have you proposed to her?"

"I'm afraid to."

"Why?"

"I know she'd turn me down. She thinks I'm too young."

"How old is she?"

"Twenty-eight."

"That's pretty old."

"I don't think so. I mean, I've had it with girls."

"I never thought I'd hear you say a thing like that."

"Well, now you've heard it," Jerry said.

After that they rode along in silence for a while. A long car ride has its own rhythms. Jerry pushed with his tongue at the tooth Begler had loosened. Phil drove. When Phil at last broke the silence, it was to say, "That place at Cresson is just ahead. You want to stop for dinner?"

"I could eat," Jerry said.

They were on Route 22 between Holidaysburg and Ebensburg. Over the years they had experimented with various routes back and forth, but by now they had settled on Route 22 to Pittsburgh, then Route 30, the Lincoln Highway, which they took all the way to Valparaiso, Indiana, where they turned north toward the lake. They even had their favorite motels and restaurants along the way, one of them being The Crest at Cresson.

The middle-aged waitress with the seamed face and dusty blonde curls was on duty. She prided herself on snappy service. Scarcely had Jerry and Phil seated themselves at the counter than she was in front of them with glasses of water and silverware wrapped in a napkin, her order pad at the ready. A plume of smoke rose from the cigarette she had abandoned in an ashtray by the door to the kitchen. "What'll it be, boys?"

"Can the *me-en-you* get together?" Jerry asked.

Without a blink the waitress dealt out menus to Jerry and Phil. "Honey," she said to Jerry, "that's the oldest joke in the book. If I had a quarter tip for every time I've heard that one, I'd be a rich woman. I could retire to Florida and live on my income. The hash is good tonight."

Jerry said, "You could retire now. Just marry someone like my friend here. He's a good worker, he'll support you."

"He hasn't asked."

"I'll have the pork chop dinner," said Phil.

"Then take me," said Jerry.

"Like a shot," said the waitress. "Pork chop for you, too?"

"No, give me the hash."

"And coffees for you both?"

They nodded, and she hustled off, pausing only to take a drag on her cigarette before she disappeared through the kitchen door. "She smokes too much," Jerry said, "but she's a great waitress."

She was back in no time to serve them their coffee. Jerry said, "Since you're marrying me, you better wear this from now on." He had fished out the Deke pin that had been burning a hole in his pocket ever since Pat had returned it, or rather flung it back at him. "Here, I'll put it on you."

Laughing, the waitress leaned forward to let Jerry fix his fraternity pin to her white uniform. Then, after taking another puff on her cigarette, she disappeared into the kitchen again. She was gone longer this time. When she returned, she had their dinners with her, but her expression had changed. She'd taken off the pin. "Honey," she said to Jerry, putting down his Deke pin beside his plate, "this looks kind of valuable."

"It's my fraternity pin," he told her.

"Well, you don't want to give that away to just anyone."

"You're not just anyone."

"Aren't you sweet," she said.

"Come on, let me put it back on you."

But she wouldn't lean forward again. "I wouldn't feel right wearing that."

"Come on," Jerry said again. He held out the pin.

She looked at it, then at his face, and shook her curls. "No, you keep it, honey," she said, "I wouldn't know what to do with a thing like that." Then she was off to wait on a heavyset customer whose buttocks overflowed the stool on which he sat.

The pin rested on the counter throughout the meal. The waitress came back several times to refill their coffee cups and take their dessert order, but her chatty manner had left her, and mostly she kept herself busy at a distance from Jerry. He had the homemade apple pie á la mode for dessert. Phil had the raisin rice pudding. When they got up to pay at the register, Jerry picked up his Deke pin. He couldn't just leave it on the counter like a tip. "Sure you don't want to reconsider?" he asked, showing it to the waitress, who also served as cashier.

She ignored it. "God bless you, honey," she said, "and drive safe."

Outside, Phil said, "What was that all about?"

"I've got to get rid of this pin," Jerry explained. "When Laura gave it back to me I buried it on Mount Nittany. Then I dug it up and gave it to a girl named Barbara that I never even told you about because she gave it back a week later. Pat's had it since May. Can you think of anyone who might like it?"

"You're a nut, you know that? A real nut," Phil said. There was affection in his voice, but also a certain condescension.

They got into the Chevy, Jerry driving now. As he adjusted the rearview mirror, Jerry could feel Phil sitting in judgment on him. He said, "You really think I'm nutty?"

"I think you're getting pretty wild."

"Wild! I'm way too tame and gentle."

"Well, you're fighting and fucking all over the place. And stealing cars, and getting picked up by the police for indecent exposure. How do you explain that?"

"I don't have to explain it. I mean, I've always been like this."

"You have not. We were brought up the same way. You behaved yourself."

Jerry said, "You remember when we were ten or eleven and your grandmother took Linda and us to see Rumplestiltskin at the Goodman Theater?" Linda was Phil's young sister.

"Yeah."

"Well, we were all jouncing around in the back of a cab on the Outer Drive, and I could see a brassiere strap at your grandmother's neckline, and all I could think about were her breasts right there under her black dress, and I began to think I *had* to reach in and feel her."

"What does that prove?" Phil asked. "All little boys go through experiences like that."

"Yeah, but I did it," Jerry said. "I felt her."

"You did not!" said Phil. "I was there. Granny would have killed anyone who groped her breasts."

"I thought so, too," Jerry said. "As soon as I touched her I thought I was a dead duck, but all she did was to slap my hand real hard and tell me never to do that again. It was over so fast that you and Linda didn't know what had happened."

"Jerry, you're making this up."

"Don't you remember her bawling me out in the cab?"

"Granny was always bawling out somebody about something."

"Well, that afternoon she was bawling me out for taking a feel."

Phil still didn't believe it. "I sassed her once, and we never heard the end of it. I hate to think what would have happened if you'd felt her breasts."

"I think she understood."

Phil shook his head. "Granny wasn't as much a Nazi as she sounded. She was nice to our Catholic maids, and she always had that old Jewish man sit down and eat coffee cake when he came by to sell his eggs."

"He came to her funeral," Jerry interjected.

"That's what I'm saying," said Phil. "Granny could be very human, but she would never have understood your feeling her breasts."

"Well, she was nicer to me after that than she'd ever been before. It was after that when she gave me *Great Poems of the English Language*."

"Making you memorize poetry is like her, but that touching business couldn't have happened. It's a wish-fulfillment memory."

"Have it your way," Jerry said.

"You had a very normal childhood. You and I did the same things. We thought the same way."

Jerry said, "You remember the night we swam way out in the lake, the night I told you I was having an affair with Rosalind?"

"Sure."

"Remember what happened out in the lake?"

"Nothing happened."

"It did for me. I panicked. I imagined something was drifting up from the bottom to wrap itself around my legs. You know—a squid, an octopus, a kraken—and we were naked, you remember."

"Yeah."

"Well, at first I couldn't swim for fear of attracting it, and when I started to swim again I was flailing the water. You thought it was a race, but it wasn't. I was terrified. I was trying to save myself."

"Jerry," Phil began . . .

"Let me finish," Jerry said. "I mean, I've thought about that a million times since then. Why was I afraid of the lake? I love the lake. It never frightened me. The rougher it got, the more I loved it. I just didn't believe in undertows and dangerous currents, and I knew it wasn't really deep at our end, and there was nothing in the lake that could harm me. I mean, I know that after I lost Rosalind I picked the lake to drown in because I knew the lake would never really hurt me, but that night I was terrified of what was drifting up from the depths to touch my balls and twine itself around my legs, and it was the same thing as when I touched your grandmother's breasts: the terror of desire."

Phil remained obstinately sensible. "I was there both times, and I don't think anything happened either time. You're imagining all this. And I don't even know what you mean by *the terror of desire*."

"I mean it's when your desires are so huge they're like monsters threatening you."

"Jerry, you're talking crazy."

"I'll tell you what's crazy. You know what the Kinsey Report says?"

"What are you talking about now?"

"The Kinsey Report. It says the average college student has intercourse zero point three times a week. That's only a little more than once a month. The rest of the time guys are going crazy and whack-ing off alone."

"We've got to do something."

Jerry felt shocked. "*We?*"

"I jack off," Phil said. "Everyone does."

"They do not!"

"Are you claiming you don't?"

"It's not a claim. I'm not claiming anything. I'm telling you."

"Well, that could be your problem," Phil said. "That could be why you're always in deep. Instead of staying home and taking care of yourself you spend all your time rutting around and getting in trouble."

"I'd rather be in my kind of trouble than yours," Jerry said.

"What kind of trouble am I in?"

"The worst kind. You know what Blake says? *Sooner murder an infant in its cradle than nurse unacted desires.*"

"Now what's that supposed to mean?"

"Just what it says. When you're whacking off you're nursing an unacted desire, and that's a terrible thing to do."

Phil disagreed. "You're being old-fashioned, Jerry. It's very old-fashioned and Victorian to get so uptight about masturbation."

"Then I'm old-fashioned."

"You?"

"But that doesn't make me wrong. You can be old-fashioned and right at the same time."

"I don't even want to try to sort this out," Phil said, letting the argument die there. After all they had the whole night ahead of them as they sped westward, and anyway closely pursuing an ar-gument on the highway was as unwise as tailgating another car.

*

After Jerry graduated from high school Mr. and Mrs. Engels had given up their Chicago apartment to live in Indiana Shores where they had sold their summer cabin and bought a year-around house which Jerry didn't really like. He preferred the log cabin on a ridge facing the Live Dune. Still, the new house had comforts and conveniences the cabin lacked, aside from being closer to the beach where Jerry and his father went walking Saturday morning, a west wind whipping at their windbreakers and turning their cheeks bright red. There was piled-up ice along the shore, but further out they could see open water where occasionally a fountain of spray shot up when a wave hit the ice just right.

"I agree with you," Mr. Engels said, "that Petroleum and Natural Gas Engineering was not the right major. I'm just not quite sure how you'd earn a living with an undergraduate degree in psychology. To be a youth counselor in the school system you'd need professional training, and with your grades I frankly don't know what graduate school would take you."

Jerry had dropped the Korea idea, or at least hadn't mentioned it to his parents, so his father was proceeding on the basis of Jerry's last letter home when he'd brought up the idea of becoming a youth counselor.

Jerry said, "I'm sure there are special camps or rehabilitation farms that could use someone like me. I can teach swimming and sailing and weight lifting and all kinds of things, and I know tree surgery and gardening. I'm good with my hands. I can build things, and paint, and do some car work. And I'm good with people. People like me. What I'd like, eventually, is to have my own camp where boys and girls live together and develop the right attitudes." He looked at his father. "You know, learn to love nature, and each other."

Mr. Engels rubbed his forehead. "Well," he began.

"Anyway, I've got to have a new major, and I'm sure psychology is right."

"I agree to that," Mr. Engels said, sounding glad to postpone talk of the future. "But now there's this problem of where you'll live."

"Begler's finding us an apartment in town," Jerry said. "We'll be able to fix our own meals. It will probably cost less than living in the Deke house."

Choosing his words carefully, Mr. Engels said, "Perhaps you could get a dormitory room on campus and take your meals at one of the cafeterias? It would save you shopping and housekeeping."

"I like shopping and housekeeping," Jerry said.

"Well, frankly," said Mr. Engels, "your mother and I think it might be better for you not to live with Jeff Begler."

Jerry said, "Why?"

"We think he's a bad influence."

"You hardly know him," Jerry said.

"You yourself admit he knocked out your tooth."

Jerry put a hand to his mouth where he had finally dislodged his own tooth. "He only loosened it. He was just trying to teach me a lesson. I mean, Jeff's a good influence on me. He won't let me use his hairbrush or toothbrush, or take his neckties and socks and underwear without asking. If I lived with anyone else I'd be borrowing everything all the time."

"Maybe it would be good for you to live alone."

Jerry shook his head. "I don't like to be alone, and anyway it would kill Jeff if I moved out on him."

"I can't believe that," Mr. Engels said. "He could find someone else to share with."

"Yeah, but I'm the only person he loves," Jerry said.

Mr. Engels frowned. "What do you mean by that?"

"Well, his mother died when he was ten, and he's never had a real girlfriend. He doesn't know anything about women, or even men. He gets along miserably with his father. I went up there once with him, and he and his father quarreled so much they didn't even speak to each other one night at dinner. Mr. Begler would say to me, 'Will you ask my son to pass the wine?' and Jeff would say, 'Will you tell my father it tastes like vinegar?' I was very uncomfortable."

"That further convinces me that he's not the right person for you to be living with."

"We're perfect for each other."

Mr. Engels dropped his reasonable manner. "I want you to get a dormitory room on campus."

"I don't think I can. Dorm space is very tight, very limited, especially in the middle of the year like this. I couldn't possibly get a room of my own. I'd have to share with someone I don't know, and it would take all my time just getting used to a new roommate."

His father stopped walking and turned to him. "We've been very lenient with you. I think I've been too lenient."

"You and Mother have been great," Jerry said. "I mean, I appreciate how good you've been."

"I haven't said all I could say about this scandal in your fraternity, or your school record, or your debts."

"That's another thing," Jerry said. "If I let Jeff down about the apartment, he'll want me to pay back what I owe him, and it's over a hundred bucks now." Though fanatically possessive about his car and his clothes and all his other possessions, Begler lent money with a liberality that made him banker to several brothers, Jerry most of all.

"I will help you settle that debt. Have you made others this semester?"

"I owe Phil for my share of the food and gas coming home, and I had to borrow from him at Thanksgiving."

"How much does that amount to?"

"Thirty. And I should really pay back a girl for what she lent me when I took her out to dinner."

"I should think so."

"And I owe a couple of other people," Jerry continued, "but I'm doing better. The money I make posing helps out."

"You know what we think of that job," Mr. Engels remarked.

"It's a perfect job for me," Jerry argued.

He saw on his father's face the sad, baffled look that came over it so frequently during their talks. It made Jerry's heart ache. He said, "I love you, Daddy. I wish you could love me the way I am."

Tears—wind whipped by the cold?—appeared in Mr. Engels's eyes. "Jerry," he said, "you must never think I don't love you. I do. You're my only son. You're very dear. It's because I love you so much that I'm concerned for your future. You need an education. You *must* learn to concentrate, and to study."

"I learn from people," Jerry explained. "I get everything I need from people, and from my own heart, not from books. And, frankly, I've just gotten to know a woman who knows English literature by heart. You'll be amazed how literate I'm going to become."

"Who is this?" his father asked.

"Now don't be frightened." Jerry put out his hands to calm his father. "She's older than I am, and she's been divorced, and she doesn't want me to marry her or anything like that. She's just interested in me, and I'm interested in her, and we're perfect for each other right now, and she's another reason I can't live up on campus, because I'll be spending a lot of time painting her apartment and fixing her car, and I'll need to live in town close to her place."

"You're not planning to study at all," his father remarked.

"Psychology is people. I already know more psychology than most fellows my age, and I'll be learning all the time from Elizabeth. She's a brilliant woman, a Harvard Ph.D. She graduated summa cum laude from Radcliffe. I mean, she's not like some girls I've brought home. She's not like Marie." Marie Promojunch had chewed gum when she met Jerry's parents, and worn blue eye-liner and lilac-colored lipstick. The meeting had not been a success.

Jerry saw the baffled look come back to his father's face. "It'll be all right," he assured his father. "If you can help me settle my debts, Begler and I will live very economically in our apartment, and I'll be working hard on Elizabeth's place, and going to class regularly, and working out, and posing, and there won't be any reason for me to get drunk and be picked up again by the police. It was that fine for indecent exposure that got me behind the eight ball financially this semester."

"We'll have to discuss this some more," his father said.

*

"Maybe you could help reconcile Daddy to what's happened," Jerry said to his mother. They faced each other across the breakfast table on the Monday morning after he arrived home. "He worries too much about me, and he's afraid I'll never be able to make a living. Actually I bet I could make a living right now posing for clothes ads. I'm a good model."

"Your father doesn't think that's a very suitable way to earn a living," Mrs. Engels said.

"Well, we can't all be scientists," Jerry pointed out.

Mrs. Engels reached across the table to squeeze Jerry's hand. "Jerry, it isn't money your father worries about most. It's your relations with women."

"I know. He's been warning me since I was thirteen."

"I worry, too," Mrs. Engels said, and on her face Jerry saw the martyred expression he'd grown too familiar with. She said, "The Inglesides have sold their house out here, you know."

"You wrote me."

"They haven't really used it since that summer."

Jerry nodded.

"And I know they're leaving the Shores because we live here."

"You mean because I live here," Jerry said.

"How you could have done that to a girl like Rosalind!" Mrs. Engels mourned. "And when I think of all Mrs. Ingleside has been through, losing both sons, I just feel like going down on my knees in front of her."

"Mother, I didn't kill Rosalind. She's fine. She's at Vassar."

"You just don't feel guilty about it," Mrs. Engels said.

"We've been over this before," Jerry pointed out.

"What bothers me most of all," his mother went on, "is your attitude. I can understand you being carried away with Rosalind. You were young, and she's very beautiful, and people can make slips. But you don't regret it. You aren't ashamed. You never said you were sorry, and you've behaved the same way about Nancy Train, and all your girls. You've never been ashamed."

The Trains were neighbors of the Engels in Indiana Shore, where year after year Jerry and Nancy had had summer flirtations.

He said, "Mama, I had nothing to be ashamed of with Nancy. You know that. I've told you. We just got carried away one night and decided to elope, but nothing happened."

"Nothing happened!"

"Nothing sexual happened. She changed her mind by the time we got to Indianapolis and I brought her home. It was Mr. Train who turned it into a scandal."

"You brought her home at dawn, Jerry."

"That doesn't justify Mr. Train in chasing me with a baseball bat and smashing the headlights of my car."

"He'd been stewing and fretting and worrying all night. Naturally he was angry and upset."

"Mother, whose side are you on?"

"You know I think Mr. Train was wrong to have made such a public stink, and to have threatened you with the Mann Act . . ."

"He had no case. We didn't cross a state line."

". . . but I simply can't understand your attitude. It's not how we brought you up. You weren't taught to indulge yourself, and to do whatever you feel like, and to brazen things out afterward. That isn't the model we set for you. That's what hurts me the most, that my son should be shameless."

"Mother, I don't think we're getting anywhere," Jerry said. "I mean, you've said all this before."

Her martyred look turned angry. "I keep saying it because I want you to listen. I want you to know how we feel each time there's some new scandal."

"I know how you feel. If I could do something about it I would, but I can't. It's the way I am."

"You don't mean to tell me you can't stop yourself?"

"I don't want to stop myself. I don't think people should stop themselves. It's wrong to be all stopped up. It's unhealthy." He stopped. He could see he had not carried her along with him. "I'm just this way, Mother."

"But it's a monstrous way to behave, sleeping with one woman after another and ruining reputations and causing pain to the people who love you."

"Then I'm a monster," Jerry said.

"But you're not!" she wailed. "I know you're not. You're a lovely person. I've watched you grow. I'm your mother. I know you. I know you're good." She was weeping now, and he knew the only thing to do was to get up and go around to her place at the table, and kiss her, and stroke her soft hair.

*

His sister, Anne, lived with her husband in an odd, half basement apartment on 57th Street in Chicago, between Kimbark and Kenwood. Out behind they had a two-room brick cottage in a wilderness of ailanthus trees and brickbats where they did most of their eating and talking. Jerry visited them there a few days before Christmas. He'd been in Whiting to see Dr. Vulmer about his tooth, and gone on into the city to finish his shopping and to see old friends.

"Have you checked what kind of psychology department Penn State has?" Anne asked. "You don't want to find yourself studying clinical or behaviorist psychology."

Jerry said, "I've got to get out of petroleum and natural gas, and Psychology will take me, and Daddy thinks it makes sense."

"He thought it made sense for you to go into Petroleum and Natural Gas Engineering in the first place. He thought Penn State made sense."

"It does," said Jerry. "There's nothing wrong with Penn State."

"It's wrong for you," Anne said. "You should have gone to Antioch or even Black Mountain in spite of the communists there. I'd rather see you anywhere than in a restricted fraternity at Penn State. I kick myself that Michael and I were in France when you were choosing a school." Her husband, Michael Goodfellow, had had a Fulbright that year. Now he was in his second year at the University of Chicago Law School. Anne was studying economics in the Social Sciences Division, though mainly these days she was pregnant.

To change the conversation Jerry said to her, "Listen, what are you getting Daddy for Christmas?"

"Two more volumes of Douglas Southall Freeman's biography of Washington."

"Maybe I could give him one of the volumes?"

"No. Figure out your own presents."

Jerry said, "I hope you're going to be some help when you come out for Christmas. I mean, they're both giving me hell."

Anne said, "Well, you've been fined for indecent exposure and thrown out of your major this semester, and your fraternity house has been closed. Then you come home with a black eye and a missing tooth, owing money right and left. Did you expect them to pat you on the back and congratulate you?"

"Still, you could help," Jerry said to his sister.

"The only good thing that's happened," she went on, "is that you've gotten rid of Pat."

"She got rid of me."

"That would have been the end if you two had married."

Jerry looked from his sister to his brother-in-law, sitting at the kitchen table with a law book and a cup of coffee in front of him. Michael had been following the conversation with a smile on his face. "Is she like this with you?" Jerry asked him.

"I have her under my thumb," Michael said, putting up a bony thumb for Jerry to look at.

Anne said to Jerry, "You told me yourself that Mr. Gaheris approves of Senator McCarthy. The worst thing in the world would have been for you to settle into that kind of reactionary, country-club-Republican environment."

"I was marrying Pat, not Mr. Gaheris."

"And you admit she said anti-Semitic things. I can just imagine what she and her father think about civil rights for Negroes."

"Anyway, it's over," Jerry said.

"Thank goodness."

Michael said, "And have you pursued your erotic survey of American womanhood beyond la Gaheris?"

Jerry hesitated. He had shopping to do. He wanted to see his old pal, Ernie Hill. It would take time if he told Anne and Michael about Elizabeth. He checked his watch. "Listen," he said, "I've got things to do. When are you two coming out to the Shores?"

Michael looked at his wife. "See? What did I tell you?" He looked back at Jerry. "I bet Anne that you'd already be involved with another woman."

"Are you?" Anne asked.

Jerry said, "I can't go into it now, but it's someone you'd like. It's not another sorority girl. She's older than I am, and a lot better educated."

"You can at least tell us her name."

"Elizabeth."

"Where'd you meet her?"

"At a ski lodge, but I knew her from before. She was my freshman English teacher."

"You mean she's on the faculty?" Anne said.

Suddenly willing to prolong the conversation, Jerry said, "She's worried about that. Is that the way things are at schools? She thinks if it comes out that she's having an affair with me she might not make tenure. She thinks she might even be fired."

Anne and Michael looked at each other. Then they both looked at Jerry and shook their heads. Michael said, "Maybe for something flagrant they'd fire her, but a quiet little affair ought not to make that much difference."

Anne had second thoughts. "Of course she's a woman, and there's a double standard."

"And State College *is* a small town," Michael agreed.

"So you think she could be right?" Jerry said.

"She probably understands the situation better than anyone," said Michael.

"How old is she?" Anne asked.

"Twenty-eight."

"Twenty-eight!"

"You see, she lost three years being married to a drunk poet who finally tried to kill her."

"Tell us more," Michael said.

"Why do you say I'd like her?" Anne asked.

"She's wonderful. She's brilliant."

"But twenty-eight!" said Anne.

"Hey, I'm twenty-seven," Michael objected. Anne was only twenty-four.

"Anyway, she's not interested in marrying me," Jerry said. "She made that clear right from the start."

"So you mean there's no future to this?" Anne asked.

Jerry looked at his watch again. "Listen, I can't stay. I can't go into all this now, but I've begun to think maybe I'm not meant to marry. Maybe I'm a kind of soldier-of-fortune type."

"Where'd you get that idea?" Anne asked.

Michael said, "Soldiers of fortune look tough. You don't have the right kind of face."

Anne brushed it all aside. "This is just silly. Why are we talking about it?"

Jerry said, "We were talking about the future. I mean, I'd be glad to marry, but what kind of woman would marry me the way I am now?"

"What do you mean by that?" Anne asked.

Jerry explained it to his sister. "I've had too much experience for girls my own age, and older women like Elizabeth are too smart to hook up permanently with someone like me."

Anne shook her head impatiently. "Jerry, you just don't realize what a wonderful person you are."

"You were just telling me what a mess I am."

"I was explaining why the parents are mad at you, but you know you're no mess. A smart woman should thank her lucky stars to get you."

"Well, so far no one's been doing that."

Anne shook her head again. "I don't want you thinking this way about yourself. You're too good, you're too sweet." Suddenly Anne's whole manner changed, and Jerry heard again the greedy, slightly sentimental tone of voice that seemed to echo back from all the intimate childhood conversations he and Anne used to have. "You're my little brother," she said, drawing close and putting an arm around him. "I want you to be happy. I want you to have a wife and children. I want you to have everything you want."

"Maybe I want too much." Then, suddenly, Jerry couldn't take it anymore—the heat of the little kitchen, the closeness, Anne's swelling stomach, Michael's law book. "Listen, we can talk about it out at the Shores. I've got to go now."

*

Like most of Jerry's high school class, Ernie Hill had gone on to the College of the University of Chicago. When school was in session he lived at Burton-Judson Court, but he, too, was home for the holidays. He was stretched out on the couch in his mother's apartment on Kimbark reading *The Daily Worker* when Jerry rang the bell.

Ernie was a communist now, or at any rate a member of American Youth for Democracy, a communist front organization high up on the Attorney General's list of subversive organizations. It pleased Ernie to be considered a subversive, but at the same time he felt blue that none of his causes ever triumphed. The Smith Act had not been repealed, the House Un-American Activities Committee rolled merrily along, and the Rosenbergs were still scheduled for execution. Moreover, Ernie had recently discerned another threat to good progressives everywhere. His great high school love, Carolyn Webster, had just gotten engaged to a law student. "You realize what this means?" he said to Jerry. "Next Rosalind will marry a doctor. Professional men are going to end up with all the really terrific girls, and you and I will have to make do with tall dames who wear black and want to talk about Jean-Paul Sartre."

"I met a girl just like that!" Jerry exclaimed. "She asked me to spank her."

"Exactly," said Ernie. "And are you getting to know women who paint and write poetry?"

"Actually, I am."

"It's as clear as day. You and I are being winnowed out of the social and sexual mainstream, while legal crooks and medical bloodsuckers glom onto the Carolyns and the Rosalinds." Ernie narrowed his eyes. "And for you, Engels, the poets and tall dames in black are just the beginning of the end. Next your life is going to be filled with pale young men in pastel shirts."

"There aren't any pale young men in pastel shirts at Penn State."

"I thought you told me your freshman roommate . . ."

"He wasn't pale. Actually, he was a high hurdler. I still see him on campus sometimes, but he'll hardly look at me now. I think he's afraid I gossip about him."

"How could he possibly think you gossip?"

"I don't," Jerry said. "I'm very discreet. I've told you, but at Penn State I've told only one person about him, and I only told her because she's afraid she's a lesbian."

"One of your new girlfriends, I presume?"

Jerry nodded. "As a matter of fact I think you're right. I do feel winnowed out of the mainstream. The girls I went out with in high school were the best girls in school, and now I hardly see girls like that. I see prostitutes, and fat ladies, and . . ." He was about to add schoolteachers to the list when he stopped himself. "I don't see anyone like Rosalind," he concluded.

"And I don't see anyone like Carolyn," Ernie said.

"Who do you see?"

Ernie pursed his lips. "Nurses at Billings. Left-wing girls. I make out, but the excitement's gone."

"That's terrible."

"It's a terrible world, Engels. So you better join the movement. Our only hope is violent overthrow of the government, nationalization of the means of production, and free love."

"Actually, what I've been thinking about is volunteering for Korea."

"Don't joke with me."

"I haven't made up my mind."

"What mind?"

"After all, Jimmy Kaplan went." Jimmy had been Ernie's oldest friend.

"And got killed. You know that?"

"Yeah. Shirley wrote me."

"I'd like to machine-gun the bastards who did it to him."

"They were just doing their duty," Jerry said. "You can't blame the Chinese."

"Who's talking about the Chinese?" Ernie asked. "I'm talking about Harry Shithead Truman and Dean Dong Acheson and the other murderers who got us into this war."

"You can't blame them, either," Jerry said.

"Nobody's to blame in your world?" Ernie asked. "Jimmy just dropped dead by accident? Maybe a brick fell on him out of heaven? Is that how you think it happened?"

"You shouldn't make yourself angry this way. That doesn't do any good."

"It does me good," Ernie said. "I like being angry."

"You don't want to become a sorehead."

"How do you know what I want?"

Jerry said, "Well, anyway, do you want to go to Shirley's New Year's party?" Shirley Hyatt had been in their class. Jerry had grown up with her both in Whiting and at the Shores because her father—like Phil's—worked for Standard Oil.

Ernie said, "I'm not invited. Shirley doesn't invite me to her parties anymore."

"She would if I asked her to. It's practically like we're all the same family—the Hyatts, the Forsons, and the Engels."

"Why should I want to go?" Ernie asked. "I've got nothing in common anymore with Shirley's crowd."

"Carolyn will be there."

Ernie said nothing.

"So will Rosalind," Jerry said. "Shirley told me Rosalind's coming."

Ernie said, "Haven't you heard that life is flux? You can't step into the same river twice."

"I think we should go."

"You go. They're still your friends."

"I want you with me."

"For moral support, or what?"

"Because we're in the same boat. I feel closer to you now than to Phil, and he's always been like my brother."

"Okay, you win," Ernie said.

CHAPTER 8

Shirley Hyatt had at last persuaded her parents to let her have her own apartment in Chicago. Unlike the Forsons and the Engels, her parents never moved from Whiting to Chicago. Shirley had had to commute to the University of Chicago High School. For a season after Anne Engels went to Swarthmore, she used Anne's room, but her presence in the Engels apartment so distracted Jerry, then fifteen, that the arrangement soon ended. Then Mrs. Yngling died and for the next two years Shirley used Mrs. Yngling's room in the Forson house. After that she had been in Kelly Hall on campus. Now, at last, she had her own two-room efficiency on Blackstone Avenue, thronged, when Jerry and Ernie arrived, with some very familiar faces.

"Jerry!" Marylynn Morris cried, letting him sweep her off her feet. "Jerry!" cried Rachel Klein, letting him kiss her. Carolyn Webster gave him her hand, and said, "Hello, Mr. J.E.P.D.Q. Engels."

Ernie was already talking to Burt Powell, Carolyn's fiancé, a medium-sized man with a big jaw, dressed in a three-piece suit. Ernie had clothed himself in the livery of campus radicals everywhere: a plaid shirt and knit tie, corduroy pants, and a worn tweed jacket with leather elbow patches. "Just how much money do you figure on making your first year out of law school?" Ernie asked Powell.

Powell shrugged. "Depends what kind of firm makes me an offer."

"Well, say a big firm like Baker and McKenzie takes you in. How much would you clear to start off with?"

"I can't say," said Powell. "Someone I know made $25,000 his first year with Gottlieb Cleary in New York."

"Well, would *you* be satisfied with $25,000?" Ernie asked.

A smile flitted across Powell's face. "Yeah, I think I'd take that."

"But not for long, I bet," Ernie said. "I mean, what do you expect to make eventually? Roughly speaking, of course, and in a good year."

Carolyn said, "Don't be a bore, Ernie."

Ernie turned to her. "It's your future, sweetheart." He turned back to Powell. "I guess you know Carolyn and I were close once. That's why I'm asking you these questions. I want to be sure she's made the right choice."

"Is this the guy you were telling me about?" Powell asked Carolyn.

"It's him," said Carolyn.

"*He*," Ernie corrected her. "We say, *it is he*, or in some circumstances, *Lo, it is he*."

"Lo, it is he," said Carolyn, with an appropriate hand gesture.

"You two are pretty funny," Powell observed.

"That's as may be," said Ernie, "but you haven't answered my question."

"I don't think I like your question."

"It's an honest question," said Ernie, "asked in a spirit of scientific inquiry. How much is a lawyer worth? Some people say shit, but I'm trying to get a more precise answer."

Powell turned away, and took Carolyn by the arm. "I *said* we should have gone to the Coconut Grove."

"Pardon me, I didn't hear that," Ernie said. "The noise in here . . ."

Still speaking to Carolyn, and without turning his head toward Ernie, Powell said, "I'm not spending the evening with this clown hanging around me."

"Clown!" Ernie cried. "Is there a clown here? He must be talking about you, Engels, you're everyone's favorite goof-up."

Powell swung around on Ernie. "If you've got a burr up your ass, let's go outside and settle it."

Carolyn took hold of Powell's arm. "You're playing up to him," she said. "It's what he wants."

"She knows me very well," said Ernie.

"Will you lay off?" Carolyn said to him.

"*Lay off?*" Ernie's voice rose almost to a falsetto. "What a curious expression! Lay off what? Lay off whom? On whom am I supposed to have been lying?"

At that point Powell punched Ernie in the breadbasket. Marylynn shrieked. Voices rose all over the room, and suddenly Jerry found himself restraining his friend while Powell punched Ernie a second time. "Will somebody please hold him?" Jerry called out.

Phil and John Williams obliged, and the fight ended. Shirley, her eyes blazing with anger, said to Jerry, "I knew when you asked to bring Ernie that something like this would happen. He ruins every party."

"I'm sorry," said Jerry. "We're going. I'm really sorry."

Out on Blackstone Avenue he said to Ernie. "Now why'd you do that? I didn't even get to talk to Rosalind."

Ernie was feeling himself where Powell had hit him. "Why'd you hold me so tight? And what the hell have you been doing, lifting weights?"

"Yes."

"Just my luck to have a muscle-bound friend holding me back."

"And just mine to have a sorehead pal getting us kicked out the minute we arrive."

"Let's go up to Jimmy's and have a drink," Ernie said.

But Jerry was not happy at Jimmy's Tavern. He had been looking forward to the party, to talking to old friends, and to the erotic nostalgia of seeing Rosalind again. After several drinks at Jimmy's he said, "I don't want to spend the evening here."

Ernie said, "Maybe I could call up Gertrude."

"Who's she?"

"She works at Billings. She shares an apartment with a couple of other nurses."

Jerry shook his head. He didn't want to spend New Year's Eve holding hands with a nurse. He said, "Let's go to the Del Prado."

"What's at the Del Prado?"

"The Colony Club party." Earlier in the evening Jerry had seen Linda Forson all dolled up for it, and the sight had awakened pleasant memories of when he himself had belonged to the Colony Club and used to escort girls like Linda to big affairs at various Hyde Park hotels. His great romance with Rosalind actually began at a New Year's Eve Colony Club party. "Come on, let's go," he said.

They had checked their coats and were heading for the ballroom when Mrs. Riefsnyder intercepted them. She had been head chaperone for longer than anyone could remember. "Jerry! Ernie!" she said. "You don't belong here anymore."

"Mrs. Riefsnyder!" they exclaimed, "you know us."

She knew them only too well. She had once caught Ernie and Carolyn Webster necking in a deserted cloakroom of the Windermere Hotel, and she had memories of Ernie and Jerry promoting fake birthday cakes for Bernard Pear. "I can't let you two in here," she said, barring the double doorway with her arms.

Just for a while, just for auld lang syne, they pleaded. "We're all alone," Jerry told her. "We've got nowhere else to go. Just let us in to see what it's like in there."

"You know what it's like."

But they wanted to see it again. The balloons. The bandstand. The paper streamers. The noisemakers. The piles of cotton snow balls stiffened with glue. "Please!" Jerry said.

Mrs. Riefsnyder weakened. "All right," she said finally, "but you're not to stay. You're not to cut in. You're far too old to be here." Then she let them pass.

Inside it was a replica of every Colony Club New Year's party they had ever attended when they were in high school. "God, they look young," Ernie said.

"There she is," said Jerry.

"Who?"

"Linda."

Linda Forson was seventeen now, slender, with her hair up, exposing her slender neck. She had on a white gown that showed her bare shoulders. Jerry knew, from seeing her earlier at the Forson's house where he was spending the night, that she had on a gold chain with an old-fashioned locket that had probably been her grandmother's. He couldn't see the chain and locket now because Linda was being held, he thought too closely, by a rather handsome boy. "Who's she with?" he asked Ernie.

"Looks like Jason Williams," Ernie said.

"That's Jason!" Jerry felt astonished. He remembered Jason as a tumultuous eighth grader. He said, "Is Mrs. Riefsnyder watching us?"

"Why?" Ernie asked.

"I'm going to cut in. Keep an eye out for me."

Linda's eyes widened with surprise as she saw him approaching. "Jerry," she said, "what are you doing here?"

"Dancing with you," he answered, tapping Jason's shoulder and dismissing him with a smile. Except that Jerry had scarcely gotten an arm around Linda's waist before he felt Jason tapping back.

"Did you see that?" he said to Ernie a moment later. "He cut right back. I don't think they're teaching them manners anymore." What was the Colony Club coming to? Its whole purpose was to teach manners—how to escort girls to parties, and how to behave with them there—and if there was one iron law it was that you didn't cut back. Cutting right back was uncouth. "Go cut that guy out for me," Jerry told Ernie. But the same thing happened again. Jason cut right back on Ernie.

That was too much. Jerry was advancing onto the dance floor to cut in again on Jason, when he found his arm held by Mrs. Riefsnyder. "I knew I shouldn't have let you in," she said. "This is exactly what I told you not to do."

"But he's cutting right back, Mrs. Riefsnyder," Jerry protested, "and I . . ."

"It's before the interval," Mrs. Riefsnyder said firmly. At Colony Club parties bands always introduced pauses partway through each dance. No cutting in was allowed until after that interval.

"Well, he should have told me that," Jerry said, "instead of . . ."

"You'll have to leave now," Mrs. Riefsnyder told him.

"All right, but that's Linda Forson. I'm staying at her house. I have to tell her something," and pulling free from Mrs. Riefsnyder,

Jerry went out onto the floor. This time Jason looked as if he were prepared to use his fists to hold off interlopers. Smiling, palms up, Jerry said, "Sorry, I didn't know it was before the interval." Then to Linda, he said, "I'll see you at home."

He hadn't known he would say that until he said it, and it had no particular meaning, but he felt satisfied as he turned away from the couple. He had shown Jason his long-standing intimacy with Linda, and maybe he had left Linda wondering what he meant.

Out on the street Ernie said, "Well, wasn't that fun? I can hardly wait to hear your next idea."

Jerry said, "Where's Jimmy buried? I mean, did they bring back the body, or is it still in Korea?"

"It was never in Korea. He died in a hospital in Japan."

"So where's his body? Is it here or there?"

"It's here," Ernie said. "He's in Woodlawn Cemetery."

"Do you know where?"

"It'll be locked up now. The whole place is surrounded by a wall."

"We can scale the wall. I think we should buy a bottle and go out there and sit on Jimmy's grave and drink with him."

"Engels, you're crazier than I am," Ernie said.

"Can you find the grave?"

"I don't know. I was there, but I wasn't paying all that much attention. There was a mob of Jimmy's aunts and uncles and cousins and grandparents all around me. Jimmy's whole *mishpocha* was there."

"His what?"

"Family, dumbhead."

"Can you find it?" Jerry said.

"I guess so."

It was after midnight before they found the grave, which wasn't the sort anyone could sit on. It was a headstone surmounted by a

Star of David. Ernie and Jerry sat down on the frozen ground beside it and opened the bottle of Black and White they had brought with them. Jerry said, "Jimmy was almost the nicest guy I ever knew. We used to fight in fifth grade, and then one day you and he were hanging together in the courtyard between Blaine and Belfield, and Jimmy said, 'Hey, Engels, want to have a sundae with us at Stineways?' and I don't think I ever even argued with him after that."

Ernie said, "Jimmy and I made friends in playschool. You know something? He had to go to the bathroom once, only he felt shy about asking to go, so he built a little house out of those great big building blocks we had, and he went in there and peed. I saw him do it."

"Let's pour some Scotch on his grave," Jerry said.

They watered Kaplan's grave with Black and White.

"May he rest in peace," said Jerry. Then he said, "Why do people say that? Do you want to rest in peace when you're dead?"

"No, I'd like some action."

"So would I. I bet most dead people want action, especially if they died young like Jimmy."

Ernie said, "A guy down the hall from me in B-J took cyanide last quarter. He telephoned me and said, 'I've just taken poison.' Then I heard a funny sound and I thought he was being cute, only when I went down there to bawl him out he was lying on his bed turning blue."

"Why'd he do it?" Jerry asked.

"Why do any of them do it?"

"One of my brothers did it," Jerry said. "He went out the third-floor window."

"You tried to do it," Ernie reminded Jerry.

Jerry said, "I thought I had nothing left to live for, but the funny thing is that there's always something more. I remembered they were altering a suit for me at Fields, and that's when I turned back toward shore."

"No kidding?"

"A vicuña suit. You remember that suit I had in twelfth grade? That's the one. My mother was mad at me for picking it because it wasn't a school suit and it was expensive, but it saved my life."

As they talked they passed the bottle back and forth over Jimmy Kaplan's grave. Jerry said, "I've been very lucky to have friends like you and Jimmy and Phil and Begler." He sighed. "Lucky in friends, unlucky in love."

"What do you mean, unlucky?" Ernie said. "I envied you. You had more girlfriends than I did."

"I envied you," Jerry said. "You went further with your girlfriends than I did."

They drank. Then Jerry said, "Who was the first girl you ever went all the way with?"

"Carolyn," Ernie said promptly.

"Mine was a prostitute in Michigan City. Phil and a cousin of mine and I all went there together the night my sister got married."

"You rich kids have it easy," Ernie said. "I never had money enough for prostitutes."

Jerry said, "I wonder who Jimmy's first girl was?" He was leaning against the headstone now, with an arm around it.

"He told me once, but I've forgotten," Ernie said. "It was at a summer camp. They were in a canoe and he was afraid the whole time that they'd tip over."

"There's a lot of fear," Jerry agreed. "A lot of anxiety."

He felt peaceful now. It was quiet there in the cemetery, and the Scotch tasted good, and it was nice to be with Ernie, and to have an arm around Jimmy's headstone. He felt like really talking. He said, "What happens to guys like us?"

"I don't know."

"I mean, do we go on having affairs for the next fifty years?"

"You tell me."

"I don't want more affairs. I mean, they're wonderful. I love them as long as they last, but I've had them. I want something else."

Ernie said nothing.

"I want a love that lasts a long, long time."

"You were always a sentimentalist."

"It doesn't pay to be cynical," Jerry told him. "You must want that too."

"What I want to is to get out of this fucking cemetery and off the freezing ground."

But they went on sitting beside Jimmy's grave thinking their own thoughts. Finally Jerry said, "At Shirley's you said I was everyone's favorite goof-up. You wrote that about me in *The Correlator*, didn't you"

Ernie said, "No, but I was on the committee and I can tell you who did. We pledged each other to eternal secrecy, but after what's happened I don't care. It was Carolyn and Shirley."

"Carolyn and Shirley," Jerry marveled, "and after all I did for them!"

"What did you do for them?"

"I loved them."

"I loved them, too," said Ernie.

"I still love them, don't you?"

"I don't know. I guess so, but it's different now."

"Of course it's different," said Jerry. "Loving them afterward is not the same as loving them beforehand. Beforehand you're always trying to get more of her, and afterward you keep trying to lose less of her. But it's still love."

"That's good," said Ernie.

"I've been learning a lot."

"At Penn State?"

"Yeah."

"I thought all those big engineering and mining schools were intellectual dumps."

"Oh no! Penn State's a great place. The only trouble is they don't teach you anything. You have to learn about love on your own, and some poor guys don't know how." He was thinking of Weigert. "I mean, that's the worst thing about school. Why doesn't anyone ever try to teach love?"

"Because there's no money in it," Ernie said. "Lovers are losers. Look at us."

"We're not losers."

"Then what are we doing out here drinking together at Jimmy's grave?"

"We're showing him our love."

"We're goofing off together because we haven't got girls, and you know it."

Jerry brooded a moment. "It always comes back to that, doesn't it? Do you know any happily unmarried men?"

"I don't know any happy people, period."

"You know me," Jerry said.

"I guess you are happy," said Ernie. "I'm sorry you went away to school. At Chicago we're all miserable. I don't have any friends here like you."

"I haven't got anyone at Penn State like you." Then Jerry added, "I haven't got anyone at Penn State like anyone. It's all different. I mean, I chose Penn State so Phil and I could go east together to college, only I hardly see him now, and when I do he's studying. I don't think he plays any games. I know he's not on any team. I'm sure he's getting out of shape, and Phil was a good athlete."

"He was your friend, not mine," said Ernie.

"We were all friends."

They had finished the Scotch and were just sitting. Finally Ernie stirred. "If I sit here any longer I'll freeze to the ground."

"We should go," Jerry agreed. He carried the empty bottle with him. He didn't want to leave it beside the grave, or anywhere in the cemetery. In fact he kept hold of it through the cab ride back to Hyde Park. He was still holding the bottle when he and Ernie parted at the corner of Kimbark and 57th. "You want this?" he asked.

"It's empty."

"I thought you might want it to remember Jimmy by."

"I don't need an empty bottle to help me remember Jimmy."

"Then I'll keep it," Jerry said.

Holding his bottle, he set off for the Forson's house. Merrymakers came pouring out of the Tropical Hut as he passed it. A girl with red bangs startled Jerry by blowing a noisemaker in his face. It unrolled and hit him on the nose, and as he shied away, he lost his bottle. It smashed on the pavement, and he said to the girl, "Look what you've made me do."

She looked. "It was empty."

"But you didn't know that," he said. "You should be more careful." Then he walked on, feeling a little sad now that the evening was ending and Jimmy Kaplan was dead and Phil out of shape and

Ernie turning into a sorehead. His old gang, the Hard Core that ate lunch every day in Scammons Gardens, had changed. It was gone, all broken up now just like that bottle.

He let himself into the Forson house with the latchkey Aunt Beth had given him and went straight to the dining-room sideboard where Uncle Fred kept his liquor. It was dark in the dining room, and he couldn't see exactly what he was doing, but when he tasted the liquid he poured himself, he realized that he had found the sherry decanter.

Then he looked around. Even when it was lit, it was a dark dining room, full of heavily carved black walnut furniture and elaborate silver pieces. The Forsons owned lots of ugly silver, probably inherited from Mrs. Yngling, who had been rich before the crash in 1929. Her silver had so much ornamentation, so many figures and so much scrollwork, that it reflected hardly any light, especially now. They should get rid of it, Jerry thought, and buy simple modern trays and coffee services and fruit bowls. Simple, modern Mexican-silver fruit bowls. That's what the Forsons should have instead of this stuff.

Then he noticed a line of light under the door to the pantry, so he wasn't alone. He pushed through the pantry door, and went on into the kitchen, where he found Linda sitting at the kitchen table eating a bowl of Grape-Nuts. "Well, hello!" Jerry said. She relaxed. "I didn't frighten you, did I?" he asked.

She said, "Is Phil with you?"

"He must be still at Shirley's." Jerry looked around for signs of Jason, but there were none except for the orchid Linda had been wearing on her wrist, and which now rested on the table beside the bowl of Grape-Nuts. "Where's Jason?" Jerry asked.

"Home, I guess." Linda sounded a trifle grim.

Jerry smiled. "Did you have trouble with him?"

"What do you mean, trouble?"

"Trouble," Jerry repeated. He sat down next to Linda. The orchid was just in front of him. Jerry could guess to within a nickel what Jason had paid for it. He said, "That will last longer if you put it in the refrigerator overnight."

"I know that," Linda said.

"It's pretty," said Jerry, touching it with his finger. He liked orchids. Then he said, "He was mad, wasn't he, that I cut in?"

Linda stopped spooning up Grape-Nuts and gave Jerry a conspiratorial look. "He was furious."

"But he should have told me it was before the interval."

"He thought you knew."

Jerry nodded. "Are you two going steady?"

Linda turned back to her cereal. "We go around together," she allowed.

"Did you let him come in when he brought you home?"

Linda said, "I don't ask *you* all these questions."

"I just want to know."

"Well, it's none of your business," Linda told him.

Jerry said, "I don't think it's wrong when a boy brings you home to let him come into the house for a while." In fact he had hated it when girls said goodbye to him on their doorsteps. "Jason's probably crazy about you," he added.

Linda took a deep, angry breath.

"What's the matter?"

"What if he is crazy about me?" she burst out. "That doesn't mean I should fall all over him with gratitude."

"I didn't say that."

"Well, *he* thinks it."

Jerry said, "Well, don't blame him. You're very pretty. In fact you're beautiful."

A blush began at the base of Linda's throat and went right up to her eyebrows. She had always been a great blusher.

"Well, you are," Jerry said.

Linda filled her mouth with Grape-Nuts and said nothing.

He watched her eat. Then he said, "Is Jason the only one?"

"The only one what?"

"The only one crazy about you?"

"I don't know." She said it as if she would be the last to know and the least interested.

"Well, who else is there?"

"Jerry, stop prying."

"Well, are you interested in anyone besides Jason?"

"Who says I'm interested in *him*?"

Jerry felt like laughing. "I do. He's good-looking, he buys you orchids, he takes you out, you let him come in when he brings you home. You like him."

"When he's not being shtupid," Linda conceded.

Jerry knew what she meant by *shtupid*. The language had not changed that much since he was in high school. "Boys can't help being shtupid," he told her. "I was shtupid. I was probably the most shtupid boy in U-High."

"Well, now Jason is."

"He gave you trouble tonight, didn't he?"

Linda exclaimed, "Honestly, Jerry, I don't see why I have to tell you everything."

"Because I can help you." He put his Deke pin on the table in front of her.

"What's that?"

"It's my fraternity pin. A girl gave it back to me, but I don't want it anymore. It's been given back to me three times already. I mean, it's used. I've used it up, but it'll be good for you."

Linda went pale. Her circulation had to be very good, Jerry thought, the way she could blush and pale at the blink of an eye. "I can't wear your fraternity pin," she said.

"Listen," he said, "I know girls who lend each other pins, and class rings they got from high school boyfriends. I mean, a girl goes out with someone she's not sure about. She doesn't know how far she wants to go, or how serious he may get, so she takes along a pin or a ring, and if things get too hot, she can slip on the ring or go to the bathroom and put on the pin and come back and show the fellow that she's pledged to someone else. It can save a lot of argument."

"That's terrible!" Linda exclaimed. "It's dishonest."

"I don't think so. I know it's been worked on me, and I don't mind it, because there always *is* someone else: your mother, your brother, your father. Everyone's pledged somewhere. Your heart's never completely free, so why not have my fraternity pin to show to Jason if he starts putting too much pressure on you? I mean, Catholic girls all have crosses they can wave at you when things get tense, but you haven't got anything like that. You need my pin."

Linda picked up the pin and looked at it.

"Shall I put it on you?"

"Who else have you given it to?" she asked.

He said, "Don't think of them. You're the first I've given it to this way. You're the first it's meant to protect."

He was breathing a little deeply now, and he could see Linda was moved. "Let me put it on you," he said, taking it out of her hand.

They stood up. Rather solemnly, Jerry fastened his Deke pin to Linda's dress. He said, "I think we should kiss each other now." Linda hesitated, and then went up on her toes, gave Jerry a quick kiss on the lips, and then left the kitchen before he had time to kiss her back.

Feeling thoughtful now, Jerry rinsed out Linda's bowl, poured the remains of his sherry down the drain, put Jason's orchid in the refrigerator, and then turned off the kitchen lights. He went back through the dark dining room into the square lobby where a light burned on the desk at which Aunt Beth wrote letters and did the family accounts. She and Uncle Fred were evidently still at their cotillion. Across the lobby he could see the dark living room where Mrs. Yngling used to sit in a wing back chair, reading the *Chicago Tribune* while lying in wait for visitors to the house. Jerry had seldom been able to escape her, no matter now noiselessly he opened the front door—no one locked up in those days—or how fast he scooted across the lobby to the stairs that led up to Phil's room. By the time he got to the first landing, below the stained glass window, he would hear Mrs. Yngling's voice, thunderous with displeasure, calling out, "Come here!" Then he would go there to be scolded and lectured. Didn't he know enough to say *hello* to the adults when he came into a house? "Hello, Mrs. Yngling," he would say, or rather yell, because she was rather deaf. Then she would sit him down and harangue him about some new atrocity committed by That Man in the White House, or by the British, or the French, or the Poles, or the Russians. Mrs. Yngling hated all foreigners except the Germans and the Dutch.

Or if she were not on politics that day, she would rattle her *Trib* at Jerry and show him the story of some child in Milwaukee or St. Louis who had fallen out of a window and been impaled on the iron railings around the house. "That could happen here," she would say. "You and Phil get to roughhousing up there on the third floor. One of these days one of you will push the other out the window," and then she would go on about how she had told Mr. Forson to have those railings removed, but he never paid any attention to

her, just as he ignored the danger of the cottonwood tree in front
of the house, a tree sure to fall one night and crush Mr. and Mrs.
Forson in their bed.

She expected the worst. Mrs. Yngling was the only adult Jerry had
known who was not surprised by Pearl Harbor. She had been expecting something like that ever since Roosevelt was first elected.
Her mind was a kind of bloody scrapbook, full of old disasters, fresh
atrocities, potential horrors, and gruesome cautionary tales. She
knew of brides who had gone up like torches in their wedding gowns,
grooms crushed in their flivvers at railroad crossings, and babies
whose eyes had been poked out by sparkler sticks on the Fourth of
July. She had a catastrophe for every occasion: boys and girls chok-
ing to death as they bobbed for apples at Halloween, whole families
incinerated by improperly wired Christmas trees . . . and yet she had
frightened Jerry into memorizing almost all the poetry he knew,
some lines of which came back to him as he mounted the stairs:

> With how sad steps, O moon, thou climbst the sky,
> And with how pale and wan a face.

He couldn't remember the rest, and he might have those lines
wrong, but he felt grateful to Mrs. Yngling that he remembered
anything, and grateful, too, that she had not insisted his right hand
be cut off when he presumed to reach in and feel her heavy old
bosoms. Because despite what Phil said, Jerry knew he had done
it, and that Mrs. Yngling had shown a surprising toleration of the
outrage. She was outrageous herself.

Jerry could remember his mother once coming home from the
Forsons' in a rare fury after being insulted by Mrs. Yngling. "Why
do you always disagree with everything I say?" Mrs. Yngling had

demanded. They must have been talking politics. Jerry's mother replied as calmly as possible that her father had been a lawyer and she was brought up to look at both sides of a question. "You weren't brought up at all," Mrs. Yngling declared. She could be outrageously rude, and outrageously prejudiced, and for that very reason, though she frightened Jerry, he always felt a kind of bond with her. In a way it was right that he should have groped her. It was a case of one outrageous person making contact with another.

Linda's bedroom door was closed. Jerry stood a minute just looking at it. His mind, after its detour through memories of Mrs. Yngling, now felt poised to deal with the question that had been hovering in the background ever since Linda had kissed him.

Did she love him? He had always been nice to her, taking her sailing in the summer, helping her with her swimming and tennis, playing cards with her, even sleeping out in the dunes with her and his cousin Joanne when they wanted male protection. Might Linda have developed a secret crush on him? After all, it was natural for a little girl to hero worship her big brother, especially a big brother like Phil, and what could be easier than for that hero worship to wash over onto the big brother's best friend, and to acquire a romantic flavor in the process?

—In which case he was in hot water again, Jerry thought, as he went on up to the room he was sharing with Phil.

He was lying in his bed in the dark, still thinking of Linda, when Phil came in. "It's all right," Jerry said, "I'm awake."

Phil turned on the light, and started to undress. "What an asshole Ernie's become," Phil said. "What did you two do after you left Shirley's place?"

"Why do you call him an asshole?" Jerry asked.

"The way he behaves—picking that fight with Powell."

"I thought he did it brilliantly," said Jerry. "He got Powell furious in no time flat."

"That's brilliant?"

"It takes skill. You have to know how to put the knife in. Ernie's good at it. Begler's terrific. He can walk into a bar in Bellefonte and get a fight started any time he feels like having one."

"Excuse me for not being impressed," said Phil.

Phil was undressed by then, and there could be no question that his whole body just did not have its former hard fitness. Most people might have seen nothing wrong, but to Jerry the situation was plain as day, but this was not the time to bring that up. "Listen, I want to tell you something," he said, "and don't get upset."

"Just a minute," Phil said. He disappeared into the bathroom. When he finally came out he had on citron-colored pajamas that further disheartened Jerry. Of course, at Haverford there was probably no one like Begler to set the style and exemplify manliness, but even so . . .

"What did you and Ernie do after you left?" Phil asked again.

"What I want to tell you," Jerry said, "is that I've given my Deke pin to Linda."

Phil had been moving toward his own bed, but now he stopped as suddenly as if he had seen a snake in his path. "You what!"

"I told you not to get excited," Jerry said. "It's all right. I was trying to help her out with Jason Williams."

"Who?"

"John's brother. He was Linda's date tonight."

"I know that. What do you mean you're trying to help her out? What are you talking about?"

"I don't know whether you've seen Jason recently," Jerry said, "but he's gotten to be very good-looking—just like John—and he's a real hotshot. I mean, you should have seen how he cut right back when I cut in on him."

"You cut in on him? Where? What have you been doing?"

"Ernie and I talked our way into the Colony Club party. Mrs. Riefsnyder threw us right out, but I could already see that Jason might be trouble."

Phil said, "Let me get this straight. You cut in on Linda at the Colony Club party and gave her your fraternity pin?"

"Not then," said Jerry. "Then we went out to Woodlawn Cemetery to Jimmy's grave. I gave Linda my pin when I got back here."

"Are you drunk?" Phil asked.

"What do you mean, drunk?"

"Stand up," said Phil. "I want to see you walk a straight line."

"I told you not to get excited," Jerry said.

"Excited?" said Phil. "You've pinned Linda? My sister? You've given your dumb pin to Linda?"

"It's not so dumb."

"You were trying to give it away to that waitress."

"I told you I needed to get rid of it, but this way it can do some good, only there could be a problem."

"The problem is that I'll kill you if you start messing with Linda."

Jerry acknowledged that brothers—also fathers—had certain rights where girls were concerned, but even so he found Phil's words offensive. "That's no way to talk to me," he said.

"I'll do more than talk," Phil promised.

"I was afraid you might be upset," Jerry admitted.

Phil said, "I still don't understand this. I can't believe it. She let you pin her?"

"Yes," said Jerry, "but it's not what you think. Or anyway I don't think it's what you think, only there's this problem."

He was about to explain it, when Phil interrupted him. "Get up! I want to see if you can walk straight."

"I can walk straight. I can walk on my hands," Jerry said. He got out of bed and began to walk across the room on his hands.

Phil said, "Where are your pajamas?"

"I don't own any pajamas now."

"Well, stand up. You look ridiculous that way."

Jerry stood up. "Satisfied?" he asked.

"I'm not satisfied at all," said Phil. "If you've really pinned Linda, you must be completely out of your mind."

Jerry said, "Linda's beautiful now. There'd be nothing crazy about pinning her, only that's not what I did."

"You said you did."

"Well, I gave her my pin. I put it on her, in fact, but that's not the point."

"Let me smell your breath," Phil said.

"I'm not drunk," Jerry insisted. "I mean, Ernie and I drank a lot of Scotch at Jimmy's grave, but that was a while ago, and I wasn't really drunk even then."

"I don't understand anything," said Phil. "What were you doing at Jimmy's grave?"

"Drinking with him, talking about him. We loved him."

Phil clutched his head. "All right, go on," he said.

"Go on where?"

"I don't know. I was feeling all right until this began. Now I think *I'm* drunk."

Jerry said, "The problem is that Linda may have a secret crush on me. Do you think that's possible?"

"With you around, anything's possible."

"I didn't mean for this to happen," Jerry said. "I mean, Linda shouldn't get starry-eyed over me."

"She certainly shouldn't."

Jerry said, "Maybe you can warn her."

"Don't worry, I will."

"Don't blacken my name too much," Jerry said, "just tell her she shouldn't pin her hopes on me."

"I'll tell her."

"My pin's really just for emergencies," Jerry said. "Tell her that. Tell her not to use it as armor to keep everyone at bay."

"Are we talking about the same thing?" Phil asked. "That little pin you gave the waitress at Cresson?"

"Yes, my Deke pin."

"What kind of armor is that?" Phil asked. "How can a girl defend herself with a pin that size? They need hatpins, or whistles. A policeman's whistle is better than some dinky little pin."

"You don't understand," Jerry said, and he explained again that he had given Linda his fraternity pin to use the way Catholic girls used crosses to keep boys from going too far.

"And you expect me to believe that?" Phil said.

"Well, what's unbelievable about it?"

"People just don't do that kind of thing. Fraternity pins are almost like engagement rings. You don't propose to a girl in order to save her from someone else."

"You might," said Jerry.

"Maybe *you* might, but I wouldn't. I wouldn't propose to anyone that I didn't want to marry."

"Well, I'd be glad to marry Linda," Jerry said, "only she's too young. I probably am, too."

"And you're in love with someone else."

"Yeah."

"And failing in school."

"Failing in my major. It's a very tough major. One of the hardest at Penn State."

Phil just shook his head. "Let's go to bed. You're making my head ache, and I'm tired of seeing you standing there naked."

"I want to talk to you about that," Jerry said.

"About what?"

"About your body."

"*My* body?"

"You're not looking the way you should. Your physique used to be better than mine, and now . . ." Jerry shrugged. "And those pajamas!" He shook his head.

Phil said, "I'm going to go sleep in the guest room. You get back in bed, Jerry, and maybe in the morning you'll seem less insane than now. Right now I don't think I want to sleep in the same room with you."

CHAPTER 9

Some holiday! Then on January 3rd, when he got back to State College, Jerry found himself faced with a new problem. The apartment Begler had found for them on Locust Lane was too expensive, but since the Deke house was about to be closed Jerry moved his possessions to Locust Lane at least for the time being. Then he settled down to write Linda.

Dear Linda, he wrote,

Phil says I've gotten you in trouble with your parents, and that the only fair thing is for me to ask you to give me back my pin. Is this true? He says you won't give it back just because your mother and father want you to, but that if I ask you to send it back, you will. Do you want me to ask you for it? If you want me to ask for it, I will. I'll do whatever you want me to do.

You can write me at this address, but I may not be staying here because the rent is too high. I don't know if Phil has telephoned home since we left, but what happened is that our old Chevy blew a gasket in Ohio, and we had to sell it for junk. The generator was about shot anyway, and we needed new tires, but it was a blow all the same. Phil got a train to Philadelphia, but I had to take a bunch of buses to get here. We were so tired of arguing with each other about you that we were glad to part, even if it did mean losing the Chevy.

So let me know, and I'll do just what you tell me to do.

He signed it "Love, Jerry," and then dashed off a note to Phil to say that he'd written Linda offering to ask for his pin back if she wanted him to ask for it. Then he wrote home to his parents to say that he had arrived at last, after an all-night bus ride, but that the rent on the apartment Begler had found for them was $110 a month, which was too high. He would find a cheaper place, maybe in a mixed co-op a few blocks away. He had already found out, as he suspected all along, that there was no dorm space available. He would be letting them know where to reach him.

He mailed those three letters, grabbed a BLT at the Corner Room, and then went to see Elizabeth.

He found her in what he thought of as her ecstatic mood. There had been a snowfall the night before and that morning she had taken a long walk across the university golf courses and out into the country. The bare trees atop Bald Eagle Ridge were etched sharply against the cold blue sky. Closer at hand fresh snow glittered on every branch of every tree and every twig of every branch. On the ground the only marks were those of squirrels and rabbits, and what Elizabeth thought might be a fox. Of course, it could have been a raccoon or maybe a possum, or possibly some kind of small dog, but she was almost sure those had been the pad marks of a fox. And then the birds! She had seen chickadees and purple finches and a cardinal and what she thought might be a pine siskin. It was glorious. That was the only word for it: *glorious.*

He loved her this way when she seemed radiant both inside and out, even though outside she was still wearing her old brown cardigan instead of the fine lamb's-wool sweater he had sent her from Marshall Fields. "Go on," he said.

She went on. Her whole holiday had been wonderful. She had spent most of it in Cambridge, staying with an old friend. She had seen her thesis director, who told her he liked her dissertation and that he was willing to schedule her defense in February between semesters.

"Defense?" Jerry interjected.

Yes, didn't he know? Every Ph.D. candidate had to defend his or her dissertation in front of a committee of professors who posed questions and probed for weaknesses.

"They have their nerve!" Jerry exclaimed.

"Why? What do you mean?"

"Well, you worked hard on that dissertation," Jerry reminded her. He had seen an impressive pile of revised drafts stacked on the floor beside Elizabeth's desk. "Why should you have to defend it to a bunch of old professors? They should mind their own business."

"This is their business."

"I bet you know more about Blake's *Songs of Innocence and Experience* than anyone."

"Jerry, don't argue about things you don't understand."

He subsided though he was not convinced, and Elizabeth went on to point out that this early defense meant she would get her degree in June. She had already told her department head, who had congratulated her and spoken encouragingly about tenure and better teaching assignments. In short, everything was looking up.

"I wish I could say the same," Jerry said.

"Why? Is something the matter?"

"Something? Everything." And Jerry launched into a recital of his current problems. He touched lightly upon money, housing, and transportation, before getting around to Linda. "Her whole family's mad at me now. They think I'm after her."

"Are you?"

He gave her a reproachful look. "You know I'm not. Would I be here if I were?"

Elizabeth paused to consider the matter before saying, "I think you might."

He felt hurt. "Is that what you think of me?"

Choosing her words carefully, Elizabeth said, "I think you're active and affectionate enough to carry on several affairs at the same time."

"All right," he conceded, "maybe I *could* carry on with more than one woman, but I'm not."

"Fine."

"You sound as if it doesn't make much difference to you."

Elizabeth leaned back into the corner of the couch where she was sitting. "I'm sorry this has come up," she said.

He was, too. "I've been promiscuous," he admitted, "but that isn't what I want to be."

"What do you want?"

He moved next to her on the couch. "You know what I want."

"Jerry . . . ," she began.

He interrupted her. "I know what you're going to say. We have no future."

"Well, look at the facts."

"What facts? I love you."

"Love comes very easily to your lips."

Why was she saying these terrible things? "You mean you don't believe me?"

"Jerry, you live in such a rush of events and feelings that it's easy for you to get swept up by your own momentum and conclude you're in love, but how long do your feelings last?"

"Forever!" he declared.

"Forever is a long time."

"All right, for the rest of my life. I mean, I still love every girl I've ever loved. I saw Rosalind on New Year's Eve. We didn't even talk. I saw her for maybe two minutes, and it was like my heart was bursting all over again."

"As if," Elizabeth murmured.

"What?"

"You should say, it was *as if* my heart *were* bursting."

"It was," he insisted. "And I know if I were to see Marie Promojunch again I'd feel the same craziness I felt for her from the beginning. And it's the same with Laura and Pat. In fact, I do see Pat. I've seen her three or four times, and each time it's like I'm kneeling again to kiss her navel."

Elizabeth seemed startled. "Who? What? Who are all these people?"

"Girls I've loved."

He had never given her the history of his love life. Now, suddenly, he wanted her to know it all. He said, "In fifth grade there was a girl named Gloria Offenbach who hid in a coat closet at school and said, 'Come here' and when I followed her into the closet she grabbed me and kissed me on the lips. It's one of the great moments of my life. I'm grateful just thinking about her. I'm grateful to them all, even when it ended badly."

Elizabeth nodded. He moved closer to her. "Listen," he said, "why aren't you wearing the sweater I sent you?"

Again he seemed to have startled her.

"Didn't you get it?"

"Yes, I got it. It's lovely."

"Then why aren't you wearing it? Doesn't it fit? I mean, I can change it if it doesn't fit."

"It fits."

"Then why are you still wearing this?" And he started to unbutton her brown cardigan.

She put a hand over his hand to stop him. "Jerry," she said, "you mustn't start giving me things."

"I want to. I mean, I can't give you the moon, but at least let me give you what I can." And despite her restraining hand he went on unbuttoning her cardigan. After a moment she took her hand off his and murmured:

> License *thy* roving hands and let them go
> Before, behind, between, above, below.

When he got back to the Locust Lane apartment late that afternoon, Jerry found Begler looking at himself in the bathroom mirror. "My hair's falling out," Begler announced in tones suggestive of high tragedy.

Jerry could have told him that. For months Begler's brush had been so clogged with dark hair that Jerry hadn't felt like using it. Now the only consolation Jerry had to offer was an unfeeling, "You'll survive."

Begler went on staring at himself in the mirror. He touched his temple. "I'm going to be bald!"

Jerry brushed it aside. "Listen," he said, "we've got to talk about this apartment."

That lack of sympathy punctured Begler's self-absorption. Recalled to the here and now, he said, "Some screwy girl telephoned while you were out."

"Did you take a message?" Jerry asked.

"She said she'd changed her mind."

"That's all?"

"She said you'd understand."

It had to be Anne, Jerry thought, deciding she wanted to sleep with him after all. Just what he needed! He left Begler facing the mirror and went to telephone the Kappa suite. When he asked to speak to Anne Player, the girl who answered the phone asked who was calling. "Jerry Engels," Jerry said.

"Jerry Engels!"

"Yeah, Jerry Engels."

There was a confused noise as if the girl might be coughing, or stifling a laugh, or something. Then she said, "Just a minute, I'll call her."

What kind of a reputation was he getting? Jerry wondered. Then Anne came on the line with a bright, challenging *Hi* that didn't sound natural. "Was that you?" he asked.

"Me what?"

"That called here to say you'd changed your mind."

"What if it was?" she said.

"You mean it was?"

"Was what?"

Jerry felt his head beginning to spin. "Was you."

"Yes, it was me," said Anne.

"Well, listen," he told her, "we can't talk now. I'll see you tomorrow. I'm posing tomorrow. We'll talk about this after class. Okay?"

"Okay," she chirped.

She sounded so unlike herself that he asked if she were all right.

"I'm fine," she said, and hung up.

More trouble, Jerry thought, as he cradled the receiver and went back to Begler, who had given up looking at himself in the mirror and was now staring out a window at the leafless trees along Locust Lane. "Listen," Jerry said, "I just can't afford this apartment."

"Why not?"

"What do you mean, why not? I don't have the money."

"Your father has."

"Yeah, but I can't ask him to raise my allowance. I'm already in Dutch with him in a dozen different ways. The least I can do is not cost him extra money—which I already have getting this new tooth." He bared his gums so Begler could see. "Which you loosened," he added.

"So sue me."

They weren't getting anywhere. Jerry tried a new tack. "If I move out, could you find someone else to share with? What about Gossage?"

"He's fixed up."

"Well, then, O'Dana. You like him."

"He's got Rex." Begler hated dogs.

"Well, why in hell did you sign a lease for a place this expensive?"

"It's not so expensive. You're just being cheap."

"I haven't got the money!" Jerry exclaimed. Then he said, "I think I know where I could make some more, but . . ." He looked at Begler. "Listen, give me your advice," and then he told Begler about an offer he had received that fall. A local businessman of somewhat shady reputation had approached Jerry one afternoon to ask if Jerry would be interested in acting. Acting? Jerry said. Well, posing. Oh, posing! Sure, he posed for the art department, Jerry told the man, who said that was one reason he had approached Jerry. "You don't mind being naked, do you?" At that point the light dawned. "I don't know where he gets the girls," Jerry told

Begler, "but he said he could use me in one of his films. What do you think? It pays pretty well."

"It's up to you," Begler said.

"Well, would you do it?" Jerry asked.

"Hell no!" Begler sounded almost angry at the suggestion.

"Then why say it's up to me? I mean, if you think it's wrong?"

"I didn't say it's wrong."

"You must think it's wrong or you wouldn't be mad."

"What are we arguing about this for, anyway?" Begler asked.

"I just think friends should help each other to do the right thing."

Begler threw up his hands. "So do it if you want."

"I don't want to. I hate pornography."

"Then don't do it."

"I don't think I will."

"Jesus, Engels. You drive me crazy sometimes."

"Okay, let's drop it. Let's go eat," Jerry said.

They hadn't bought any supplies or set up housekeeping in the apartment, so they walked down to the Tavern.

At the Tavern, Jerry said, "Maybe I could get a job here." Tavern waiters were all male, all roughly similar in size and general looks. Jerry fitted the type. "I bet they'd hire me here," he said, "I know some men in Acacia who work here. They could vouch for me." So after dinner he asked to speak to one of the owners, who took note of Jerry's references and then asked Jerry if he had any experience.

"No, but I mean how much experience do I need? I'm deft. I'm not clumsy. I don't drop things."

The man laughed, and said he would check Jerry's references and get back to him. "I'll probably give you a call tomorrow. I can always use good waiters," he said.

"So that's that," Jerry reported to Begler. "I even get meals there on nights when I work."

"So you're going to stay?"

"Yeah. I can't let you down."

The apartment was really very nice. They had a living room with windows on Locust Lane, a kitchen-cum-dinette with a table beside a window looking out toward Phi Kappa Psi next door, and a bedroom with two windows from one of which they could actually see a corner of the roof of the Deke house over on Thompson Street. Begler was particularly pleased that a garage came with the apartment. He had hated leaving his MG exposed to the weather in the Deke parking lot. It was some compensation for losing his hair.

Jerry settled in on Locust Lane that night, and in the morning started going back to classes for the first time since Weigert's death. He had missed a week and a day in all his classes, but since he was going to do poorly anyway, and since all his courses were requirements in PNGE, it hardly made any difference so long as he managed to get at least D's.

After his last class he went over to the art building to pose. He tried to catch Anne's eye as he took his position on the platform, but she was looking at her sketchpad. She was half-hidden as usual behind her easel, and he somehow surmised that her bright chirpiness had leaked away. He wasn't surprised. He could remember the year—years, really—when he'd hovered on the brink of sexuality, wanting to take a plunge, afraid of what was down there in the deeps. He'd blown hot and cold in the same breath. He'd spun like a pinwheel, throwing out sparks sideways, never getting anywhere. Anne must be like that. He really sympathized with her.

Later, at Baroutsis, she seemed subdued. "Why don't you come to dinner?" Jerry said. "I'll fix us dinner. I want you to see the apartment."

"I've been thinking . . . ," she began.

"Now wait a minute," he said. "Don't say that."

"You don't know what I'm going to say."

"You're going to say you've changed your mind again."

"Well, what if I have?"

He said, "Listen, I know what you're going through. I went through it myself. Everyone goes through it."

She didn't reply.

"It's natural."

"Jerry . . . ," she began.

"I mean, don't let me pressure you into doing something you don't want to do, but you've got to go ahead sometime with someone, so why not with me? I mean you like me. I'm nice. You said so."

"I just . . ."

"I mean, yesterday you had your mind made up, so why chicken out now?"

That got her. Her chin came up, her eyes met his, and she said, "I'm not chickening out."

"Good. Great," he said. "I'll pick you up tomorrow around six."

Their dinner date had to be postponed, however, because the next day Jerry got a call from the Tavern and went to work there on Thursday, Friday, and Saturday. Sunday he spent with Elizabeth. They drove out to Shingletown Gap and walked up behind the reservoir. Rhododendron leaves hung stiff in the cold. The stream was sheeted with ice. In a pool they could see an immobile fish frozen in place. *No motion has she now*, Elizabeth said. "Do you know that poem?" Jerry didn't, and so as they tramped onward Elizabeth taught him some Wordsworth. It was not until the following Monday that Jerry was in a position to entertain Anne Player on Locust Lane. Begler had agreed to get lost until after midnight.

In the meantime Jerry had a letter from Linda in which she said that she didn't want him to ask for his Deke pin. Her mother wouldn't let her wear it to school, she said, but she had told her best friends that she had Jerry's pin, and her best friends had blabbed it around so that Jason now knew and was not speaking to her except to make cutting remarks in the corridor, and to write her letters in study hall saying that he hadn't done anything to deserve being treated the way she was treating him, and that unless she relented and acknowledged that she was in the wrong he would start to go out with Phyllis Pope. Furthermore he wanted her to return Jerry's Deke pin, if she actually had the pin, which he doubted. He knew she was just being mean. "I hate him," Linda concluded.

To this Jerry replied that he was glad she wanted to keep his pin, but sorry it was causing her so much trouble with everyone, particularly Jason, who was more to be pitied than hated. "He's just sore that you threw him out New Year's Eve and he thinks you're trying to punish him and make him jealous by saying you have my pin. Tell him I gave it to you because I've always had a crush on you, and that you had to accept it from me because you didn't want to hurt my feelings, but that you think of me as just a very good friend. That should make him realize that if he behaves better he has a chance with you. What you want is for him to be good, and act like a man, so give him some hope." That fine, faintly Machiavellian advice was on its way to Chicago when Jerry played host to Anne Player.

The repeated postponements of their date had had the effect of restoring her confidence to some extent. When Jerry unlocked the door and offered to carry her across the threshold, she said, "Are you crazy?"

He explained it was the first time he had ever entertained a girl in his own quarters. He felt almost as excited as if they were just married. "I have champagne for us," he told her. "And filet mignon." There were potatoes already baking in the oven. He had gone to some trouble and expense. The apartment was immaculate, and he had even bought candles for them to eat by. He had two long-stemmed roses arranged in an empty beer bottle on the coffee table. "What do you think of the place?" he asked her.

She looked around with the same indifference she had displayed at La Villa. "It's all right," she said.

"Let me show you the bedroom."

"No."

He picked up a record—"Begin the Beguine"—and gestured at the phonograph. "You want to dance?'

"No."

This was heavy going, he thought, as he opened his bottle of champagne and poured her a glass. Anne accepted it without enthusiasm and drank without any apparent pleasure. When he asked whether she'd like her filet rare or medium, she told him she wanted it well done. He tried to argue her out of that, telling her this was good meat that he'd bought at Temple Market. It shouldn't be well done. All she said in reply was that's how she liked her meat. Well done. So he overcooked her filet and served it up with a baked potato and some canned peas. "I wish you could enjoy this," he said.

"Enjoy what?"

"Being here. Having dinner with me. We should be enjoying ourselves."

She gave him a dark look.

"Aren't you sort of excited?" he asked.

"No. I'm scared."

"There's nothing to be scared of."

"Maybe for you there isn't."

This was heartbreaking. He said, "Well, if you'd rather, we could just go out to a movie after dinner."

She considered the possibility, and then like a convicted prisoner accepting punishment said that they might as well go through with it.

What an attitude! he thought, as they left the table and moved toward the bedroom. He had envisioned an evening of bubbly, rising intimacy, not this last-supper march to the gallows. What should he do? Argue her out of it, or argue her into it? Neither alternative made sense. This wasn't an occasion for argument.

In the bedroom he said to her, "Now you go in there," he pointed to the bathroom, "and get undressed. And I'll be waiting for you here."

"You want me to take off everything?" she asked.

"Yes, everything."

She went into the bathroom and closed the door. He turned down the bed. He put some preservatives on the bedside table. He changed the record in the living room to Tchaikovsky's *Nutcracker Suite*. Then he turned off the lights, and brought in the candles from the kitchenette. Finally he undressed. "Okay," he called out to Anne, "I'm ready." She didn't answer. Water continued to run in the bathroom, muffling whatever other sounds she might be making. He wondered what she needed all the water for? Could she be taking a bath? "I'm ready," he called again. Still no answer. Only the steady thrum of water. He began to grow concerned. He had heard of girls in similar situations passing out in bathrooms from a combination of stress and fear and drink. He hoped Anne hadn't locked herself in. When she didn't respond to his third call, he tiptoed over and gently tried the doorknob. It was locked. How would he get her out if she had collapsed in there? Then he wondered if the water was running to hide the sound of her escaping through the window. He had heard of that happening, too. Anything could happen. Probably everything *had* happened. "Anne?" he said, his mouth right against the door. "Are you all right, Anne?"

"Go away," she replied, "don't come in."

So she hadn't escaped or collapsed. He went back to the bed and sat down and tried to be patient. At last, after what seemed like half an hour, the water stopped running, and he heard Anne's voice saying, "Have you put out the lights?"

"You want it to be dark?" he asked.

"Put out the lights," she replied.

He snuffed out his candles. "The lights are out," he called back.

"Do you have any clothes on?"

"No. I don't have anything on."

"Put on something," she replied.

"No," he said, "now come on out."

"Jerry," she said, "I want to go home."

It was too late to go home, or rather, too early. "You can't go home," he told her.

She took her time thinking that over. Then she said, "Are the lights really out?"

"Yes, they're really out," he called back. "It's totally dark here."

"Where are you?" she asked.

"I'm sitting on the bed."

"Well, don't move," she told him. Then she turned out the lights in the bathroom, and he heard her unlocking the door.

"I'm here," he said, when he heard the door opening.

His eyes had adjusted to the dark, but hers hadn't. "I can't see you," she said.

"Just take a couple of steps forward," he told her, "and put out your hand." There was enough light coming in from the street for him to see her as a white figure against the darker black of the bathroom. "Just put out your hand, and you'll feel my hand."

"You're not going to do anything?" she said.

"I'm going to take your hand," he told her.

"Jerry, I just can't do this," she said.

He decided this was killing him as much as it was killing her. "Just shuffle forward," he said. She moved slightly, and he shifted his own position further down the bed so as to be able to reach her sooner.

She heard him move and in a voice filled with alarm she called out, "What are you doing? Where are you now?"

"I'm still on the bed. I just shifted a little closer to you."

"I'm frightened," Anne said.

"I know you're frightened.

"What am I going to do?" she asked.

"Take a step."

She took a step, and at last he was able to reach out and take hold of her hand. He felt it was like the first meeting of Adam and Eve. He'd had whole nights of lovemaking that now seemed like superficial encounters compared to holding Anne's hand. He drew her to sit on the bed beside him. He said, "You're cold."

She said, "I don't know what I am."

He put an arm around her. "We're just going to sit here," he told her, "until you stop shivering."

"Am I shivering?" she asked.

"You're trembling." He edged against her, his leg against hers, his body next to hers, his arm around her shoulder. "You'll feel warmer," he assured her.

Out of the dark she said, "You must think I'm a fool."

It reminded him of Weigert looking up hopelessly and asking his brothers what they thought of him. But Anne had a spark that

Weigert lacked. "No," he told her, "I think you're great." His hand moved on her shoulder, softly stroking her smooth skin. "Put your head on my shoulder," he said. When she didn't do it of her own free will, he put his hand on the side of her head and pressed until he could feel her head resting against his chest, her cheek on the skin above his heart. "That's better," he said. He took her hand. "Here, touch me." He guided her hand to his thigh, and felt cold fingers brush his skin. "Put your hand on me," he told her, releasing her hand and waiting, but only her fingertips remained in contact with his skin. At that he stirred, "This isn't going to work," he said.

Anne raised her head and drew away from him. "You're telling me?"

He let her move away, though he took her hand. They sat for a while like children holding hands in the dark. Jerry felt almost sexless, as if he were a little boy again. It felt odd, but not unpleasant. He squeezed Anne's hand.

"Jerry," she said, warningly.

"I'm not trying anything," he told her. "I couldn't," he added. Then he felt her stir beside him. "No, let's stay this way," he said. He wanted to go on enjoying this curious intermission of desire. "Would you like some more cake?" he asked her. He had bought a chocolate cake for dessert.

"No."

They remained on the bed holding hands. Then he began to play with her hand, and to feel each individual finger, and that somehow awakened him to new possibilities. She had strong fingers. She was an artist. The professor was always complimenting her on her drawings. "Why don't you sketch me?" Jerry said.

"Now?"

"Stay right here," Jerry told her. He found his way into the living room, turned on the light there, and found a tablet of paper and a pencil. Back in the bedroom he said, "We'll light the candles, and you can sketch me," and before Anne could protest, he'd struck a match and lighted both candles.

"Jerry, please, I'm embarrassed," Anne said.

"I'm not looking at you," he told her. He sat on the edge of the bed with his head turned. "I'm looking away over my shoulder. You've got my head in profile."

"I can't do this," she said.

"Sure you can. This is something you're good at. You draw very well. The professor is always saying so. Go ahead. Sketch me." After a minute or two of silence he could hear her stirring on the bed. Then he heard the scratch of pencil on paper. He sat quite still, as if he were posing in class. When the pencil sounds stopped, he said, "Now let's try this pose." He hopped to his feet and stood with one foot up on the bed frame, leaning forward with his elbow on his knee.

Anne said, "Do I have to go on?"

"Just a quick sketch."

"I can see your thing," she said.

"So if you don't like it, leave it out of the drawing."

After a while the sketching sounds began again. Finally he heard paper being ripped from the tablet. Anne announced she was going to go dress.

Jerry turned to smile at her. "Okay, fine."

"You said you wouldn't look."

"There's no reason for you to hide," he told her. "You have nice breasts. You have nice, creamy skin. You have nothing to be ashamed of." Then he dropped to his knees in front of her and began to kiss the smoothly stretched skin of her belly. She stood it for a moment, and then ran for the bathroom.

He was dressed by the time she came out. He said, "I think we should do this again."

"Why?"

"I don't know why, but I think it's right. You don't want to spend your whole life in the dark. You should at least see me."

"I see you in class."

"It's not the same. It's not personal."

She said, "Why did you kiss me there?"

"I wanted to."

She sighed. "I'm tired," she said. "Take me home."

"But you'll come back?" he said.

"I suppose so. I always do what scares me."

Linda's reply to Jerry's second letter came three days later. This time she reported more on her family dilemma than on repercussions at school. "Mother understands better than Daddy does, but she thinks I'm spoiling my senior year by keeping your pin. She says I'll miss going to all the parties and the prom if I sit at home writing you letters and thinking of you as my boyfriend. Daddy just says the whole thing's impossible, and that I should never have accepted your pin in the first place. He keeps reminding me of Nancy Train. I hate him."

Jerry wrote back to say that she shouldn't get in the habit of hating people, and that it was true that he had created a scandal with Nancy. "I don't want you to put me on a pedestal," he wrote Linda, "because I'm not immaculate, and I sure don't want you to miss your senior parties and the prom. Have you made it up with Jason? You should. He's the right kind of date for you, you just have to keep the upper hand with him, and not let him have his way too much."

He got that off on a Sunday morning, along with his usual letter home telling his parents about his new job at the Tavern, on the basis of which he had gone ahead and settled in with Begler. He mailed those letters on his way up to Rec Hall for a workout. He couldn't remember when he had felt so good. He liked the cold wind blowing in his face, the ring of his footstep on the pavement, and the prospect of hard exercise ahead.

CHAPTER 10

Before the semester ended he found himself carrying on three quite different love affairs, and far from this taxing his resources it seemed to increase them. It proved what he had always believed, that love strengthened you in every way. He felt more alert mentally and physically than ever before. He waited eagerly for each letter from Linda, he looked forward with fresh enthusiasm to posing in front of Anne. Most of all he looked forward to weekends with Elizabeth. When classes ended he felt torn. He dearly wanted to go with Elizabeth to Cambridge for the defense of her thesis. The long drive in her Hudson appealed to him. The nights they would have to spend together on the road and in Cambridge excited his imagination. He even wanted to see Cambridge and to walk around Radcliffe and Harvard. He had been taken there as a boy, but except for the glass flowers nothing had made much of an impression on him. Now, because Elizabeth had lived there, he wanted to see it all—her dormitory in the Radcliffe Quad, the church on Massachusetts Avenue where she married Whittington, the apartment building on Story Street where they had lived. He wanted to go out to Concord to see where she used to ride and picnic with Elmer. It was as if by visiting those spots he would make them his own, and thus retroactively absorb that period of her life and knit together in his own person whatever stray feelings Elizabeth retained for her earlier lovers.

Yet if he went with her he would lose what they agreed was his best opportunity to paint her apartment. She was willing for it to be painted, but she had resisted him throughout January because she hated the smell of paint and did not want to have her books and papers moved about while she was teaching. Even when they decided he would stay in State College and paint while she was away, she had misgivings over the upheaval this would cause. She said, "I know it doesn't appear to you as if this is organized, but I do know where to look for things." She stood by her desk, gesturing at the top deep in papers and books, and at the piles of papers on the floor. "There's a system here," she insisted. "I know all my tax papers are in that pile, and those are mainly letters and some clippings I want to keep, and *that*," she pointed to a great pile of paper on the floor, "*that* contains all the different drafts of my thesis."

"Well, at least we can get rid of that now," Jerry said.

"No! no!" she cried. She seemed genuinely agitated. "You must promise me not to throw away anything. I can't leave you here, I can't let you do this unless you promise to keep all the piles separate, and to put them back in the same place. Otherwise I'll never find anything again."

He promised.

"I mean this," she told him. "When you paint this end of the room move all the books and all the papers to the far end, and put them down there in the order they're in at this end, and then put them back in the same order. I mean it, Jerry. You've got to do it that way."

He promised again, but she still didn't quite believe he meant it. Before she left on Saturday morning she went over it again, and made him promise a third time. Then she said, "Now I've talked to Mrs. Lutz. She knows you'll be working up here. She may come up to see for herself, but that's perfectly all right with me. I've told her I've hired a young man to paint the place, and she was quite nice about it, and she's giving me something off my next month's rental."

"She should give you a month off at least. This place hasn't been painted in years."

"She's giving me something off," Elizabeth went on, "and I've told her what color the walls will be. It's all arranged, and all you have to do is to leave the key with her when you're finished today, and pick it up from her tomorrow, only you'll have to come before she goes off to church. She spends most of Sunday in church. It doesn't matter when you leave at night because you can just drop the key in her box, but to get it from her you'll have to be here before 9:30 tomorrow."

"I better just keep the key myself," Jerry said.

"No!" Elizabeth cried. "Heavens! I can't let a young man have my latchkey. Mrs. Lutz would think that's very strange."

How could she live with this hypocrisy, he wondered. How could she bear to pander to Mrs. Lutz's snoopy and suspicious mind? But rather than start Elizabeth off on her journey with the taste of an argument in her mind, Jerry promised to leave the key with Mrs. Lutz. Then he put his arms around her. They would not see each other until Thursday. "I wish I could be in both places," he said.

She was patting him on the back a little distractedly. "I wish you could, too," she said, but he could tell her mind was now on the drive ahead of her.

After she left, he stood at her front windows and watched as she came out of the building and went to her car. He could see her expression as she unlocked the Hudson. She had a preoccupied, half-anxious look that wrung his heart. He should be driving her, he thought. He should have gone with her in spite of the cost of the trip and the lost opportunity to paint. It was just wrong, he thought, for someone like Elizabeth to be preoccupied and worried about petty matters. He should take over all that part of her life so that she could think and write and recite poetry to her heart's content. He felt almost like running downstairs and chasing after the Hudson in his old jeans and sweatshirt, but instead he watched Elizabeth back and fill several times before she pulled away from the curb. Then she drove off, and he turned away from the window to survey the work ahead.

He began just by cleaning the place. He washed every glass and dish and bowl and scrubbed every pot in her kitchen. He scrubbed the tile around the sink, he cleaned the stove inside and out, and virtually emptied the refrigerator in order to clean it. Mrs. Lutz encountered him as he deposited trash and refrigerator remnants in the garbage bin behind the building. "You're the young man working in Miss Grant's apartment?" she said. Jerry replied that he was. He looked at her impassively. He would not smile at her small face and colorless eyes. "There's a lot to do up there," said Mrs. Lutz. Jerry nodded. "Miss Grant doesn't keep house the way other people do."

Goaded, Jerry said, "She probably has better things to do." Then he left Mrs. Lutz to mull that over.

By late afternoon he had gotten rid of the dirt and prepared the walls, except for the wall of books in the main room. He would leave that wall for last. The work left him feeling raw inside, as if all his scraping and scrubbing had rubbed him thin. Time after time he had come across little makeshift arrangements and botched repairs that broke his heart as being signs of Elizabeth's poverty, and of the fact that she had no one, until now, to take care of her. It seemed to him mere luck that she had not shorted out and burned down the whole building with her system of frayed extension cords.

He left the key with Mrs. Lutz and said he would be back early on Sunday morning. Would 7:30 be too early for her? "No indeed," she said. "I'm glad that apartment is getting the work it needs."

He walked back to Locust Lane feeling a little more friendly toward Mrs. Lutz. He found Begler in their living room, smoking a cigar with his feet up. Begler had wanted the two of them to go up to Split Rock again, but Jerry said he couldn't afford it and didn't have the time. So Begler had spent the day skiing at Moshannon. "What are you doing tonight?" he asked.

"I'm on the late shift at the Tavern," Jerry said.

Begler made a face. He was finding the new arrangements less satisfactory than he expected. Jerry wasn't available for excursions to Split Rock, or night rides to Altoona, and there was not the usual crowd around to provide Begler with someone to shoot pool with or toss a ball to. Begler yawned and took his feet off the coffee table. "I should have gone up to Stowe," he remarked.

"I told you I'd be busy."

"Fixing up The Schoolteacher's apartment," said Begler. He always referred to Elizabeth as The Schoolteacher. He was jealous of her, whereas he thought Anne was simply a joke. He called her The Virgin, or The Virgin Queen, or sometimes The Queen of the Fairies. Jerry refused to discuss his relationship with Anne, but Begler was no fool. He knew something had been scheduled to happen that Monday night, but that it had led to the sketches Anne left behind, not to the use of the condoms Jerry had left out on his bedside table.

"So what the hell?" Begler said. "I might as well eat at the Tavern, too." He waited while Jerry washed up and put on a good pair of dark trousers. Then they strolled down together.

Even though it was semester break, Saturday night at the Tavern was still a busy time. Begler had to wait for a table. Jerry went right up to change into the regulation short-sleeved white shirt that all Tavern waiters wore. When he came down and was assigned his station, he found Begler seated at one of his tables. "What do you want?" Jerry asked.

Begler said he wanted the chopped steak. Then he said, "Look who's found himself a girl at last." He nodded toward Paul Richter, who had been Jerry's roommate in Irvin Hall. Paul was a nice-looking, fair-haired fellow. He was sitting with a girl, also fair-haired and nice-looking. They made a handsome couple. They were already eating. They were not at one of Jerry's tables, but he had to pass near them, and it seemed to Jerry just uncivilized not to stop and be friendly, even though he knew he made Paul uncomfortable now. But, after all, they had shared a room. They had even shared a bed a few times. How could you just ignore someone after that?

He stopped, and said, "Hi! Hello! How are you?" Paul said he was fine. Paul's girlfriend looked up, expecting to be introduced, but Paul looked down at his plate and took a bite of veal. Jerry smiled at the girl, felt like shrugging, looked down at Paul's head, and said, "Well, see you around." Paul nodded without looking up, and Jerry went off feeling sorry for him. Elizabeth's frayed extension cords and badly glued cups flashed back into his mind, and her chair whose leg fell off when he moved it. Elizabeth ignored things, and shoved them out of sight. Paul did the same with certain events in his past. The truth was that everyone had ugly, broken, messy stuff to deal with, and some people—most people— just could not deal with it, and would not think about it, and kept things in the dark, like those fantastic potatoes in Elizabeth's cupboard. They had white tentacles and dark eye-spots like little undersea monsters. Jerry felt almost sorry to throw them out they were so extraordinary looking. What would potatoes like those taste like, he wondered, as he served up helpings of good French fries and baked potatoes at the Tavern. He should have saved one to eat.

—Because he was not like Elizabeth or Paul. He revisited every part of his life, explored all his own crannies and cupboards and dark spots, left nothing untouched, or untasted. His worst deeds and most immoral acts fascinated him, and gradually lost their ugliness as he thought them over, just as his most painful losses had acquired a beauty and glamour of their own.

He was not like other people.

For years he had turned away from the slow dawning of that truth, but nothing could stop the sun from rising or the truth from shining through at last. It shone through now. He didn't want to be different. He didn't feel different. Yet he wasn't like Begler or any of his fraternity brothers, and he wasn't like Phil, and he wasn't even like Ernie Hill. In fact he'd never met anyone quite like himself. So he must be different. The conclusion left him feeling a little strange and isolated as if he were all by himself up on some platform with a spotlight trained on him. Yet since everyone seemed to see him as an ordinary young man with a quick step and a bright smile, maybe his difference didn't make any difference?

"Well, you *are* early," Mrs. Lutz said approvingly when he turned up shortly after seven the following morning. She still had on her wrapper. "I went up last night and looked at it," she went on. "You keep it up!" And she gave him an encouraging nod.

He kept it up all day Sunday, sometimes whistling while he worked. Mrs. Lutz looked in on him when she got back from pot-luck lunch at her church. "I brought you some scalloped pota-toes and ham and deviled eggs and jello," she said. "I knew there wasn't much in the refrigerator up here." Jerry thanked her quite genuinely. While he ate the food she brought him, Mrs. Lutz in-spected his work. "Now you're going to have to get these paint spots off my woodwork," she said. Jerry assured her he had plenty of turpentine and rags. She didn't have to worry about her wood-work, or her floors. "You can get it off faster if you clean it now," she told him. He said it would come off fast enough when he cleaned up at the end of the day. That marked a dip in their re-lationship, and Mrs. Lutz went off saying, "Well, mind you do clean up."

He was drinking a bottle of beer and taking a well-earned break when Mrs. Lutz checked in after evening service. Evidently she regarded Elizabeth's absence and Jerry's presence as a God-sent opportunity for her to pry around upstairs. The beer bottle in Jerry's hand drew first fire. "You shouldn't drink on Sunday," she told him. He said he was thirsty. "Drink water. It's better for you, anyway." Then she walked through the rooms, paying as much attention to Elizabeth's possessions as to the state of the walls and the woodwork. "I don't know how she can live the way she does," Mrs. Lutz observed aloud. She looked into the bedroom, and even opened Elizabeth's closet. "This needs cleaned," she said. Jerry felt like strangling her. What right did this old snoop have to look into Elizabeth's clothes closet? But he kept his face smooth and said he would start on the bedroom after he finished the kitchen and the main room. "How much does she pay you?" Mrs. Lutz wanted to know. Jerry said Elizabeth had tutored him in English, and he was paying for those lessons by working for her. "What do you charge normally?" Mrs. Lutz asked. Jerry gave her a sum off the top of his head. "I could use a good worker," she said. "Can you do repairs?" He could do some, Jerry said. "I don't suppose you know electricity?" He'd taken electrical engineering courses, he said. "Well, when you're finished here, I'll pay you to do the little apartment in back. It needs repaired and cleaned before I rent it out again. Can you plaster?" He could try, Jerry said. Mrs. Lutz nodded several times. "I like a boy will work hard and try," she said, and when he left the key with her several hours later, she offered him coffee.

Her living room was filled with china. "I collect," she said, as Jerry stared around. Every surface in the room was covered with china, every wall space in the room had a corner cupboard or a china cabinet filled with plates, cups, saucers, and bowls, all of different patterns. Then there were Toby jugs, and china birds, and china toadstools and elves and Bambis and cats—lots of cats— and a group of minstrels, men in capes and top hats. "In here," Mrs. Lutz said, leading Jerry to her kitchen, which was plain and strictly functional. She served him coffee from a big aluminum pot sitting on the burner. She poured the coffee into a plain white cup, chipped in one place. "I generally sit in here," she said, sitting down across from Jerry and filling her own cup, also chipped. "The things in there are too valuable," she explained.

Over coffee she grilled him about his past. Why had he come to Penn State instead of going to Indiana? Jerry had told her he lived in Indiana. "I wanted to go east with a friend," Jerry said.

Mrs. Lutz sniffed disapprovingly. "It's not much further east here, anyway," she said. Jerry realized she was thinking of Indiana, Pa., but it didn't seem worth trying to straighten her out. Her apartment was so hot that he was already sweating, and her coffee tasted as if she had been heating and reheating it all day long, which she probably had.

He drank it stoically like an Indian brave undergoing torture, or a noble Greek drinking hemlock. Then he thanked her and got up. "When will you be back in the morning?" she asked. He said he would be back at the same time. She nodded her tightly permed head and ushered him out through the collection.

It was seven o'clock by then and he hadn't eaten dinner yet, and Mrs. Lutz's coffee made him feel giddy. Snowflakes were drifting down out of the sky. He opened his mouth and caught a snowflake on his tongue. He felt somehow in touch with the whole world, as if he could embrace it with his arms, or let it melt on his tongue like that snowflake.

What had become of Mr. Lutz, he wondered. Were his ashes in one of those Toby jugs, or did she keep him in the kitchen in a plain white cookie jar, chipped like those coffee cups? He hated Mrs. Lutz, and he loved her at the same time. All those plates! All those fancy cups and saucers that she never used! If he were a different sort of person, Jerry thought, if he were evil instead of good, he would set about seducing Mrs. Lutz and then make her use her good china. She could be had, he thought; she was susceptible. She had an eye for a bargain when she saw one, and a good worker when he crossed her path, and she was undoubtedly upstairs in Elizabeth's apartment at this very minute, checking to see that he had removed every last trace of white paint from the woodwork. Abruptly he turned and headed back to Fraser Street. Yes, the lights were on in Elizabeth's front room.

"You didn't leave me any tip last night," he said when he got back to the apartment on Locust Lane, and found Begler idling around, clearly at loose ends.

Begler gave him a serious look. "This is no joke," he said. "I don't know what to do with myself." Clearly he was shocked to discover how dependent he had become on having Jerry at his disposal so much of the time.

Jerry felt shocked himself to see Begler in such a state. "I've told you before," he said, "you should get a girlfriend."

"So I can be pussy-whipped like you?"

"Well, look at you now."

"Look at you," Begler said. "Painting The Schoolteacher's apartment and romancing The Queen of the Fairies."

"Which of us is having a good time, and which of us is bored to death?" Jerry asked.

"I am bored," Begler admitted. "Let's do something tonight."

They went bowling. Then they went to the V.F.W. on Calder Alley, one of the few places in town where a man could get a drink on Sunday night. You had to be a member, of course, but then Begler had somehow managed to acquire membership. It was just another example of his genius. He said to Jerry, "So how's the Pen Pal in Chicago? She solved the pin problem?" The Pen Pal with her pin problem seemed as ridiculous to Begler as The Schoolteacher or The Virgin Queen.

"Here, listen to this," Jerry replied. He took out Linda's latest letter. She wrote him almost every day now, and not just about his pin. Her letters had expanded to take in every aspect of her life.

"Listen," he said. But first he had to explain. "Linda's on *The Correlator* staff—that's the high school yearbook—and they're composing write-ups now for all the seniors. It's a very big deal." Then he read. *"We've been arguing about Janet Ewing. They want to call her bright and talkative, and I say it makes her sound like a parrot. What do you think?"*

Begler just stared in response. "Yeah?" he said at last.

Jerry said, "Well, I think it's cute." He folded up the letter, however, and put it away. He should have known better than to try to charm Begler with high school gossip. He said, "You could turn into a lonely old man."

"Better than living with a Pen Pal."

"Listen," said Jerry. "Do you know any happily unmarried men?"

Begler considered. "Faggots excluded?" he asked.

"No. Why exclude them?"

"Well, the chaplain at Lawrence was having a ball. I guess he was happy."

"It's strange, isn't it," Jerry said, "how they enjoy it? A man once told me I had the most beautifully shaped prick and balls he'd ever seen."

"Let's get out of here," Begler said. Outside he explained. "The bartender was listening to you."

"Well, let him listen," Jerry said. "Who cares?"

"I care. I want to go back there."

Jerry said, "This country is just lousy with fear about sex. Elizabeth thinks she could be denied tenure if the Liberal Arts Dean finds out she's sleeping with an undergraduate. And look what the Dean of Men did to us just because of Veronica."

Begler looked, and for a while they walked along in silence. Finally Begler said, "Why do you think Weigert did it?"

The moon was out now. The few flakes of snow that had been drifting down earlier had stopped. It was a high, cloudless winter night open to the stars. Jerry said, "Bob was loveless."

Begler said, "I think he must have been queer."

"Who cares about that?" Jerry said.

"A lot of guys."

"Houser!" said Jerry with scorn.

"I care," said Begler. "Faggots give me the creeps."

"I don't give you the creeps," Jerry said, "and I've had a lot more homosexual experiences than Bob could ever have had."

"*You* have?"

"Sure, haven't you?"

"*Me*?" said Begler.

Jerry said, "Most guys have had at least some experiences."

"How many have you had?"

"About a dozen blow jobs, and then Paul and I used to hug each other in bed and come on each other's bellies."

"Holy shit!" Begler exclaimed.

"It was a mess," Jerry agreed. "That's one reason I was glad to move in with you when a room opened up for us at the Deke house that winter. Paul thought I was deserting him, and I probably was."

"It's a good thing no one ever knew this."

"You know something?" Jerry said. "I wouldn't mind the whole world knowing. I think all this hiding is very bad." Begler started to say something, but Jerry interrupted him. "Only of course if it got out it would be the last straw for my parents. It would wreck me with half my friends. I'd be ostracized." Again Begler tried to say something, but Jerry went on. "And all because of something that gives some people pleasure and doesn't hurt anybody."

Begler finally got out what he'd been trying to say. "If you want my advice, Engels, you'll shut up about this for good and all."

"I understand. I don't tell everybody."

"And you'll cut it out, too."

"I don't do it so much."

"Don't do it at all."

Begler, the incorruptible, had spoken.

"Oh, Jerry!" Elizabeth said. "You've worked miracles." She was back from Cambridge, her thesis successfully defended, and her anxieties over the Hudson happily misplaced. Now she was inspecting her transformed apartment.

"I bought you all new extension cords, and I took that broken chair to a repair shop."

Elizabeth was looking at a framed print of Van Gogh's "Sunflowers," a gift that Jerry had put up in place of all the postcards with which Elizabeth had covered her walls. "*Ah, sunflower, weary of time*," she said.

"I thought you'd like that," Jerry told her.

"No, I hate that picture," she said, turning away from it and going on with her inspection. She had a way of landing sucker punches just when he least expected them. "It's all so clean and white," she said. "It even smells clean."

"I used a lot of Murphy soap on the floors and the woodwork."

"Oh, Jerry," she said, looking at him, "how can I ever thank you?"

She was particularly pleased to find that he had obeyed her instructions about her papers. Against the wall on either side of her desk there were neat stacks of papers. "All I did was straighten them up," Jerry said.

She kissed him. "You're an angel."

Either she didn't notice or it didn't bother her that he had rear-ranged all her books, putting the short little paperbacks all on the top shelf, and the big heavy anthologies and Modern Library Giants on the bottom one, and the in-between books on the in-between shelf.

"And you did the bedroom, too!" she marveled, taking a peek in there.

"Except for the closet," said Jerry. The closet had really defeated him.

"Good," said Elizabeth. "I wouldn't want anyone looking in my closet." Then she just stood for a moment, a smile on her face, breathing in the scent of wood soap. "Oh, this is blissful," she told him.

"Come see the kitchen."

"This room is just so different-looking," she said as she followed him to the kitchen. "Look at the table," she said, stopping in mid-track. "Look at the sun on the table!" Jerry had shelved all the books that usually encumbered the table, and polished its surface so that the pale oak shone in the winter sunlight. Elizabeth ran her hand over its smooth surface. She looked at Jerry, her face lit up with pleasure. "I've always loved this table," she said. "I found it in a junk shop in Potter's Mill, and I bought it because of the feet." He hadn't had time to clean up and polish the lion's-paw feet, but then she didn't look at them. She went on dreamily running her hand over the tabletop.

"Come see the kitchen," he said again.

"Why, you've done all my dishes!" she exclaimed, taking a quick look around.

"I've done a lot more than that," he told her.

She said, "Did Mrs. Lutz give you any trouble?"

Jerry crossed his fingers. "Mrs. Lutz and I are like that. She's hired me to paint the back apartment."

"She's not a bad person if you know how to deal with her."

Jerry nodded. He knew ten times more than Elizabeth about how to deal with the Mrs. Lutzes of the world. He said, "So, come on, tell me about your trip."

She sat down on her couch and began to tell him about it. After a while she eased off her shoes and stretched out. Jerry put a pillow under her shoulders, and she threw back her head to get rid of the driving kinks in her neck. Her skirt hiked up so he could see the full line of her legs from knee to elegant ankle. "Want some tea?" he asked her, as she paused in her recital.

When he brought her tea, she said, "You're spoiling me."

That was exactly what he wanted to do. She deserved to be spoiled. He said, "I'm waiting tonight at the Tavern. If you come, I can see that you get a table at my station, and all the vegetables and salads that you want." Elizabeth loved vegetables and salads.

A smile hovered around her lips as she considered the matter. "That sounds very attractive," she said, and so that night Jerry waited on the woman he loved. Later he shared her bed.

Anne Player came back from semester break with a new hairdo. In place of those fluffy curls, her hair was now straight, and cut straight in bangs across her forehead. "That's *much* better," Jerry said, as soon as he saw her.

"Mother was against it."

"Mother doesn't always know best," Jerry said.

"Mother thought I seemed happier."

"Is Mother right?"

Anne heaved a great sigh. "I don't know, Jerry. I just don't know."

He said, "Happiness isn't something you know. It's something you feel."

"Well, that's my problem, isn't it? My feelings don't work right."

They were at the Corner Room, having coffee on Monday morning. Anne was on her way up to the Armory for registration. Jerry already had his course cards. He was registered for The Crusades, to fulfill a liberal arts History requirement, and for three psychology courses: Professor Kingisiepp's General Experimental Psychology, Rowell's Human Development, and Measly's Dating, a popular gut course that Jerry's new adviser had put him into. "We don't want to overload you with tough courses to begin with," he said. Jerry's fifth course had been left open, pending the results of his placement test in French.

When Anne went off to register, Jerry went down the street to buy his textbooks. Their weight appalled him, also their cost. The text in Human Development set him back six dollars. It seemed to weigh a ton, and when he got back to Locust Lane and checked, he found it was 1,001 pages long. It was called *PERSONALITY: A Biosocial Approach to Origins and Structure*. The author was somebody called Gardner Murphy. Jerry began to leaf through the book just to see what it was like.

"Listen to this," he said when Begler came in for lunch. To illustrate how individuals emphasize their place in the group, Murphy referred to a Deke song that had a line that went: *It takes a slick man, it takes a damn fine man to make a jolly DKE.* "Have you ever heard that song?" Jerry asked.

"Maybe they sing it at Yale," Begler said. Yale had the parent chapter of Delta Kappa Epsilon.

"I'm not sure this guy is right," Jerry said. "He says Teddy Roosevelt was an asthmatic weakling who was taunted by other boys when he was a kid, and then spent the rest of his life trying to show the world that he was really strong. I mean, I think Murphy's got it in for Dekes."

"He's probably a Sigma Pi," said Begler.

They had lunch together. Afterward Begler suggested they get out their lacrosse sticks and sling the ball around. Jerry said, "Later, hunh?" He went back to Gardner Murphy. After a while Begler left, saying he was going over to SAE to see what the guys there were doing. Jerry continued to read Gardner Murphy.

Murphy was certainly wrong about Roosevelt, and after due consideration, Jerry decided he was probably wrong about Lord Byron, too. Murphy said that Roosevelt and Byron—and a Greek named Demosthenes—were all examples of men who overcompensated for childhood weaknesses. Byron hadn't been loved by his parents, and had infantile paralysis as well, so he forced himself to become a great swimmer and lover and poet just to show the world that he wasn't handicapped, and that he could be loved. But he hadn't achieved happiness because he was driven to do all he did. He was a neurotic, like Roosevelt, and like that Demosthenes. They had all been driven men, unable to freely enjoy their own performances.

This didn't ring true at all to Jerry, because in the first place a kid with infantile paralysis would have a much better chance to enjoy himself in the water than on land. His handicap didn't make as much difference there. President Franklin Roosevelt swam a lot after he had polio. Byron must have loved the water because he didn't limp there, and naturally he got to be a good swimmer. And as for Byron's not enjoying his own love affairs, or his own poetry, how did Murphy know?

Jerry got down *Great Poems of the English Language*, which Mrs. Yngling had forced on him years ago and which he always kept with him, and began to read the Byron selections. There were some good, resounding lines like *Roll on, thou deep and dark blue ocean, roll*, and some funny rhymes like *ladies intellectual . . . hen pecked you all*, but what impressed Jerry the most was a poem that went:

When we two parted
   In silence and tears,
Half broken-hearted,
   To sever for years,
Pale grew thy cheek and cold,
   Colder thy kiss;
Truly that hour foretold
   Sorrow to this!

The dew of the morning
   Sunk chill on my brow—
It felt like the warning
   Of what I feel now.
Thy vows are all broken,
   And light is thy fame:
I hear thy name spoken
   And share in its shame.

They name thee before me,
   A knell to my ear:
A shudder comes o'er me—
   Why wert thou so dear?
They know not I knew thee
   Who knew thee too well:—
Long, long shall I rue thee
   Too deeply to tell.

In secret we met:—
   In silence I grieve
That thy heart could forget,
   Thy spirit deceive.
If I should meet thee
   After long years,

> How should I greet thee?—
> With silence and tears.

Strange, Jerry thought, that a man could regret that a woman had been too dear to him when obviously she hadn't been dear enough. He had parted from her only *half* brokenhearted. That was the problem. He'd let her go, and she'd gone bad for some reason. Maybe just because he'd let her go. Anyway she'd become the town floozy, and now all he could think about was how embarrassing and painful it was for him to hear men talking about her. He had no thoughts at all of what she might be going through. In fact he was planning to cut her dead if they ever met again, and at the same time he expected people to sympathize with his silence and tears. Some lover! But even though the speaker was a poor excuse for a man, the poem was fascinating. So where did Gardner Murphy get off? If Byron had been driven to write bad poetry, Jerry could understand how he might have been miserable, but this was good poetry. And anyway, when Jerry came to think of it, men could enjoy composing bad poetry. Jerry got pleasure from his own poems.

Stimulated by Byron, Jerry put aside *Great Poems* and got out the manila folder where he kept copies of his own poems. He began to read his more recent ones:

> She was new at the oldest profession
> Didn't know all the tricks of the trade
> Seemed sort of fresh and unspoiled
> How was I to know she had crabs?

Not bad, he thought, but too short. All his poems were too short. And prosy. Maybe they weren't poems at all, just sort of random notes on his erotic experiences? He read what he'd written about Sandra:

> Fat Sandra fell on me, pinned me flat.
> I was down for the count till her clock rang.
> But she drilled it, and pinned me again.
> I was getting the upper hand when the cops came
> And I had to scram. No one won that one.

Oh well, he thought. Not everybody could be a poet. He sighed, and went back to *PERSONALITY: A Biosocial Approach to Origins and Structure*, where he read that Byron's life showed that Byron lacked serene self-acceptance, which might have been true, but who was to say that serene self-acceptance meant happiness? Bill Houser was a fine example of a serenely self-accepting person. He liked everything about himself, he thought everything he did was right, and that anyone who did differently was wrong. But did that mean Houser was happier than everyone else? No. He was just more of a jerk, that was all.

Jerry took Gardner Murphy with him to Elizabeth's apartment that evening. "What's that?" she asked.

"It's the textbook in one of my psychology courses. I want to ask you something about it."

Elizabeth looked at the cover, and said, "Oh, Geoff Rowell's course."

"You know him?" Jerry asked.

"We've met," she said. "He was a student of Gardner Murphy's at Columbia."

"Well, listen to this about Byron," Jerry said, and he read Murphy's analysis of Byron's life.

Elizabeth said, "Byron had a clubfoot, not polio."

"So he's even wrong about that," said Jerry.

"He's wrong about that detail. I think Byron was driven."

"Is that bad?" Jerry asked. "I'd rather be driven than stand still."

Elizabeth waved it aside. She said, "Jerry, I'm afraid there's something I have to ask you about. When you straightened up my papers, did you find some old love letters of mine?"

"No."

"They were in that pile," she said, indicating a now much disarranged stack on the floor. "I can't find them. They were held together by a rubber band. It would have been easy for you to notice them as you straightened up."

"I didn't see them," he said.

Elizabeth sighed. "I thought of them as I was driving up to Cambridge. They've been on my mind. That's why I looked for them."

"I'm sorry you can't find them," Jerry said.

"You're sure you didn't see them?"

"Do you want to search me?"

She said, "There's nothing in them I'd be ashamed for you to read. They were quite eloquent in spots. It's just that . . ."

"That I shouldn't read them."

"Well, you shouldn't," she said.

"I haven't."

They stared at each other. Finally Elizabeth sighed. "Well, I just don't know what could have become of them."

He said, "You have a way of knocking people over without noticing it, and strolling on their remains while you admire a sunset or think of a poem."

That description of herself made Elizabeth smile. "Have I done that to you?"

"Just now. And Thursday, too, when you told me you hated Van Gogh's *Sunflowers*."

"But it's just all wrong!" Elizabeth exclaimed, turning toward the picture, which still hung on her wall. "I've been staring and staring at it. He's made them into horrible, writhing, tortured things, and they're not that at all. They're simple, upright flowers with their heads modestly inclined. Blake saw what they're really like." And again she repeated the line, *Ah sunflower, weary of time.*

"Even so, I gave you the picture, and hung it up for you, and instead of saying thanks, you said you hated it."

Elizabeth smiled contritely. "Oh, Jerry," she said, "what must you think of me?"

"If I could tell you all I think of you, you wouldn't need to hunt any more for those love letters."

Her eyes moved searchingly over his face. She reached out to touch his lips with her fingertips, like Helen Keller learning to communicate. "I think I'm very lucky," she said at last.

"How do you think I feel?" he said.

"In spite of being knocked down and trampled on?"

"In spite of it."

Or did he love her so much precisely because she could be so outrageous? In bed with her that night, he nudged her as she was going to sleep. "Did you really suspect me of taking those letters?"

"Oh, don't hold my sins against me," she said.

He said, "If I were in your place, I'd be the first to suspect myself."

"Would you?"

"I could have taken them and read them."

"But you didn't?" It was a real question.

"No. The reason you can't find them is that all your papers are in a mess. You're a slob."

Elizabeth made a plaintive sound.

"Well, it's true," he said.

"I know," she said. "I don't deserve you. I don't deserve this happiness."

"Neither do I." Then it occurred to Jerry that here again Gardner Murphy was wrong. He apparently thought people pursued happiness, but they didn't. They went after tangible things. When he'd chased Elizabeth from Split Rock to State College, he had been after *her*, not happiness, and yet here he was in her bed, happy as a lark.

CHAPTER 11

Jerry had been prepared to dislike Professor Rowell even before class met. To his surprise he found that he liked the man a lot. Rowell was young-looking, energetic, and enthusiastic about his subject. He moved restlessly around the podium as he explained the course and described the work he expected students to do. He told a joke or two. He had short, curly hair and bright eyes that crinkled at his own punch lines. He held a pointer in his hand and gestured with it frequently. It looked suspiciously like a sawed-off broom handle. He kept one hand in his trouser pocket much of the time, jingling the change there. He wore a good tweed suit. On the surface Rowell looked very much like the kind of teacher Jerry liked best. Jerry left class the first day feeling that he had probably mis-judged Gardner Murphy. If Rowell looked up to the man, and used his book as a text, then Murphy must be okay after all.

But he wasn't. Wherever Jerry dipped into *PERSONALITY*, he found things he disagreed with. Murphy thought selfishness was the ultimate human emotion. He wrote, "Whatever the self is, it becomes a center, an anchorage point, a standard of comparison, an ultimate real. Inevitably it takes its place as a supreme value." Murphy realized that some people could love things other than themselves, but he wrote, "The normal lover needs to be loved and to *know* very clearly that he is loved; he needs to share fully in the process by which his own image is bathed in love."

Now that was just plain wrong. Jerry could remember being bathed by his mother. He had liked it (a lot of little boys didn't), but even in the midst of his soapy splashings under his mother's loving eyes Jerry had been aware that there was a price to pay for these tender moments. He was supposed to keep his ears clean and be a good boy from then on, and since he knew that wouldn't happen he had always felt a little sorry for his mother. She loved him so much, and wanted him to be so good, and he just wasn't.

Murphy didn't seem to understand this. He didn't know that love could be a burden, which was why so many normal lovers were leery about being loved in return. They didn't want to bear the beams of love. They wanted good wives who would keep house and cook and bring up the children. Almost the last thing a normal man wanted was to come home in the evening to find his wife all charged up with love for him. Love was active, and after a day at work a lot of normal men weren't up for that. They wanted peace and quiet at home.

What was the matter with Murphy that he didn't understand obvious things like this? Who were these normal lovers who were supposed to *need* to be loved, and who needed "to share fully in the process by which their image was bathed in love"? Jerry considered himself a fairly normal lover, and he could testify from first-hand experience just how embarrassing it could be when a woman went overboard about you. He treasured his memory of that truck-driver's wife who had told him this would be a better world if there

were more men like him, but he had never called her up or tried
to see her again because in the first place he would probably end
up disillusioning her, and in the second place he could take only
so much praise. You had to be a movie star or somebody like that
in order to enjoy constant adulation. Is that what Murphy thought
normal men were like? Movie stars? If so, Murphy was nuts.

Jerry was not sure he himself fully understood love, but at least
he knew that love was a kind of possession. A lover was possessed.
He was driven and ridden and goaded by desires he could not resist.
That he did not want to resist. Lovers welcomed love, and let it
take over and guide their actions. They enjoyed being possessed
by love. Their prayer, if they had one, was for love to possess them
yet more fully. Love was a sort of god for lovers, who willingly
surrendered to it and asked only that love make as full a use of them
as it could. Lovers were crazy.

Murphy seemed to have no inkling of all this. Either he had never
been in love, which seemed unlikely, or else he had paid no attention to love when he experienced it, and that did seem likely. It
happened all the time, in fact, that people gripped and possessed
by love failed to recognize what was happening to them, failed to
honor love, or even to know that they were in love. Mrs. Lutz, for
instance, was clearly possessed by a crazy love of china, but she
would be horrified and insulted if anyone were to suggest that she
was in love, or that her passion for china had anything in common
with a young man's passion for girls. Mrs. Lutz had probably spent
her whole life denouncing and opposing the passions of young men,
only to give way completely to a different version of the same force.
Jerry was willing to bet that the sight of a ceramic bluebird for sale
gave Mrs. Lutz the same kind of concupiscent thrill that he himself felt daily just walking across campus looking at all the wonderful girls in their long coats and saddle shoes, their loose hair

blowing in the wind. He didn't have to have every girl he saw, in fact he knew he couldn't have them. He was just glad they were there. They kept him on his toes, happy to be alive in a world so full of desirable girls. Their presence added spice to his life, just as Mrs. Lutz must get spice from the idea that she would find some great bargain in china in the next antique store or junk shop she visited. Everyone needed that spice. You couldn't live without wanting something more, something you didn't have.

That was the funniest thing about love. It was for something you didn't have. What he loved about Linda was her innocence, which he didn't have himself and would never recover, but which he loved and wanted. And what he loved about Anne was her bravery, another quality he lacked. He was sure that if he were beset by Anne's fears and problems, he would not have shown half her guts. Life was just easier for good-looking people interested primarily in the opposite sex. They should thank their lucky stars every day of their lives, and get down on their knees before people like Anne. Sometimes when he heard Begler call her The Queen of the Fairies he wanted to say what he really thought, but what was the use? And anyway he didn't have the words or the courage it took to stand up for others. He had tried, but he knew he was no good at it. You had to be more eloquent and passionate and powerful than he would ever be.

Which brought him to Elizabeth. Jerry suspected a mistake had been made in the fourth dimension when Elizabeth had not been born as rich as Rosalind Ingleside. Elizabeth should have servants to take care of her. She was queenly. He loved that quality in her, and was quite willing to become her servant—he already was—but how could he support her the way she should be supported, even assuming she would want to keep him as her servant, which wasn't at all clear to him. Elizabeth was the sort of woman who could, and maybe should, fall madly in love with someone she considered a prince among men. In which case it would be "Good-bye, Jerry." Jerry felt he had some valuable qualities, but he wasn't princely. He would never be able to satisfy Elizabeth's need to fling herself into the arms of some superior being. He himself could be thoroughly happy serving her, but could she ever be thoroughly happy just being served by him? She probably needed more than he could offer.

—All of which made reading *PERSONALITY* a real trial, because it had so little to do with what made people tick, which was love. Murphy was trying to explain human development without having the key that unlocked the mysteries. Love was the key. If you lacked the key, then you were just slipping your gears. Murphy spent 1,001 pages slipping his gears, and, for reasons Jerry could not understand, Professor Rowell thought well enough of the book to have students buy it and read it.

He went up after class at the beginning of the second week. Over the weekend he had spent quite a lot of time reading *PERSONALITY*. With a smile, he asked Professor Rowell if students had to believe that book.

Smiling himself, Rowell said, "What do you mean?"

Jerry explained what he meant. Murphy didn't understand love and therefore couldn't explain human development. Jerry said, "There are only eight references to love in the index, compared to thirty-three references to selfishness and narcissism."

Smiling even more broadly, Professor Rowell said, "So you've been using the back of the book?"

"Well, why not?" Jerry asked.

"Have you read the assigned pages?" Rowell asked.

Jerry admitted he hadn't. They had not looked as interesting to him as the passages about love.

Rowell said, "Maybe when you've read them you'll understand." He went on to point out that books had to be read in the way they were composed. You shouldn't dip into the middle just because you found in the index a reference to your favorite subject.

Jerry objected, "But it's such a big book! If I read it from the beginning I'll never to get to what interests me."

"What's your name?" Rowell asked.

"Jerry Engels."

Speaking in friendly, even genial tones, Rowell said, "Well, Jerry Engels, if love is all that interests you, maybe you're wasting your time in school." Then he turned to a girl who had a question, leaving Jerry with several retorts on the tip of his tongue.

He voiced them a few evenings later to Anne Player who was again visiting the apartment, though not for dinner this time. Jerry's budget couldn't stand regular champagne suppers. Anne came after dinner, bringing her sketch pad with her. Begler was playing poker at Acacia.

Over coffee, Jerry asked Anne if she had ever been taught anything that helped her to understand herself and what life was really like.

"Have you?" she said.

"No, and that's what I'm complaining about. What every kid needs to know about is love, and so they teach you French and Latin and algebra."

"How could they teach love?" Anne asked.

"I don't know, that's their business. They should figure out how to teach love instead of cramming kids full of French verbs. We learned to conjugate in twenty-two different tenses. What good was that? I didn't even exempt French here. I'm in French 3 now. I think my whole education has been a waste of time."

He got up and began to undress. "Love could be taught," he told Anne. "I know it could be taught if teachers just understood it themselves, but that's the real trouble. Our teachers don't know enough. And their teachers don't. Look at Professor Rowell. He's a good man. He could be teaching us all kinds of good things about love, but instead he's using Gardner Murphy's book because Gardner Murphy was his teacher, and Gardner Murphy doesn't believe in love at all. He thinks Freud and Plato were all wrong to put love in the center of life. He thinks selfishness belongs in the center. How do you like that?"

And so saying Jerry whipped off his jockey shorts, stretched them like a slingshot, and let them fly toward the couch where he had discarded his other clothes. They sailed off, and landed on his pants. He turned to Anne, smiling. "Okay, what will it be tonight?" he asked.

"Whatever you want," Anne said. She was not enthusiastic about these posing sessions. She had refused to undress after their first experiment, and Jerry had given up trying to persuade her. Posing for her without anything on in these intimate surroundings made him feel naked enough for them both, and as Anne ran her eyes over him and translated what she saw onto her sketching pad he felt she was getting to be as familiar with his body as if they were really lovers.

"Okay, this is *Glad Morning*," Jerry said, assuming a pose he had seen in one of Elizabeth's Blake books. He stood in front of Anne, his legs together, his arms slightly spread. "There should be rays of light shooting out of my head."

"Yeah, yeah," Anne said, "I've seen the picture." She set to work sketching Jerry.

He had always wondered what would happen if he got a hard-on while posing. In class it had never happened, but this evening it did. Maybe it was the pose, maybe it was the fact that he hadn't seen Elizabeth since Sunday. Whatever the reason, up it reared its rosy head.

Anne quit sketching. "Stop that," she said.

"I can't stop it," he told her.

"I don't believe you." She looked away.

"Well, I'm not going to try," he told her. "Go ahead. This is probably how Blake's picture ought to look anyway."

"It's horrible."

"It most certainly is not," Jerry replied.

Anne's response was to go, "Yech!"

Jerry said, "How'd you like it if I made sounds like that about you?"

"I make those sounds about myself."

"You shouldn't, but anyway that's not the same," Jerry replied. "People can't hurt their own feelings as deeply as they hurt the feelings of others."

Anne refused to argue about it. She turned her back on him. "Jerry, I just can't. You'll have to cover up or go down."

He did neither. He grabbed her from behind and held her tightly against him, feeling all his frustrations converge toward a single point. It was as if by grabbing Anne he had gotten a grip on Professor Rowell, and Gardner Murphy, and the American school system. "Don't yell," he told her, "I'm not going to hurt you." He realized, too late, it was what rapists usually said. If anything, it seemed to galvanize Anne in her silent struggle to free herself.

She tried to elbow him. She stepped on his bare feet with her saddle shoes. She fought him tooth and nail without being able to use her teeth or her nails. Her arms were imprisoned by his arms. Her head faced away from him. Then he *did* feel her teeth. She was trying to bite his biceps! And now she was kicking his shins! She amazed him. He could feel her swelling with anger within the prison of his arms and gathering strength as she swelled. Abruptly he let go of her, but now *she* was not finished with *him*. She grabbed Begler's lacrosse stick, leaning against the wall, and turned on Jerry like a fury. He dodged the stick, which connected with a standing lamp. He heard a light bulb explode like a bomb, and almost at once he felt glass fragments, like shrapnel, underfoot as he backed away from her toward the door to the bedroom. Again Anne attacked him with the lacrosse stick, which slammed this time against the door frame. She had gone mad. Her face, changed by fury and by her new hairdo, looked like the square face of some wide-eyed stone idol. He had never seen her—he had never seen anyone—so transformed by passion. Pat's anger when she heard he had exposed her to crabs was nothing compared to this, and again the poem flashed through his mind:

> Or if thy mistress some rich anger shows,
> Imprison her soft hand, and let her rave,
> And feed deep, deep upon her peerless eyes.

That was just playing with anger, this was the real thing. Anne's breath came harshly as she stalked him, lacrosse stick in hand, through the bedroom until he took refuge in the bathroom with the door locked. This was fantastic, he thought, as Anne delivered a smashing blow to the door. Next she would summon him to come out and fight like a man.

Instead she seemed to calm down. At least she didn't batter the door a second time, and when he ventured to look out, he saw her sitting on the edge of his bed, lacrosse stick in hand. "Is it safe for me to come out?" he asked her. She didn't reply. He emerged and stared down at her with more admiration than he had ever felt before. "You could have knocked me cold," he said. He was reminded of Mr. Train chasing him with a baseball bat. "You could have killed me."

She gave a jerk of the head as if to say that was the least of her worries.

He watched her for a moment, not sure what you said to someone in her state. Then, limping slightly and leaving a trail of bloodstains, he went to the kitchen and fixed her a drink. "Here," he said to her, holding out the strongest highball he had ever mixed. She accepted it and drained it as if it were a glass of water. Then she choked slightly and said, "What was that?"

"How do you feel?" he asked her.

"Funny," she said.

He sat down on the bed beside her and said, "You've had a real upheaval." She nodded. "Want me to take you home?" he asked. She shook her head. "What do you want?"

"Give me something to drink."

This time he brought her a glass of water from which she sipped delicately. "I wish you could have seen yourself," he told her. "You were magnificent."

"Why'd you grab me that way?" she asked, a faint return of anger in her voice.

He said, "It's very wounding to have a woman go 'Yech' at the sight of this," and he gestured at his now peaceful piece.

She glanced at it and said, "Poor you."

"All right," he said, "I'm just telling you why I did it. I'm not complaining, even though you tried to kill me."

Anne took another sip of water. He wished she would talk, but probably it was too soon. He didn't want to hurry her. Again he sat down beside her. He took her free hand, and held it. She sipped water again, and they sat together for a while saying nothing. He had never felt closer to her. After another sip of water she stirred and said, "Maybe I better go."

He offered to accompany her, but she turned him down. She wanted to be alone. "Anyway, you've hurt your foot," she remarked, and it was true that a sliver of broken light bulb had cut his sole deeply enough for it still to be oozing blood. He let her go off by herself.

Begler said, "What the hell's been going on here?" He surveyed the wrecked lamp, and the marks of Jerry's blood on the living room carpet.

Jerry said, "The worst is in there." He pointed toward the bedroom and bathroom. Anne had splintered the upper panel of the bathroom door, and cracked Begler's lacrosse stick.

Begler went to check, and came back holding his ruined stick and looking outraged. "How did this happen?" he demanded.

Jerry told him.

"*She* did it?" Begler exclaimed, looking down at his stick.

"I'll buy you a new one," Jerry said. "I'll pay for the damage."

"That little girl? She did this? She did all this?" Begler looked around at the havoc Anne had left behind, and then at Jerry, sitting at the dinette table, his foot up on another chair. He had bandaged his foot, but done nothing to straighten up since Anne left. Instead he had been reading *PERSONALITY*.

"She did it," Jerry said.

"What did you do?" Begler asked.

"All I did was to get a hard-on."

"And she went berserk?"

It wasn't that simple, but sometimes you couldn't put it all into words. Jerry nodded, and Begler shook his head in disgust. "Your women!" he said, instinctively promoting Anne from Virgin Queen to Woman. Jerry noticed the promotion and felt it was probably the best way to summarize the evening.

On Saturday when he saw Elizabeth, she greeted him with an apology. "I've found those letters," she said. "I'm very sorry I ever questioned you about them. They were in a dresser drawer. I'd forgotten I put them there."

He nodded. "Whose letters are they?"

She said, "I'd just as soon you didn't ask."

But he had asked. People were always doing that—telling him he couldn't say something he had already said, or shouldn't ask something he had already asked. "They're not from Elmer or Tony?"

She said, "No."

He said, "The only other man you told me about was one of your colleagues here. Are they from him?"

Elizabeth gave him a long considering look as she decided whether or not to rebuke him, or to ride roughshod over him, or what. Finally she said, "Yes. They're from Geoff Rowell as a matter of fact."

"Professor Rowell!" Jerry felt thunderstruck. Horrified. "You would have married Rowell?"

"If he'd asked me to." She sounded unrepentant.

Jerry stared at her. How could she be so smart about some things, and so dumb about men? Elmer. Tony Whittington. And now Professor Rowell. At last he said, "Well, why didn't he propose?"

"He has to take care of his mother."

"His mother! What's the matter with his mother?"

"She's all alone except for him, and in frail health and financially dependent. Geoff felt that he couldn't ask her to move out of his house, and that he couldn't ask me to share it with her."

"And you believed that?" Jerry said.

"Certainly." She was beginning to sound annoyed. "We can't always do what we want. Sometimes people have to make choices like Geoff's."

"Not people in love. They don't make choices like that."

Elizabeth said, "I think we've talked about this enough."

Jerry shook his head. They hadn't even begun. "I still can't believe it," he said. "Professor Rowell!"

"I think you're jealous."

"I think so too."

"Well, there's no need to be. It's all over. We're simply friends now."

"But you wanted to marry him. You're keeping his letters. You idealize him."

"Jerry . . . ," she began.

"You think it was noble the way he chose his mother over you."

"It's a decision I respect him for," she said.

"Why?" Jerry demanded. "Aren't you worth more than some poor old lady? Aren't you more lovable?"

"That's not the way to look at it," Elizabeth said.

"It's the way I look at it. If I had a chance to marry you I wouldn't let anything stop me."

A funny look came over Elizabeth's face. "Why do you say that?" she asked.

"Say what?"

"*If* you had a chance to marry me you wouldn't let anything stop you."

"Well, I wouldn't."

"And why do you think you have no chance?" she asked.

He shrugged. "You've been telling me all along we have no future." He felt embarrassed to say it, but he went ahead. "Besides,

I know I'm not what you really want. You'd like to marry someone nobler than I am."

She said, "I've made you feel that?"

"Isn't it true?"

She looked around her apartment. She gestured. "You've done all this for me? You've been so good, you've made me so happy, and I've made you feel you're not what I really want?"

"Well, don't blame yourself," he said, "it's just how you are. You want to look up to your husband. You want to idealize him."

Abruptly she sat down. "You understand that!"

"Well, why else would you have married Tony if you hadn't thought he could be a great poet?"

She nodded.

"And why else did you try to get rid of me?" he continued. Then he answered his own question. "Because I'm hard to idealize."

She shook her head. "I'm not sure I agree with that."

"Well, you can bet I wouldn't give you up just to take care of a dying mother."

"Mrs. Rowell wasn't dying."

"I know. And Rowell isn't noble. That's your trouble. You fall for men who don't love you enough, and then kid yourself into thinking it's because they're so high-minded or something."

She nodded.

"Rowell's not bad," Jerry went on. "In fact, he's a nice man, but he's just a professor. You can do better than that."

"Maybe I have done better," she murmured.

"What?"

"I said maybe I have done better."

"You mean with me?"

"Yes, you."

He felt oddly embarrassed. "Well, I don't know about that."

"Come here," she said, and behind or maybe within her voice he could hear a whole chorus of female voices saying the same thing: Come. Come here. Come. He moved toward the straight chair in which Elizabeth was sitting. He felt very strange. Almost frightened.

She said, "Will you marry me?"

"Do you mean that?" he asked.

"I think I do," she said, "only I should warn you I want to have children."

He thought of his sister and her baby. "Children are all right," he decided aloud.

"Do you realize what you're getting into?" she asked.

"Do you?" he replied. "Do you really want to marry me?"

"If you'll ask me."

"I'll ask you. I'll ask anytime you want."

"Then ask."

"You mean, now?"

"Yes, now."

"You mean we could get married now?"

"If you'll just ask," she said, her voice showing a touch of impatience at his stupidity.

He said, "Wow!" Then it seemed to him wrong to be standing over Elizabeth, so he got down on one knee. "Will you marry me?" he asked.

She didn't answer at once. They looked at each other. Jerry felt as if he'd done this before, as if he'd been doing it all his life. Kneeling. Looking up. His heart in his mouth. Waiting. Wanting. He felt a little breathless. He repeated his question. "Will you marry me?"

"Yes, I will," Elizabeth replied.

Two weeks later they honeymooned at Split Rock Lodge. Elizabeth had student papers to grade, and Jerry brought PERSONALITY with him, thinking he might find time to read some of the assigned material, but in the event he never cracked the book, and Elizabeth never got out her red pencil. A cold, drizzling, late winter, early spring rain ruined the skiing for them, though they hardly noticed their loss. Jerry could still hardly believe his good luck, and Elizabeth seemed unable to get used to her happiness. "Am I going to feel this way all the time now?" she asked him. They were in the lounge where they had met in December.

"How do you feel?" he asked.

She reached across the table to cover his hand with hers. "Grateful."

"Grateful?" That surprised him.

"Oh, let's go out anyway," Elizabeth said, "I can't stay inside without bursting."

Outdoors a wet wind blew the rain in their face. They found the shelter of a line of trees and walked there. Presently Elizabeth said, *"Therefore let the moon shine on thee in thy solitary walk; And let the misty mountain winds be free to blow against thee."* Suddenly she turned on Jerry, her eyes blazing. "Why solitary? How could he have been so blind as to think his blessing on her solitary walks would be happiness enough for a lifetime? It wasn't! She got old and cantankerous and queer." There were tears in Elizabeth's eyes. "I just can't bear to think of what finally happened to Dorothy Wordsworth!" Then she had him in her arms. "Oh, Jerry," she cried, "you've saved me from that. I might never have married. You've saved me from solitary walks, and all the horrible things that happen to lonely people."

That was Saturday. On Sunday morning, conscious that he had some explaining to do, Jerry said, "I'm going to write my parents."

Elizabeth, still in bed, stretched her arms voluptuously and said, "I'll just watch you write."

So Jerry sat at the little desk in their room, and on a sheet of Lodge stationery composed a letter home.

Dear Mother and Father, he wrote,

On Friday I got married to the woman I told you about at Christmas. I hope you'll forgive my doing it this way, but we're so in love that we didn't want to wait, so we just went across the street from where she lives and had it done by the Justice of the Peace. We're up here at Split Rock for the weekend. It's our honeymoon. I don't think I've ever been this happy.

Elizabeth's mother is dead, and her father lives out in Boise, Idaho, and she doesn't really have any close relations anywhere, so for her this seems like a normal way of getting married. It was how she married her first husband. So you mustn't blame her for how we did it. She isn't used to the kind of family we have, and doesn't know what a shock I'm giving you, but for once it should be a good shock. I've found the most wonderful woman in the world, and now the long search is over. When you meet her you'll know what I mean because anyone who sees her can tell right away that she is a great woman. I can't tell you how lucky I am to have her. I know when you get used to this and when you've gotten to know her yourself, you'll agree we're all very lucky to have Elizabeth in the family now. I can't be sure, especially since her car is sort of old, but right now we're talking about coming to see you at spring break.

I'll write you again just as soon as I have time. My new address is 123 Fraser St., Apt 3. That's where Elizabeth lives, and I will be moving in with her on Monday.

He signed that "Your loving son, Jerry," folded it up, slipped it into an envelope, and sealed it before Elizabeth could ask to see what he had written. Then that letter made him think he should

write Linda at the same time so that the news wouldn't come to
her via her mother. Jerry knew his mother would get on the phone
to Mrs. Forson almost as soon as she had time to recover from his
letter. His mother and Mrs. Forson shared everything. Jerry knew
obscure details about Phil that he got from his mother via Mrs.
Forson rather than directly from Phil. So, taking another sheet of
Split Rock stationery, he wrote this to Linda.

> I've married a woman who's eight years older than I am. I've
> been in love with her since December. We met up here at this
> ski lodge, but I knew her before because she was my freshman
> English teacher.
> I hope you're not too disappointed. I would never have been a
> good husband for you, or even a good boyfriend for you to see a
> lot of. I really only gave you my pin for the reason I told you, to
> help you keep Jason under control. I never expected you to love
> me, though I've loved having your letters and I really do love
> you like a big brother, and I hope I haven't messed things up for
> you or made you too unhappy. Hearts heal. I know yours will.

That letter, too, he sealed up before Elizabeth could ask to see
it. Then he got up and went to the window. The snow had been
melting all night. A thick white mist surrounded the lodge. He
could see nothing, neither the sun, nor the slopes, nor the dark
trees. It made him think of the steam room in Rec Hall when you
first walked in and saw nothing through the mist. Then shapes
emerged, and soon you could recognize particular faces. He had
seen Moomaw there on one of his last visits. It felt odd to meet
him naked, face to face, with the idea of Pat somehow between
them, keeping them apart. Otherwise he might have felt close to
Moomaw, almost brotherly, because Ken and he had so much in
common from their brush haircuts on down. Pat had merely changed

from one fraternity man to another, whereas he had moved on, he thought, turning toward the bed where Elizabeth sat watching him. He had moved on, and up, and out.

"You look so serious," she said.

He was serious. "Can't I be serious?" he asked her.

She said, "I've been watching you write your letters. Your lips were moving as if you were talking."

This was marriage, he thought. Someone to watch you and tell you things you didn't know about yourself. He said, "Did you know that you talk in your sleep?"

"I've been told that."

She had been married before. He could think of Tony without jealousy now. Soon he might even be able to think of Rowell that way. "Where is Tony?" he asked.

She seemed not to be surprised by the question. "Back in California. He's found someone else to take care of him."

"Is he writing poetry?"

"I suppose so. I haven't seen anything of his recently, but I don't read all the magazines he might publish in."

"When people meet us are you going to be embarrassed that I'm so young and that I haven't done anything yet?"

"Come here," she said. A royal command. An Yngling command. He went there, and she put her arms around him. "I wouldn't have married you," she said, "if I didn't think you'd already done wonders."

CHAPTER 12

News of the wedding spread rapidly through the different circles of Jerry's friends. As the Deke most directly affected Begler was naturally the first to know, and the most deeply shocked. "I knew he was crazy," Jeff said to Gossage, "but I didn't think he was this crazy."

"Why did he do it?" Gossage asked. "Did he knock her up, or what?"

"No, I don't think she's knocked up. Jerry would have told me that."

"What did he tell you?"

"He told me he loved her."

Gossage puffed out his lips. "That doesn't make sense. He's been in love a dozen times. Why marry this one?"

"That's what I said," Begler replied. "She's got no money. She teaches school. She's way older than he is, and I don't even think she's good-looking."

"You've seen her?" Gossage said.

"I was there when they met at Split Rock. I saw her first, in fact."

Gossage shook his head. "It's very strange. Jerry was having a ball. Why would a fellow with all his opportunities go after a woman like that?"

"It's what I said," said Begler, "he's crazy."

Gossage nodded thoughtfully. "Well, this sure leaves you up the creek without a roommate."

"That's no problem," Begler said. "I'm even sort of relieved." When Gossage expressed surprise at that, Begler lowered his voice and said, "Don't spread it around because I still like Jerry, but he's queer."

"What do you mean, queer?" Gossage asked.

"I mean flitty."

Gossage said, "That's absurd."

"I'm telling you, he's got wings."

"Engels?"

Begler nodded.

Gossage said, "That's impossible."

"He told me himself."

Gossage said, "Well, if he's that way, why is he marrying?"

"Like I said, he's a complete lunatic." Then Begler put it all together. "Jerry will do anything. I haven't even slept well since he told me what a fag he is."

"And you and he were such good friends," said Gossage.

"I know. It makes you wonder who you can trust."

"You could knock me down with a feather," Gossage said.

*

Harold Collins, hit by the dual catastrophes of the closing of the Deke house and the end of his football career, had withdrawn from school. He wrote Jerry from McKeesport.

Dear Jerry, he wrote,

    I want to congratulate you on your marriage and wish you and your bride the best of everything. I'm sure you'll be very happy. Please let me know where I can send a wedding present.
    Everything's going fine here. I'm working for my uncle again, and the old knee hardly hurts except at the end of the day. Wishing you the best again,

Your brother,
Harold Collins

*

Houser said, "I don't see why we should give him a wedding present."

Mildenhall said, "Well, I'm collecting for the chapter."

"What did you give?" Houser asked.

"Two bucks."

"Okay," said Houser ungraciously, "I guess I can spare fifty cents. What are we buying him?"

"A vacuum cleaner."

"Why that?" Houser asked.

"It's what he says he wants."

*

In the Kappa sorority the news that Jerry Engels had run off with a married woman created a three-day sensation. "She wasn't married, she was divorced," Anne Player kept saying, but it was hard to scotch that rumor, or any of the others that got started. Jerry was supposed to have seduced his English teacher in order to get a good grade. On the other hand he had to marry her because you know why. Pat Gaheris said, "I pity her." Other Kappas with fewer grudges against Jerry were inclined to pity him. Elizabeth was supposed to be forty. One girl who had actually had Elizabeth as a teacher described her as a witch. The general consensus held that the marriage was a tragedy, unless it was a scandal, or perhaps a farce. In any case no one expected the marriage to last or to be happy. No one except Anne. "I think they'll be very happy," she said. Her sisters all looked at each other and privately raised their eyebrows. What did Anne Player know about marriage, or happiness? And besides, what was making her so opinionated and assertive these days?

*

Further afield the reactions were equally diverse. Shirley Hyatt wrote to Rosalind Ingleside at Vassar. "You won't believe what's happened. Jerry Engels got married secretly to one of his teachers at Penn State. He wrote his parents from a ski lodge where he was honeymooning with her. They don't know anything about her except that her first husband tried to kill her. Isn't that fantastic?"

Rosalind wrote back, "I hope they'll be very happy. I've always liked Jerry."

Shirley shook her head over this evidence of Rosalind's incurable niceness. In Shirley's book Jerry had goofed again.

*

Ernie Hill ran into Carolyn Webster in Woodworth's Bookstore. She was in the back buying colored paper. Ernie thought she hadn't seen him and was about to scram when she spun around gracefully and said, "Lo, look who's here."

He said, "Hello, Carolyn."

"I haven't seen you since Burt hit you in the stomach. Are you all right?"

"Yeah, I've recovered," Ernie said, "how's he?"

"You never touched him."

"I mean in general. Is he doing all right in school? First in his class and all that?"

Carolyn said, "He's all right."

"I'd hate to think of you married to anyone who comes in second."

"I know how you feel," she said. "Have you heard about Jerry?"

"What about Jerry?"

"He's married."

"Who told you that?" Ernie demanded.

"Shirley. She got it from his family."

"Married!" said Ernie.

"Married," said Carolyn.

Ernie felt genuinely moved. "I can't believe it. He's almost the last person I expected to take the plunge."

"She's a Radcliffe girl," Carolyn said. "Summa cum laude, I hear."

"You're making this up."

"That's what Shirley says."

"Shirley's on nutmeg if she thinks that. I can believe Jerry's married, but not to a brainy Radcliffe girl."

Carolyn shrugged, and shortly after that they parted. Ernie was sufficiently exercised by the news to write Jerry a postcard that night.

What's this I hear about you marrying a bluestocking? Or getting married at all? If true, guarded congratulations. If untrue, please deny by next post. Save the Rosenbergs!

Ernie

He mailed that to the Deke house and got it back a week later stamped "UNDELIVERABLE." He thought at first the post office was refusing to handle his communist mail, but then he met Anne Engels in the corridor of Wieboldt and found out from her that the Deke house had been closed and that Jerry was indeed married to a Radcliffe girl with a Ph.D. from Harvard.

"Jesus!" said Ernie. He eyed Anne's stomach. A dozen different things occurred to him to say. At last he backed off muttering that he would have to send the newlyweds a subscription to *The Daily Worker*. He went his way, and Anne went hers.

*

Anne had been less surprised than her parents by Jerry's news, and far less shocked. Michael had been telling her for some time that when or if Jerry married, he would do it suddenly and without warning. "He's not your bridegroom type with a flower in his buttonhole." Of everyone in the family, Michael probably had the most realistic view of Jerry. Once, after hearing one of Jerry's stories, Michael told Anne, "Your brother is totally erotic, the most completely erotic person I've ever met."

Anne had shaken her head then, though rationally she knew Michael was probably right. Emotionally, however, Jerry would always be to her the sweet little brother she'd encouraged to get in bed with her at night to play Orphans. Anne couldn't help but feel that no matter what he had done, Jerry would always be an innocent in need of her more experienced and politically mature view of life. When news of the marriage came, Michael told her she should be glad Jerry had found an educated woman to marry him. Anne said, "I hope they'll be happy," but it was hard for her to believe that a step like this, taken without consulting her, could work out well.

*

Mr. Forson's reaction to Jerry's marriage was to say devoutly, "Thank God!"

His wife said, "Don't let Linda hear you say that."

"Just the same, I thank God," Mr. Forson said.

"I don't think Jerry ever meant to do Linda any harm," said Mrs. Forson. "I think he meant well."

Mr. Forson said, "Whatever he meant, it's over I hope."

"Linda's feeling very blue," Mrs. Forson reported.

She was up in her room composing a letter to Jerry. His Deke pin lay on the desk in front of her. In the wastebasket were several sheets of pink stationery, crumpled up after false starts. She had always known Jerry would never be hers, but she loved having his pin. It gave her a superior, comfortable, proprietary sense, not so much over Jerry as over girls who didn't have the fraternity pin of a college man, and over boys who didn't have such pins to give and were jealous that she had gotten one from someone else, especially someone else like Jerry Engels.

He was a hero to her, a somewhat Byronic figure coated with scandal and trailing dark secrets. She knew something had happened between Jerry and Rosalind Ingleside. She had actually seen Marie Promojunch with her jingling charm bracelet and her mascara and lipstick and fingernail polish and chewing gum. She had heard Phil complain about Jerry's use of the car at night, and the stink—Linda supposed of perfume—Jerry's outings with Marie left behind. And then, of course, there was the Nancy Train episode, held up for Linda's inspection by her father. But in Linda's eyes that only gave a dramatic, basically innocent covering to the solid edifice of Jerry's reputation, because he hadn't really done anything. He had just driven Nancy to Indianapolis and back one night, and for that quite pardonable excursion everyone talked about him, and pointed him out, and pretended he was dangerous. Linda knew he was not, at least where she was concerned. With her he had always been good and straightforward and helpful and friendly, and then suddenly he offered her his pin, and she accepted it.

And now the question in her mind was whether she should send it back to him. Twice she had started her letter by writing, "Dear Jerry, I'm returning your pin," and twice she crumpled up that beginning, and now she started a third time by writing, "I hope you'll be very happy," but that was as far as she could get. She did hope he would be very happy, only that wasn't the point. The point was the pin, and as she looked at it for the thousandth time she realized she was not going to give it back to him. It was hers. He said he didn't want it, he had given it to her, and nothing would make her give it away, even to him. She looked down at her one-sentence letter, crumpled it up, and, taking a fourth sheet of stationery, quickly completed the following letter.

Dear Jerry,

I know you'll be very happy. Congratulations. Don't worry about me. I have your pin, and I'm just glad you gave it to me.

Linda

Phil wrote with almost equal brevity to say that he honestly hoped everything would work out well. He ended, "Let me know when I can come see you and meet her. You and I have been through everything together. I don't want this or the trouble over Linda to start separating us."

*

As Jerry anticipated, his announcement of his marriage burst upon his parents with much the same effect as his suicide attempt or his semi-elopement with Nancy Train. He was wrong, however, in thinking his parents would quickly come to see it as a pleasant shock, though his mother was to some extent willing to look upon it that way. She said, "Do you think we should invite them to come here so we can get to know her?"

"No," said Mr. Engels. "I don't want to know her."

"Now Henderson."

"Harriet," he said, "I've had enough. This is the absolute limit," and he almost crumpled up Jerry's letter.

"Well, we've got to make the best of it."

Speaking very loudly, Mr. Engels said, "I don't intend to. He's done one irresponsible thing after another, and I just . . ." Mr. Engels couldn't find words to express his disgust with his son. He looked at the letter in his hand. He looked at his wife. He had seldom felt so angry in all his life. "To write us something like this!" He looked at the letter again, and then he did crumple it up.

Mrs. Engels retrieved the letter and smoothed it out, but she could do little to soothe her husband, who had sometimes allowed himself to hope that Jerry's one undoubted asset, his good looks, might eventually lead to a fortunate marriage. Given Mr. Engels's opinion of his son's earning potential, Jerry would have need of a well-to-do wife. Now Mr. Engels said, "To marry a woman eight years older than himself, with no money, no family, no position—to throw himself away like that, and then to sit down and write us that he's at last found the most wonderful woman in the world . . . !" He looked at the letter in his wife's hands as if it were a personal enemy, and shook his head violently.

Mrs. Engels said, "You can't be sure about the woman. She *is* very well educated, and . . ."

"She's divorced. She's had a husband who tried to kill her." He had learned that from Anne. "The man was an alcoholic. What does that say about her judgment? What does it say about her that she's gotten married a second time on the spur of the moment to a young man in Jerry's position? Does she sound mature and thoughtful to you?"

"They shouldn't have gotten married," Mrs. Engels agreed.

"We can be sure they've been carrying on an affair," her husband said.

Mrs. Engels had no doubt of that herself.

"A faculty member who sleeps with her students—that's Jerry's idea of the most wonderful woman in the world!" And in his anger Mr. Engels said, "I think he's brainless."

"Henderson!" his wife exclaimed.

"It's no good, Harriet. I am fed up and sick to death of Jerry's idiocy. It's gone on for years now. He's not an adolescent anymore, he's of age, and he's chosen to get married without even discussing it with us, and from now on he can take care of himself. I will not support him. I will not send him another red cent. He's made his bed, he can lie on it."

"You've got to help him finish college."

"Why should I? What good has he ever gotten out of all the schooling I've paid for?"

"It's not that bad," Mrs. Engels said.

"Harriet, it's worse. Jerry has had every advantage. We sent him to the university schools. He's grown up in a home full of books. Everyone in this family and even his chosen friends have done well in school, and what effect does this have on Jerry? None. Neither good examples, nor good teaching, nor a good home have had any effect. He's practically failing out of Penn State. He's not stupid, but he doesn't use his head. He's unintelligent."

This was very terrible for Mrs. Engels to hear. "Well, we can't just cut him off."

Mr. Engels, after stamping around and letting his anger rip, felt relieved enough to say, "I won't let him starve."

Mrs. Engels looked at the letter in her hand. "We have to acknowledge this in some way. We can't just ignore it."

"He's ignored us."

"That's what hurts me the most," said Mrs. Engels, "that he just doesn't seem to care what we think." She had what Jerry thought of as her martyred look. "But we have to answer this."

"You answer it," said Mr. Engels. "I don't want to write him. I don't want to hear from him. I'm sick to death of him."

So it fell to Mrs. Engels to write Jerry the following letter:

Dear Jerry,

We're very sorry you've chosen to get married so suddenly to someone we don't know. It seems to both of us that since you've ignored our opinion so completely in taking this step, you really cannot expect us to congratulate you on what you've done. Your father is too upset even to write to you about it. He wants me to tell you not to expect any checks from now on. He considers that since you've declared your independence in this way you should learn to live from now on without our financial help. I wish I didn't have to write you this, and maybe [Mrs. Engels knew she shouldn't add any maybe clauses, but she couldn't help herself] he will change his mind on this point.

For the time being we think it best not to meet and try to get to know your wife [how she agonized when she had to write that word *wife*]. You mentioned in your letter to us that you might visit during spring break. I'm afraid as things are now we simply can't welcome you. It almost breaks my heart to have to write this to you, but I won't go on about my feelings. You've shown that they don't carry much weight with you.

That last sentence seemed to her too bitter when she reread it, but rather than rewrite the whole letter, she added some final lines that went far toward erasing the effect of everything that had gone before. "Your happiness," she wrote, "will always be important to me. I love you dearly in spite of all this."

*

On March the 28th, shortly before 2:30 p.m., the subject of all these reactions, the recipient of these various letters, filed into 12 Sparks Building along with his fellow students in Human Development and took his accustomed seat in the second row between a young woman named Ebersole and a young man named Day. Carol Ebersole greeted Jerry by saying, "Feel how cold my hand is." Jerry felt her cool hand. They had a friendly flirtation going. Carol said, "Your hand's as warm as toast." Jerry said it was because he was so well prepared. Then Professor Rowell arrived, called the class to order, and began to distribute his midterm exam.

"Do we have to use Blue Books?" someone in the back called out, panic in his voice.

Rowell said, "You know very well you need Blue Books. Can anyone sell Mr. Soll an extra Blue Book?" Someone could. Rowell finished passing out the exam. Then he jumped back on the podium, took off his watch, laid it on the table there, and gave the class a friendly, direct look. "Okay, begin writing. If you don't understand a question, raise your hand, and I'll come see if I can help you out."

Someone in the back said, "Can we write on both sides, or do you want us to use every other page?"

"Do what you want," said Rowell.

"Is pencil all right?" the same student asked.

"Yerkling, will you just start writing and stop asking questions?" Rowell said.

Yerkling stopped asking questions, and the class settled down. Some students pored intently over the questions. Others began to write at once. One girl started to get out her notebook. "Miss Rubicon," said Professor Rowell. "You were here Friday. You heard that it was a closed-book exam."

"You didn't say closed notebook," she said.

"Yes I did," said Rowell. "Yes?" he said in a different tone of voice, evidently in response to someone with his hand up behind Jerry.

"Will you write the time on the board?"

"Yes, I will," said Rowell. He wrote 2:32 in large numerals with a piece of chalk that squeaked horribly as he drew the 3. A girl squeaked in response and covered her ears. Several students laughed. Then calm of a sort descended.

After reading the questions, Jerry took out his fountain pen, opened his blue book, and wrote:

Dear Professor Rowell,

I'm sorry I can't answer any of your questions. I was married four weeks ago, and ever since then I've been too happy to study or to get ready for tests.

After class one day you told me that if love is the only thing that interests me I was wasting my time in school. I think you're right. Schools don't teach love, though it's the one subject young people want to know about and need to understand in order to have a good life. But in high school you learn about it from dating, and from listening to locker-room talk, and in college it's more of the same, and no matter where you are most of what you hear is wrong because no one really knows anything. And if there are teachers who do know, they can't tell you the truth because they'd lose their jobs if they did. The truth is that love is everywhere, not just between boys and girls where everyone thinks it's supposed to be, but between everyone and everything. Men can love each other. Women can love each other. Boys love cars, girls love jewelry, women love china and children, and men love their families and their work. Love holds life together, like gravity holds matter. Love is the greatest force in life. Without love you're just a piece of matter being flung out into space. One of my fraternity brothers was like that. He went flying out the window last semester, and naturally he smashed on the ground because if love doesn't have a grip on you, gravity takes over.

What I've learned about love is that if you follow it, if you give in to it, if you obey it, if you let it fill you and guide you and master you, you will end up all right no matter what happens. My parents are outraged that I got married without telling them, and to a divorced woman older than I am. My father has stopped sending me my allowance. They don't want me to bring my wife home to meet them. My father won't even write to me now. He'd like to cut me out of his life, but he won't be able to because he's a loving man and when he finally meets my wife he'll see that I've done the best thing I've ever done.

I've been very promiscuous sexually for the last four years, and even earlier I used to daydream about making love in all kinds of ways to every kind of woman. I used to be ashamed of my thoughts. I didn't want anyone to know what was going on in my head, but then I started to do the things I'd only thought about, and after that at least one other person had to know, and having a partner at last, and sharing what had only been in my head up to then made me feel so much better that it was as if I were released from a prison. The winter I was seventeen, my last year in high school, I spent all the money I could scrape together on prostitutes. We lived in Chicago then, and I found out where to go, and I even got to be friendly with some of them, those who'd let me do all the different things that I'd imagined doing. Then that summer I picked up a girl on the beach at a state park near where my family has a summer home. She was painting her toenails when I first saw her, and when we went for a walk together down the beach I carried her across a little stream that runs into the lake there. I did it so she wouldn't ruin her new nail polish by getting her feet wet, but I wanted to hold her, and as soon as I held her in my arms I knew she'd let me make love to her, and that's really all we did for the rest of the summer. I'd fall asleep sometimes on the way to work in the morning, and the friend I commuted with and owned the car with used to complain about that, and about the smell in the car, and not being able to use it at night because I was taking Marie out in it every night. We'd make love on the ground, or on the beach, or in the dunes, or on picnic tables at the edge of parking lots, or wherever we could find a place, and we did it in the car a lot because of the mosquitoes. I made love to her one-hundred and seventeen times that summer. I kept count in those days. Her mother was a long-distance telephone operator, and in July she went on the night shift, and after that Marie and I could use their house in Porter, Indiana. Marie's father wasn't around. In fact, Marie didn't have a father. She was illegitimate, but I loved her and gave her a platinum pin at the end of the summer. I wanted her to have something really great, and I thought maybe that pin would hold her to me, but it didn't. She never answered any of the letters I sent her from school, and when I telephoned to find out why, her mother told me she was going around now with a steelworker. It was my second week at Penn State.

My friend at Haverford that I'd commuted to work with had our car that semester, so I walked around campus looking for an unlocked car, and when I found one I managed to start it by crossing the wires. I planned to drive back to Indiana and do something. I don't think I would ever have hurt Marie, or even that steelworker if I'd made it back home, but I never got there. I ran out of gas near Nanty Glo, and I had only about two dollars with me, which I thought I'd need for coffee and donuts, so I left the car and started to hitchhike west, and the first man to pick me up put the make on me. This had happened to me before, and it always frightened me and made me angry. I hit a man once because of it, but that night I needed money, so when he said he'd give me five dollars, I agreed. And after he blew me he said, "That's a dandy prick you've got." Up to then it had been the ugliest experience of my life, but when I heard him say "dandy" I realized he had really enjoyed it, and that made me feel so much better that I got out of his car and hiked back to the car I'd stolen, and bought gas for it, and drove it back to campus and left it exactly where I'd stolen it.

What that shows me is how love can come popping up where you least expect it, and change everything. Love has no false pride. It can speak through the mouth of a cocksucker as much as through the mouth of the greatest poets. It has a million forms and shapes, and I think having that experience taught me something worth knowing, and something most people never learn.

But I went on being promiscuous. In fact, I got worse, because I was no longer afraid of men, only I found out that relations between men aren't all that happy. There's a lot of guilt and misery there, though for that matter relations between men and women aren't always so great. I've had a woman ask me to spank her, and another wanted me to tie her hands to the bedposts and say terrible things to her. Rotten things go on between men and women, and when I listen to what some of my fraternity brothers say about girls I think people who collect stamps, or china, or tropical fish are better lovers.

I became a good lover, but not the best because of all my promiscuity. It worried me, and I began to think I had spoiled myself for anyone except the kind of woman who doesn't really expect men to be great or good. I thought I would have to marry someone like myself, someone a little spoiled and mediocre, but nice-looking and presentable. I got pinned to a girl like that from Wilmington whose family has a summer house at Rehoboth Beach. We were going to get married when we graduated. Her father was going to use his pull to get me a job at Dupont. It was all arranged. Pat had even decided how many bridesmaids she would have, and where we'd honeymoon, and then it all blew up because I gave her crabs I'd picked up from a prostitute in Philadelphia.

I think now I may have done it almost on purpose, but when it happened I thought I'd lost my last chance for a respectable marriage. I thought maybe I would never marry at all. I didn't know what would become of me. And then out of the blue I met the woman I'm now married to.

You know her because you were once in love with her yourself, but you never asked her to marry you because you felt you should take care of your mother. I'm glad you never asked her, because she would have married you and I would have had no chance. But I'm sorry for you at the same time.

I probably shouldn't put this in a Blue Book and hand it in to you, but I'm going to anyway. Your course has been a big disappointment to me because I haven't learned anything I wanted to know. You should not be teaching a book like Gardner Murphy's *PERSONALITY*. I know he was your teacher at Columbia, but that doesn't mean you should go on the rest of your life accepting him and his ideas, anymore than you should spend your whole life taking care of your mother. People have to break free and live their own lives, even if it means giving pain to people they love and respect. I love my parents, and I respect them, but I would never let that stop me from marrying a woman I love, even if it were a woman like Marie. The most important thing in life is to be true to your deepest needs, and the deepest need of every living person is to join with another human being. We are nothing by ourselves except fragments and imperfect bits of human beings, but together with the person we love we can become whole. Love heals the scars of isolation. Love completes us.

You missed your chance once, but there's always hope. God does not turn his back on those who love. He only forsakes those who won't love, or can't love, or deny love. That leads to death. Love leads to life.

Sincerely yours,
Jerry Engels

He handed that in at the end of the hour. A week later Professor Rowell returned the exams. He gave Jerry an F and wrote below the grade "See me after class," but by then Jerry had dropped out of school to work full-time cleaning, painting, and carpentering. He planned to incorporate himself as Engels Enterprises and go into business. State College was growing. He could see a lot of opportunity for anyone who wanted to work at fixing up, maintaining, and maybe even building houses. But that is another story. This one is done.